Spirit Talker

Rebecca Laffar-Smith

Spirit Talker

First published in Australia in 2021
by Experience Possibility Publishing.

National Library of Australia
Cataloguing-in-Publication entry:
Author: Laffar-Smith, Rebecca, author.
Title: Spirit Talker / Rebecca Laffar-Smith
ISBN: 978-0-6451140-7-2 (Paperback)
            978-0-6451150-2-7 (eBook)

Cover illustration by Cristina Puscas
http://ckleinnn.deviantart.com/

For all the teens,
and those who once were,
seeking their truth
through the shadows.

Trigger Warning

While Spirit Talker is a work of fiction it deals in a couple of things that might be emotionally triggering for some readers. This story delves into mental illness, specifically major depression and schizophrenia, and documents aspects of grief, hallucination, and suicide.

If these topics will disturb you then please seek support before reading this book. While I feel the message is ultimately empowering, I know from personal experience how raw these topics can be and want you to feel in control of your personal mental wellness journey. Please, stay safe and know that you are loved.

1

He isn't really there.

I can tell, because surely if there were an old man with only half a face sitting in a rocking chair on our new porch my father would say something. I don't even think we own a rocking chair. But who can tell these days?

I pull another box out of the back seat of my dad's work truck. His company had comped him one. It was nice and clean. New, like this house, and his job, and the school I'll be starting on Monday. There's nothing to remind us of Mum.

The box isn't heavy. I can remember what I'd packed in it. My bedspread made up the bulk, but a few precious knick-knacks were in there too. Some photographs, the little bag of my gaming dice I usually kept close for when my hands needed to fidget, my favourite skate laces from the first pair of skates my parents had bought me for Christmas when I was seven, and the memory box where I keep the quarter dollar Erica had given me to remember her by. It was one of those mangled, pressed coins from the time we'd hung out at the Sydney Royal Easter Show last year. It was the first time my parents had let me go alone. Well, I was with my friends, but Mum and Dad had both stayed home. It's one of those bittersweet memories because going with my Mum and Dad had been a tradition since I was smaller than I can remember. There's a photo of me in a stroller under the wave swing with Mum. Last year was the first time Mum had been too sick to go. The last time she had been alive. Cancer is like that, slow and fast at the same time.

"Sara!" Dad calls. I wonder if he was getting sick of snapping me out of my mental blanks. Was mind-wandering a crazy person thing? Mine definitely wanders more now than it did before.

This new house, sans the weird old guy on the porch, looked like a recent winner of a home renovation show. I imagine my dad critiquing the design when his boss showed it to him online a few weeks ago. The new house was part of the package deal in moving out here to the dog's end of the world.

Perth isn't really the dog's end. As cities go it is actually kind of beautiful. We'd driven along the water a little as we'd headed to the house. The highways are quiet and the water, they say it's salt even though it's apparently a river, looks clean and blue. Not the turquoise blue of the reef waters in Northern Queensland where we'd holidayed before Mum got really sick, but a darker blue, like it's holding dark secrets.

But this city is so far removed from the rest of the world. Compared to Sydney, where we'd lived since I was little, it feels isolated. Lonely. But maybe that's because we are practically fresh off the boat. Aunt Tara won't be back from her France tour for months. She's photo-journaling buildings in true Brooks' family fashion. There is something about my father's side of the family that has always been obsessed with buildings.

"Come on, Sara! It won't unpack itself," Dad calls again.

I startle, realising I'm still standing in our new driveway looking up at the grey stucco walls of our new house but not really seeing them. I head for the double doors, both held open as Dad and I haul boxes and bags back and forth from his truck.

SPIRIT TALKER

The front entry opens into a brightly lit living room. The furniture is kind of arrayed, kind of scattered, as if the movers had guessed at each location in that 'good enough' fashion, and then dumped the mountain of boxes in the midst of all of it. I move past them, heading upstairs instead. To my new cell. Den. Room. I nudge the door open with my foot.

The room itself is simple in a pretty way. There are two windows, both huge, and both with no blinds or curtains so strangely stark. The whole room is really. The only redeeming factor is the beech wood feature wall and skirting. I like wood. It has an understated elegance that brings outside in. I like the outside.

I push the window frame up and let the spring warmth into the room. The breeze has a tang of salt on it. I draw a deep breath of the fresh air before turning back to face the gentle elegance of my new room.

The head of the bed is pushed up against the feature wall which is as good a spot as any. Especially since, with two walls taken by windows, there are few choices when it comes to down drafts and getting woken up by the rising sun. One of the two windows looks out over the river to the north which meant a few extra hours sleep after sunrise.

Instead of the bed, I put the box on the dresser underneath the other window. This one looks over our fence, right into the neighbour's yard. "I bet they love that," I mutter. If I had curtains, I would pull them shut. Instead, I open the box and begin unpacking. Holding out won't keep Dad happy and keeping my dad happy has become the central point of my life since, you know, my 'breakdown'. I say it with inverted quotes because it's one of those words. The big words. The ones that mean I'm actually a crazy person. What teenager has a breakdown? The freak one. That girl. And now I'm that girl. Although I guess here, I don't have to be and that's part of the point. No one knows me here. I'm the new girl, not the crazy one. Hopefully.

I lift the photograph that rests on the top of my blanket. The frame is simple wood too. The picture, less simple. I feel like I'm already losing the face inside the frame. My mother's face. Well, the three of us really. Six months is a long time to no longer be the three of us.

I pull the stand out and rest the photo-frame next to the box on the dresser. Then I pick it up again and move it to the side table next to the bed. It feels better there, but still not quite at home. Nowhere my mother hadn't been could feel like home. Maybe, nowhere my mother could never be ever will.

"Six cans of honey jam, two melon pies, seven sides of salted soup, another for the blind. Eighteen weights of cannon fodder, cream of soured goat, maybe in a haystack heap, they'll find the blooded bloat."

Sometimes there are all kinds of crazy in my brain. This has to be one of the strangest. I look out the window down to the front step. Dad is hauling another box out of the car, completely oblivious to the old woman that stands beside our new letter box. She rants on with her list in a voice that booms with thirty-year-old strength from a body that was probably closer to ninety.

The words are gibberish. I can't decide if that is better or worse than when the hallucinations make sense. Hearing and seeing things that aren't really there is crazy either way.

And yet, the gibberish feels more comforting, somehow. Like I don't really have to pay attention to it. It's more like background noise. Like the soft wash of water on the shore. I can hear that too. In the part of my brain that isn't broken. In the part that still knows what's real.

The foreshore is walking distance and while the waves don't ride up like the surfer waves on the beach at Bondi it still laps the sand in white froth. I can't see the white from here, but I trust it's there. Inevitable. Like the ocean. Much more inevitable than my mind.

"Can you give me a hand with my desk, Sare-Bear?" Dad calls, catching my eye as he looks up to my window.

I roll my eyes. He can't see it, probably, but then he knows me well enough to know I'd do it.

"Come on, you know how impossible it is."

"Yeah, I know," I call down to him, "I'm coming."

By the time I get outside again there are people with him. Real people. People he can see and hear because he's talking to them.

"Hey, Sara," he calls, waving me over. "These are our neighbours."

They look like ordinary people. The dad, at least I'd guess he's a dad because he has that dad look about him, is broad shouldered. He has a weathered face and glasses that don't quite counter the slight squint of his eyes. Maybe it's because he's out in the sun. There's a day's growth of hair on his lip which looks like he just didn't have a chance to shave yet rather than an attempt at growing a moustache. His hair has that slightly weathered look too. Like he'd spent part of the day running his hand through it while he obsessed over something.

SPIRIT TALKER

The boy, his son I'm guessing, looks about my age. He's got the same brown hair with the same harried look. He wears a pair of black jeans that fit him just a little bit too well. I try not to notice.

I force a smile, trying to remember the easy way I used to smile at people, when I was normal. "Hi," I say, "I'm Sara."

"Your Dad tells us you'll be going to Perth Modern on Monday," the dad-guy says. "Will goes there too. He's studying computer science."

I glance at the boy, Will, who won't meet my eye. Instead, he scuffs his sneakers on the driveway and looks like he'd rather be a million miles away. Clearly not the welcoming party and clearly not keen to talk about school or computer science. Then again, I'm not exactly volunteering my own study history either. I guess that's what Dads are for. "Sara's doing visual arts," mine says. "Maybe you'll have some of the same classes."

Will shrugs. His dad glances at him and sighs. He turns his attention back to my father "Anyway, we wanted to offer some help. Sounded like you've got a monster to bring inside."

My dad nods. "Yeah, you could definitely call my tiltable that." He motions to the bed of the truck. The standing table is strapped down with thick moving ropes. Dad unhooks it from the truck and climbs up on the back. "It's on wheels but getting it down off the truck might take a few hands."

"Fortunately, we've got a few," our new neighbour says.

Together, we manage to lift the desk down from the truck and wheel it over the uneven paving and up the front step. Dad positions it in his new study. The bookshelves in here had already been stacked with Dad's favourites. Most of the shelves were covered in architecture and design books and magazines. There were some old textbooks from his university studies, but our neighbour manages to find the fiction section. Will rolls his eyes at his dad's wry smile. "You have good taste."

"Oh?" Dad asks, "You know Rich Saint-James?"

Even as clearly disinterested and underwhelmed as Will had appeared, he manages a chuckle. His dad fixes him with a look and says, "You could say he's well known to us."

"That's amazing. I heard he lived out this side of the country."

"Pretty close actually. He's your neighbour."

Dad looks flabbergasted. "No way?" Then he does a double take. "No way!" he cries again. "You're Richard Saint-James? The mystery author? THE Rich Saint-James?"

SPIRIT TALKER

"Honestly, I'm only big here in Australia. The rest of the world has no clue who I am. Not really."

Will shakes his head. I wonder if it's because his dad is flat out lying, even I knew how big the latest Saint-James mystery had hit it in the UK last year, or if he's embarrassed full stop. Probably both. If it were my dad I'd be mortified. Just having my dad fan-girl all over the guy was embarrassing enough.

Dad starts pulling books off the shelf. "This was my favourite. But then this one is brilliant too. Oh, you wouldn't mind signing them for me, would you?"

I shake my head, "Dad, we're not at a convention. You can't just get him to sign your books. It's like walking up to a celebrity in a restaurant and asking to take their photo. You know, rude?"

"Oh," Dad says, looking deflated, like I'd burst the bubble of his happiness. I kick myself. I wasn't supposed to do that. "No, of course," he says, "I'm sorry, Rich. Can I call you Rich?" He doesn't wait for Rich to respond, "I mean, you're already doing us a solid helping me get this desk inside. I don't want to put you out. Sara is absolutely right."

"Not at all. I mean, she's right about the restaurant thing. That drives me nuts. But honestly, I don't mind. It's good to know people love the books. That's kind of the whole point, right?"

Dad grins, bubble reinflated.

"But let's get the rest of your stuff inside first. Before the kids abandon us in favour of hard rock and closed bedroom doors."

It doesn't take much longer before Dad's truck is completely empty. With eight hands instead of four it gets handled and the pile of empty boxes start to outnumber the ones full of stuff.

Dad and his new friend seem pretty content to unpack the kitchen as the kettle boils. Will has done his best to ignore me the whole time. I'm not sure if I'm impressed by his stubbornness or put out by the snub. I guess it doesn't really matter. And at least I'd been able to pretend I didn't see some old guy that isn't really there ranting about the mountain of boxes in the living room. Or the cat that seemed to streak past the kitchen window, six times in a row, in exactly the same way, like a demented déjà vu. The crazy was firmly under wraps, for now.

And, since they didn't seem to need me, I figured it was safe to head upstairs again. "I'm gonna go unpack my room," I tell my dad by way of excuse. Will glances at me but I return the favour and ignore him, dashing up the stairs before Dad can insist I invite the guy to join me. At least, in my room, maybe I could be alone for a little while. Since my mother's death, the world had become a very crowded place. It wasn't getting any quieter, even here.

2

*P*erhaps it's because the rooms are still mostly empty, but Dad and Rich's voices carry up the stairs and follow me to my room. The conversation in other parts of the house is actually kind of reassuring. It's nice to hear a semblance of normal. It makes it easier to tune out of the other sounds. The strange ones that may or may not actually be there.

I return to the box on my dresser, pulling out the blanket and fresh sheets to dress my new bed. I'm already loving this bed because its frame is made from recycled wood pallets in an arty way. The dresser and side table are made from the same kind of wood. I wonder who picked it and suspect my Dad had probably given strict instructions. He was amazing like that. He could coordinate an army of workers and end up with something absolutely beautiful despite being constructed by tradies who knew nothing about design.

I unpack a few of my other boxes too. I hang my roller-skates in my closet next to the new school uniform. Dad had assured me there were rinks here. He'd promised to get me signed up for lessons before the week was out. Still, seeing my skates opens the hole in my heart a little more. It was the hole where my mother should be but isn't. Skating was always the thing she and I had shared.

As I flat pack the box, now empty of my knick-knacks, my gaze strays out of the window again. The afternoon sun is a beautiful golden orange as it heads for the horizon to the west. It makes the large tree in my neighbour's yard cast a long shadow over our fence.

There's an old swing strung up on chains in our neighbour's yard. It hangs from a thick branch. A young boy, maybe seven or eight years old, swings his feet back and forth as he rocks the swing. Rich never mentioned another son, but we'd only just met him so it's not surprising he didn't give his whole life story.

For a while the rhythmic pattern of the boy's movements helps me feel calmer. My mind wanders away from my mother, from my skates, from the things we'd left behind. The simple motion, the simple memories of swinging back and forth, is easier.

Then, the boy looks up at me. A moment of confusion seems to cross his face as he realises I'm watching him. I smile and lift my hand to wave, but he disappears. The swing continues to rock back and forth, now empty.

My chest is suddenly tight again. "Damn," I mutter, realising. Hallucination.

I swear it's getting harder and harder to tell the difference between what is really there and what isn't. Ever since my mother had died, I'd seen more and more, but when my crazy brain gut punches me like that it's the worst. I'd really believed what I was seeing.

My mind replays it in my head, looking for the clues, searching for the secrets so that I'd know how to understand what is real and what isn't next time. As I play it back, I notice things.

If I'd really been paying attention, I'd have noticed his hair didn't move with the breeze his motion should have caused. I should have noticed the fuzzy edges of his clothing. I should have noticed the strange sadness about him because all of my hallucinations have it. But then that could be anything. Odds are people say the same thing about me. I definitely think it about my Dad. I'd even seen it a little in Rich and Will. So perhaps it's not an indicator of the real or not real after all.

My neighbour's back door swings open and Will comes outside. I step away from the window so he can't see me. I hadn't realised he and Rich had gone home but the quiet clatter of dishes downstairs only just masks a scratchy mutter that crawls like spiders up my back. The old man ranting at the pile of boxes was still down there. The not real old man.

So that made how many today? Easily more than yesterday. Maybe it was this place. Or maybe it was just feeling so out of place in this place. Or maybe I was just getting crazier and crazier.

3

inner was increasingly successful. When it comes to learning new skills, Dad was starting to master the kitchen. He approached cooking with the same sense of proficiency as he approached life. Strategic, precise, and following the rules. That was Dad to a tee. In fact, perhaps the very act of being able to follow the exact measurements, time, and temperature in a recipe made cooking something he would really come to love. I wondered if it made him think of Mum. But I won't ask him.

After eating, we'd spent the evening unpacking the living room. I ignored the old man who never seemed to leave although his rants became less obsessive the smaller the mountain of boxes became. Eventually, when the last box had been flattened, we'd nudged the couch into alignment in front of the television screen, and pulled the rocking recliner forward a little, the old man fell silent, smiled, and sat down as if everything we'd done was to set up his favourite chair. The chair rocks a little but Dad doesn't seem to notice.

"It's getting late," Dad says, glancing out of the window. "We're going to have to get some curtains."

I smile. "This rustic, everyone can see what you're doing, look not appealing to you?"

He runs a hand through his hair, stroking the stray strands of his fringe back onto the top of his head. "Well, a little privacy is never underrated." He sighs. "Time for bed?"

I nod. "Yeah, okay." I head for the stairs but pause before stepping up. "Dad?"

"Yeah, Sare?"

I swallow, suddenly not really sure what I wanted to say to him. "Um, thanks, you know?"

There's a weight separating us because we're both in that space between where we were supposed to be and what life had become. I love my dad, but we both knew the gap was where my mother should have been. She glued our family together. Not having her here, even with her pictures on the mantle, felt like trying to build a house of cards outside. Every little wind was threatening.

I could tell Dad wanted to reach out. His body turned toward me as if he was about to take a step forward. But he didn't. Instead he gave me a gentle smile. "We'll be okay, Sara. Things will get better."

"I'm sorry." I'm not sure what I'm apologising for. All of it feels like my fault. Dad doesn't seem unhappy about moving but that was my fault too. Mostly, I guess I was sorry for being broken.

Dad shakes his head. "None of this is your fault. And you had a good day today." He smiles then and I push down the guilt because that smile was the whole point of holding it together today. Letting him believe I was getting better was more important than actually getting better. This move needed to matter, for both of us. It was the only way we'd be okay.

I nod and smile back. "Bed then," I say.

He flicks the living room light off. "I'm headed that way myself. Just let me lock up for the night."

I leave him behind and head up the stairs. Even here feels a little more normal now. I flick the switch on my wall and the overhead light almost blinds me. When I flick the second switch on the wall a scatter of smaller bulbs and fairy lights gives the room a soft glow, so I turn off the overhead and let the mood lighting do its job.

After visiting the bathroom to change and brush my teeth, I lay back on my new bed and look up at the ceiling. The scatter of lights across the roof are like stars brought inside. That would have been another Dad touch.

I let the day fall away. We'd left my world behind, but it wasn't so bad. By now Erica, and all of my old friends, would be asleep. The world turns slowly.

Thinking of them, I pick up my phone and angle the camera at the scatter of lights. "Starlight inside," I post to Instagram. They'll wake up and at least know I was still alive.

The soft strum of an acoustic guitar drifts through my window with the night breeze. With no curtains to stir I hadn't noticed that I'd left it open. I wonder for a moment how many mosquitoes would be eating me alive while I tried to sleep tonight.

I get up and pad over to the window. I grip the frame in my hands, about to push it down, but pause as I see the little boy in my neighbour's yard again.

This time, he's sitting on the step of the back porch. The guitar in his arms is only a little bit smaller than he is. His fingers move along the strings, tracing cords on the frets. He strums with his right hand, letting the sound play in a soft pattern. The tune is familiar, but I can't name it.

The boy's yard is softly lit by the moonlight and the warm glow from an upstairs window. I can't see who is inside, but I imagine Will or Rich, or maybe Rich's wife, if he has one.

The sound of the guitar has an eerie echo to it. It's as if the moonlight, the breeze, and the night air touch the notes, not just the strings of the guitar. It's like the world passes through the music. I stand, watching the boy, noticing this time the little tells that he isn't real. The way the moonlight passes through him, casting no shadow. The way his fingers both touch and don't touch the guitar at the same time. The way the breeze gusts up through the trees but doesn't seem to touch him. The little things.

But mostly, again, I notice his sadness. There's a weight on his shoulders that doesn't belong there. Little boys aren't supposed to be so heavy.

Deep in my gut I feel the urge to talk to him. I push it away, because it's part of the crazy. Only crazy people talk to people who aren't really there.

I nudge the window, intending to lower it carefully, then gasp as a chill brushes my arm. I step away and the window clatters down in the frame. The glass wobbles slightly but I barely notice because there's a young man standing inches from me. He's right here, in my bedroom, looking directly at me.

I swallow, feeling the racing of my heart.

"Hello and well met, my fair Sara Brooks," the young man says.

I shake my head. He knows my name. It creeps me out because even though it's the first time I'm seeing him, and I know, in that deep gut way you just know things, that he isn't really here, if he knows my name it's because he's been here longer than I'd noticed. Could hallucinations do that? Could they be there even when I can't see them?

Or maybe he knew my name because he was just in my head. Maybe all of my hallucinations knew my name. Because aren't they just part of my brain? The broken part, but still technically the me part. I don't know how all this works.

"Grayson White, at your service, ma'am," the young man says. He steps one foot forward and dips in a half bow. A feathered hat appears in a hand that moments ago had been empty. He tips the hat forward. The hat matches the whole look of him. It's as if he's stepped out of my favourite

Jane Austen novel. He reminds me of Knightly, with his clipped accent, polite speech, and gentlemanly manner. "Though," he continues, "you might prefer to call me Grae as seems to be the more accepted form of my name in this day."

There's a charm about it but I try not to let my hallucination glamour me. Instead, it's better to ignore it. Odds are I was just seeing this, in my new room, because I was tired. And in a strange place. And alone.

"Sara?" My dad knocks on my door before opening it. "You okay?"

I glance at the young man, swallowing. My dad's gaze narrows and I quickly cover my mistake by saying, "Yeah, sorry. The window got away from me." I wave at the window behind my shoulder. I can tell Dad isn't fully convinced. His gaze rests on me a little longer. I try not to look at the hallucination and, instead, focus on my dad.

Eventually Dad nods. "Okay, g'night then."
"Night dad."

As soon as my door closes, I glare at the young man. Grayson. I try to step around him. He straightens, tilting his head.

"Well, you might neglect the niceties of a polite society but since I already know your name you need not give it in return for mine."

SPIRIT TALKER

"You're not really here," I mutter, then grimace. "I'm talking to myself." I'm not sure if I'm reassuring him or me because I'm not supposed to talk to the hallucinations. That's how this whole thing got out of hand to begin with.

It's one thing to see things other people don't see but when you're talking to people that don't really exist it starts raising eyebrows.

"I'm going to bed," I say, again, to myself not to him because talking to him would be crazy.

"Suit yourself," he says. The hat disappears from his hand and is replaced by a quill pen. "I don't suppose you've a fresh supply of ink?"

He glances around my newly made up room.

"No, I don't suppose," he says again. "But I do like what you've done with this abode. The previous owners were in no way creative. They didn't own a book or desk between them." He admires the covers of the books on my desk. I didn't have a bookshelf in here, so my personal stack of urban fantasy, old school mythology, and magic were strewn in several haphazard piles.

I want to tell him not to touch anything but instead try to pretend he isn't here. I march over to my bed, pull back the blankets, and slide inside. "He's not here," I mutter to myself. I pick up my phone, setting the alarm. Then, just because I can't resist, and because I hadn't tried it before, I snap a photograph at him. Except, of course because he's a hallucination there's nothing in the picture but my desk, my books, and the scatter of light from the soft bulbs.

I close my eyes and reach blindly to put my phone on the bedside table. "See? Not really there." My skin crawls as I imagine him watching me, but I keep my eyes tightly shut and try to convince sleep to come. It doesn't.

From time to time I blink my eyes open hoping he'll have disappeared, but he doesn't. Instead, he settles into the seat at my desk. He gazes out of the window, then leans forward and scrawls on pages of parchment that appear and disappear on the desk.

I turn under my sheets. They're crisp and fresh. They weren't new, we'd brought them from the old house, but they were clean, so they added to the out of place feeling of being in a new room, a new house, a new town. They added to the feeling of being a stranger in my own skin.

The strangeness of a stranger in my room wasn't helping.

After tossing and turning for what feels like hours, listening to the occasional chatter or the lines of poetry muttered by the soft baritone of the strange young man, I give up and sit up on my bed.

"Do you have to do that? I'm trying to sleep."

He swivels in my desk chair and grins at me. "So, she at last acknowledges me. Well met!"

"Not really," I mutter. "You're not even here. You're a hallucination. But you're making it very hard to sleep."

He looks pained, as if my words had wounded him. "Not here? Aghast! What a thing to say. You belittle me, ma'am, and I am bereft."

I shake my head. "What are you even doing here?"

"Ah, now that is a tale and much too long in the telling of it. But to speak a shortened term I'd say that when I saw your likeness today, I was so reminded of my sweet Ella-May that I couldn't resist penning a new poem to my love."

I felt the prickle of my forehead as I raised an eyebrow. "And they say I'm crazy." I lay back on the pillow again, pulling its edges around my face.

"Well, as must needs," he says. The pillow does nothing to drown out the sound of his words.

"But why in my room?" I ask as if he hadn't spoken.

"Where else?"

I groan, turning to my side. The moonlight catches against the panes of glass in my window.

"Not a line of verse worth the ink it's written in," Grae grumbles. He picks up the smeared parchment, crumples it in his hands, and tosses it at the moon. The paper seems to pass right through the glass and disappears outside. He puts the pen down and turns back toward me. "You've a tale of your own telling, don't you Sara Brooks."

I close my eyes again, squishing the pillow against my ears. If I pretend to sleep maybe I will.

"Have you any idea what an age it's been since I last conversed with the living? Well with anyone really because even the dead aren't particularly conversational."

I feel the breath freeze in my chest. The tightness hurts and I force myself to gasp rather than hold it. I drag air into my lungs and will the hallucination to leave me alone.

It's the first time one has actually talked to me rather than at me. It's the first time it feels more like a conversation than overhearing. This is different in so many ways.

It is also the first time my hallucinations had claimed to be anything else and I couldn't let myself begin to believe. The whole idea is crazier than a loony bin. My father doesn't need this right now. I have to get this under control. Sleep would help. Surely.

So, even though I can still hear the flutter of parchment and the scratch of Grae's pen, I focus on listening to my breath. I focus on tuning everything out. I focus on finding the dreams because although they were almost less comforting than seeing things that didn't exist at least they brought sleep with them. And I tell myself that tomorrow will be a better day, but I don't really believe it.

I swear, morning comes before my eyes even have time to gather sleep dust. Fortunately, the rising sun doesn't force me awake at the break of day and by the time I crack my eyes open it's well and truly up. So is Grae, still sitting at my desk, head buried over another page of parchment as he scrawls away. I groan, wishing he wasn't there.

I toss the blanket aside and swing my feet out of my bed. The floorboards are cold and I make a mental note to ask Dad for a rug before padding over to the dresser.

I pull out fresh clothes, then glance again at Grae. He's watching me, blue eyes following me as I move. I glance down at the clothes in my hand and then at my pyjamas before raising my gaze to his again.

"A merrily good morn to you, Sara Brooks," he says with a smile.

"I need to get dressed," I say, looking at him pointedly. He doesn't seem to get the point. I'm not sure if he's just oblivious or if he's a jerk. Either way I stomp over to my door. "I'm going to change," I say, again, definitely talking to myself and not my hallucination. I storm out of the room but carefully close the door before crossing to the bathroom. I change quickly, brushing my teeth and swilling a cold glass of water before going back.

Maybe Grae did get the point because when I get back to my room it's empty. I smile, but as I pull a brush through my hair, I feel a strange pit of sadness. I squash it as quickly as it flits through my belly. I can't go being sad when my hallucinations disappear. It's a good thing. No hallucination is always way better than being crazy.

And you know, maybe the whole thing was just being tired. It had been a long day, after all. I let myself pretend that's all it was but I'm not really fooling myself.

Still, he definitely isn't a ghost, no matter what he implied. That is just the wonky part of my brain looking for excuses.

And I definitely don't need to tell Dad about him. Having a young man in my bedroom all night will not make Dad happy, even if he is just a figment of my brain chemistry backfiring. In fact, that's all the more reason Dad doesn't need to know. My last psychiatrist would probably have had a field day with that.

Besides, things will get better now. They have to.

I put the brush down on the dresser, slip on a pair of shoes, and head downstairs, looking for Dad. The first place to check is always the kettle. Even before Mum got sick we had a habit of leaving notes there and this morning there was a short one. "Gone to get groceries."

I pull open the fridge. Yep, we need them. I shake my head as I grab an apple from the bowl on the table. Breakfast of kings.

I grab the marker and scrawl my own note beneath Dad's. "Gone to the beach."

4

Our street is just two blocks up from the foreshore. It's lined by a mixture of old and new homes that create an odd but beautiful, eclectic feel. Even our own shingle-style house alongside the ultra-modern Saint-James house next door creates a strange disparity, but some of the houses on the streets leading to the foreshore could have been built back in the sixties. Their asbestos walls are whitewashed and the wooden window frames are slightly warped and aged to grey under crumbling paint jobs. They look strange against the glass and concrete constructions of new buildings. And yet, somehow, the combination of old and new gives the area a warmth. It's as if we could walk through history without giving up everything that makes us who we are today.

The foreshore is fronted by an expanse of lush green lawns and a scatter of trees. There are families in small clusters up and down. And a short distance away a children's playground is filled with laughter, chatter, and at least a dozen kids. As I head toward the water, I can't help wondering who is real and who isn't.

I keep walking over the lawn, aiming for the stretch of white sand where the blue water rushes up in gentle lapping waves. Even this stretch of water feels odd. It's not like the true ocean, but it's not quite a river either. Out over the water a ferry sounds its horn and a pleasure yacht crests the ripples heading up the river to the east.

As I cross the lawn, I pull off my shoes and hold them in my hand. The grass prickles beneath my feet but I'm glad to be barefoot when I step onto the white sand. It squishes, warm beneath my feet. The grains crumble over my toes and I kick it up a little as I walk.

The shoreline stretches for a good kilometre in both directions so even scattered with people everyone is relatively well spaced apart. If we were in Sydney, almost every inch of sand would be covered by bodies, towels, and beach umbrellas. It would be noisy with chatter, shouting, laughter, and seagulls squawking. Here, even the seagulls seem to understand social distancing. The sounds seem ambient, giving the foreshore a hint of life rather than smothering it.

A way up the sand, a group of girls about my age laugh together as they lay on beach towels in the sun. They look out over the water, flicking flirty gazes, tossing their hair, and slathering sun cream on every inch of skin not covered by their bikinis. I follow their gaze to boys, probably about the same age, skimming back and forth as they paddle body boards in the water. The waves aren't anything worth surfing but the guys seem content to toss froth at each other and work their arms through the water. They tip each other off their boards, dunking each other in the water with bouts of laughter and back slapping.

At least these are real people and not the fake ones my mind liked to create.

I walk up to the wet sand where the waves splash in soft ripples. The water is cool as it touches my feet. It's stepping into shade on a hot day. It's the kind of cold that is refreshing rather than chilling.

I gaze out over the water, seeing the city in the distance and wondering how, even hearing the laughter and chatter of the other kids, even knowing I'm surrounded by a city full of people, it still feels small, and quiet, and peaceful.

The water had always been that for me. Even after Mum, the beach had been a safe place. The waves didn't stop the hallucinations, although I guess I'd been lucky in not seeing ancient pirate ships and cannon fodder out over the Pacific Ocean. If Captain Cook had graced my shores I really would have been locked up in a loony bin.

But no, the water reminded me that I walked in the world. Feeling the sludgy wet sand between my toes was grounding. And I could feel myself here, in this moment, and nowhere else.

I let my mind wander, just being here and letting go of everything that brought us here. I let go of everything that had pulled us down, out of our happy lives, in the past couple of years. I let Mum be alive again in my mind. I let everything be okay. And for a little while at least I could pretend.

I gasp as a cold, wet, yellow orb splashes past just inches from my face. I step back as something significantly bigger, heavier, and wetter, bounds behind it. My foot catches, having sunk into the sand and I flail, dropping my shoes as I fall backward. I land on my butt, feeling the drench of water up to my hips. I gasp, because it actually is chilly. Colder than I thought.

I glare at the smelly, wet bundle of fur. It dives on the tennis ball, turns in the water, and drops the ball almost in my lap.

The golden retriever hadn't, technically, knocked me over but that didn't make it any less guilty of causing my wet butt. "Hey!" I cry, then gasp again as the dog, tongue lolling, shakes off its fur. Water droplets fly everywhere, covering me head to toe.

Behind the dog, a familiar guy with light brown hair comes racing up the beach. "Oh man, sorry about that," Will says, reaching a hand down to help me up. My anger shifts from his damn dog, to him. The jerk is laughing at me. I can tell he's probably trying not to, but his eyes sparkle with it and he can't wipe the grin from his face.

I shove his hand away. "I'm fine," I snap. My hands sink into the sand as I push myself to my feet. My clothes are drenched.

"I'm guessing you hadn't planned on swimming?" Will asks. It's not really a question, it's another jab. He's making fun of me.

I glare at him. "I wasn't planning on the idiots at the beach."

He chuckles, raising both of his hands, palms up. "No harm intended. We were just playing fetch, weren't we Nikki." He reaches down as his dog nudges him in the leg. He's wearing board shorts and I realise his chest is bare.

It's a nice chest, but I'd rather not have noticed. Especially not with me standing beside him in jeans that cling in static wet against my legs. My shirt, once pristine white, cut in a bodice-style with laces, is now splattered in the grey sludge of wet sand and is probably clinging in ways that would draw way too much attention. I cross my arms over my chest because I definitely don't need to start my reputation with a wet shirt competition.

I shake my head and turn my back on him as I storm off up the sand toward the grass. "Hey Sara," Will says, chasing after me, "I really am sorry." This time he sounds more subdued, the laughter faded, but I shake my head again.

"Just leave me alone."

I can feel his gaze on me as I walk away. I bite my lip, fighting back the threat of tears. I have no idea why I want to cry. And I didn't mean to be a bitch to him. I mean, it's just water and it's not even like these are my good jeans. Then I realise it's not really Will or his dog, just reality. Because for one moment everything was calm, and quiet, and peaceful. Now, I'm back in a world where I can't trust what I see and hear. Now, the street ahead is filling up with everything I wish wasn't there.

The grass is sharp on my feet as I sprint back across the lawn. Despite the heaviness of my wet clothes, I keep up a punishing pace. I hear Will call out behind me again but ignore him because in front of my eyes more and more 'not really there' things keep appearing. The park along the foreshore that had been littered in a scatter of families fills up with people and flashes of scenes that vary in age and expanse.

As I turn up the road toward our houses, a man in military uniform steps into my path. I freeze and almost stumble as I try to avoid colliding with him. Then I step back, gasping, as I see the way the skin hangs and almost melts off his face. He groans at me, reaching for me with his hand. I weave around him, shaking my head, and stride on.

As I race past another letterbox, I see the same old woman who had stood by ours yesterday. I remember her chanting about some strange ingredients or what not for her impossible stew. She is ranting again now, but I ignore the repetitive gibberish. I want to close my eyes but need to see the footpath stretching out in front of me. Instead, I lift my hands to cover my ears, hoping to drown out her screeching voice but even my palms pressed tight against my ears don't diminish the sound.

SPIRIT TALKER

And through them I hear the piercing cries of a newborn baby. My chest, heaving with rapid breaths, feels tight and I gasp for air. A big part of me wants to rush to the old boxy pram. It lays, abandoned on the side of the road with its contents tipped all over the floor. The baby cries, and cries, and cries.

"It's not real," I mutter to myself, running past and ignoring the urge to stop, to help. Finally, I see my new house just a hundred metres or so further up the road. I race for my driveway, weaving around the startled face of a young woman who had been jogging down the street. Maybe she was real. It was getting harder and harder to tell.

Just before I reach my front door I stop. Blocking the path is the young man, Grae. "Sara Brooks!" he cries. A grin spices his features. He's clearly happy to see me. "Well if it isn't the lovely Sara Brooks."

"Leave me alone!" I shout at him. Even I can hear how loud my voice carries.

"But you've yet to hear the latest swooning of my heart. I penned another ode to my fair Ella-May just this morn. I finished it while you slumbered but you seemed not of a mood to receive me this morning."

I try to step around Grae but, as if we're in a demented dance, he weaves from side to side with me. "Get out of the way!" I shout again, pushing my hands against him. My fingers slip through, tingling. I gasp and snatch them back.

One of the wooden doors open and Dad steps out. "Sara?" he asks, clearly concerned. I feel more then see my neighbour's door opening too. I imagine Rich standing on his doorstep, watching the crazy girl next door. "Sara, calm down. It's okay," my dad says. His voice is soothing, as if being calm and sensible would somehow make the hallucinations go away. But nothing makes them go away.

I can tell my eyes are wild. I swallow, then shake my head. My breath is ragged and even the short run has left me feeling wiped out. I bend, crouching, and grip my knees to breathe between them. I rock on my feet, only just realising how cut up they are from running, shoe-less, all the way home.

Dad steps forward. Half his body passes right through Grae. The sight of his hand reaching through Grae's stomach makes me heave. The apple doesn't taste the same coming back up.

"Well, really," Grae says, a mask of horror on his cultured face. I'm not sure if he's dismayed by my unladylike retching or my father moving right through him. He steps aside.

I spit, clearing my mouth as I push myself back upright. Dad stands on one side and Grae on the other. I shake my head and shove my way past Grae. My hands pass straight through him and I feel a cold shiver as I run past, push through the door, and race up the stairs to my room. I slam my bedroom door. It shudders on its hinges.

I lean back, then sink in a wet puddle against my bedroom door. The tears won't stop now. I rock, wrapping my arms around my knees. I let my head tip forward. The tears stain down my cheek, dropping in damp patches on my grubby shirt.

"Sorry about that Rich," I hear my dad say to our neighbour. The hiss of water from the garden hose reminds me of the sloshing sound of the lapping waves at the beach.

"Is she okay?" Rich asks.

I can imagine my dad nodding as he hoses my vomit off our front step. "Just going through some stuff."

I wish I could bite back the sarcastic chuckle that escapes my throat. 'Going through some stuff'… Like it's that simple. And 'going through' implies an end to get to on the other side of it all. Except if there was another end to this it was probably inside of a padded cell.

The soft click of the front door closing echoes up through the house. I brace myself, knowing my dad won't leave me alone, even if I beg him, but time ticks away. Eventually, I start to think maybe he won't come.

My heartrate, slowing now, still echoes in my ears. Each breath is a shudder spawning another streak of tears. A chill starts to set in on my arms. My jeans stiffen on my legs as they dry. I sit there, letting myself drift as I try to figure out how to get out of my own head.

When Dad's voice finally does come it makes me jump. "Sara?" he says. His voice is soft with concern. It's followed by a gentle knock on the door behind me. "You okay?"

I swallow, then draw a deep breath. I swipe away the tears as I try to pull myself together again. I shake my head, but he can't see me. "I'm a mess," I whisper.

The shadow under my door seems to grow and Dad's voice, lower, gentler, and closer to my head, responds, "I made an appointment for you to see someone."

A wry snort shakes my chest. "Bring on the white coats," I mutter. It's the kind of thing I would have said with a smile if I could have mustered one. Instead, it sounds darker and more defeated then I intended. I sigh. "Sorry," I add, tipping my head back. It rests on the wood. I close my eyes.

"It's going to be okay, Sara. We'll figure this out."

We sit there, his back to mine with the door between us. There was a strange comfort in it, but as the minutes tick past I can sense him growing impatient. My dad loves me, but he's never been the kind of guy who could sit and do nothing. Booking an appointment with a psychiatrist was his proactive way of taking this bull by the horns. And who knows, maybe it will help.

Eventually, I hear him shuffle as he gets to his feet. "Tuesday, after school," he says.

I nod again then croak through a now sore throat, "Okay."

I listen as the soft pad of his feet fades down the hall. The longer I sit the more I feel the discomfort of my damp clothing against my skin. My eyes are puffy and my hands feel full of grit. The salty smell of stale river water wafts from my clothes.

I open my eyes, seeing my new room come into fuzzy focus. I sigh, because he's there again, Grae, watching me. He sits at my desk and balances his quill pen between his fingers.

I groan. "Just leave me alone."

A sad hurt passes through Grae's eyes. It sends a pang of guilt through me.

"My deepest and most humble apologies, Sara Brooks. I have caused you pain and for that I am filled with regret." He glances around my room, then sighs. "I will leave you," he says.

And just like that he's gone.

A strange emptiness fills me in his absence. And, in the quiet that now seems to fill the whole house, I finally stretch my body and push myself up to my feet.

A hot shower, a hot meal, and an early night puts me in bed well before nine. Grae doesn't come back again.

As I lay, drifting on the edges of sleep I hear the soft strum of the acoustic guitar next door. It lulls me into sweet dreams. I sleep, long, deep, and heavy.

I wake with the morning sun, feeling it warm my face through the window. I smile as I stretch under my covers, realising that, for the first time since we lost my mother, I'd slept through the entire night.

5

*T*he stiff white blouse and black dress pants of the Perth Modern uniform are freshly starched and new. They're easily both two sizes larger than me as well. That's Dad, pragmatic as ever, planning for the future and my finishing out the last few years of high school here without having to buy new clothes. Still, I'm glad for the uniform because as we walk into a growing sea of teenagers headed into the school it helps me blend in.

We head to the admin building which is clearly marked with easy directions from the carpark. Dad is full of smiles, greeting students and teachers alike. As we reach the reception desk, he introduces us both.

"Hello there. Mitchell Brooks with my daughter, Sara. She's transferred from Dulwich High School in Sydney. We registered her for classes two weeks ago."

The middle-aged woman behind the desk smiles and nods. With a few swift keystrokes she pulls up my record and hits print. The top-of-the-line printer behind her kicks into action and within a minute the receptionist passes us a handful of welcome pages.

"This is a map of the school to help you find your way around," the receptionist, her badge calls her Veronica Stanton, tells us. She points to a section of the map. "This is us here." Then she takes a highlighter and marks out two other sections of the map. "This is your year's lockers and your advocacy room."

I nod, noting each location but already knowing I'd have trouble navigating the maze of classrooms. Just the fact that the school has designated areas for each year level was a sign of how big it really was.

"And this is your class schedule. Welcome to Perth Modern, Sara. We hope you'll enjoy your time with us."

"Thank you, Mrs Stanton," I say, taking the pages from her.

Dad and I step outside and I turn to him awkwardly.

"All set?" he asks.

I swallow and release a tight breath. "I guess."

"You'll do great, Sara. You're easy to like. You'll be making friends in no time. You always do."

"Yeah," I mutter, "let's just hope they're not figments of my imagination." I regret the words as soon as I say them because of the tense crinkle that creases the edges of my father's eyes. "Sorry," I say, "No, you're right. I'll be just fine. I'm great with people." I grin at him and wonder if he believes my smile or if he can tell how much I'm totally faking it.

"You'll be great," he says again. He glances back to the door that leads out to the carpark. "I guess I better get going too. First day of work and all."

"As if you haven't been checking in all weekend."

He grins. "What can I say, I'm dedicated. But I'll wrap up early today to pick you up."

I shake my head. "You don't need to do that, Dad. I'm sure I can figure out the public transport system."

"It's not the same as in Sydney, Sara. Perth's a bit more laid back."

"Dad, stop worrying. I'll be fine," I tell him again.

He doesn't look convinced but eventually he nods. "Okay but keep your phone on. I'll check in with you to see how you're going and if you change your mind just say so. I'll come get you wherever you need me to. Even if it means crossing the narrows back and forth all day."

That bridge had already caused me nightmares. It was bumper to bumper traffic on the way into the city and I'd started wondering what the weight capacity was for a bridge like that. It was nothing like the Sydney Harbour which was so much steel and concrete it could probably withstand a hurricane, if Australia ever had such a thing.

I'm about to say so when a bell chimes. It rings loud in this part of the school as if a speaker for it is on one of the most immediate walls. Veronica smiles and says, "That's the first warning. Let's the kids know they need to get a move on if they expect to get to class on time."

I return her smile and nod. "Go Dad. I'll be fine and I'll give you a call if I need you to pick me up. Otherwise I'll see you at home when you finish work."

SPIRIT TALKER

He sighs and leans forward, tugging me into a quick hug. "You have a good day. I'll see you later."

The admin door swings closed behind him and I head in the other direction.

As suspected, the map leaves much to be desired when it comes to actually being able to find my way. Spatial skills were not one of my strengths and the only reason I had passed orientation in primary school was because of Erica. Sure, her dyslexia meant she might not have my fluency with the written word, but it gave her spatial superpowers. That girl could find true north by instinct.

A pang of homesickness sweeps through me at the memory. I itched to pull out my phone and text her but knew we'd both be in trouble if a teacher spotted me.

The passages between buildings start to clear as more time passes following the first bell. I turn another corner, looking for the maths wing that should have been here but through door after door all I see are science labs set with long tables decked out with Bunsen burners. I jump, as an aged wooden chalk duster flies out of a classroom door just inches from me. It clatters to the ground with a loud thud but when I look down it's gone. I glance into the classroom. At the front, standing in front of a state-of-the-art electronic white board is a nun. She's in full habit with squinty eyes that glare at me. "Tabitha Myers, you're late, again. Six demerits!" she snarls at me.

This is not a catholic school.

I step back from the door and into another student. She reaches out to catch me and we almost both go over. She's quick though, stepping out to correct our balance.

"Sorry," she says, "didn't mean to bowl you over." Her smile is warm and the golden flecks in her hair look sun-warmed, but the darker roots and eyebrows are proof of chemical alteration. She glances down at the map and timetable in my hand. "You new?" she asks.

I nod. "Yeah."

"Where you headed?" We stand together, just a few feet from the science room where the nun still glares at me. I try to tune out the scrape of her discontented voice.

I point down at the timetable. "Math, 2A. It says Andrews, AU8."

"Great, you're headed the right direction. I'm right next door, come on or we'll be late." She tilts her head in the direction she wants to lead me and we fall into hurried step together. "I'm Georgia, by the way."

"Sara," I tell her.

"Where are you coming from?"

I smile. "That obvious that I'm a transplant?"

She laughs. "Not at all, but then everyone new is, right?"

"Yeah, I guess."

"So?" she asks again, probing.

"East Sydney."

"Man, that's so awesome. I'm Perth-bred. I wish I'd seen more of the world but the only claim to fame I have is airports. Then again, I've seen quite a few of those."

"If you've seen airports then you must have been places."

"Sometimes I think my parents go places just for the airports. I mean yeah, we're always headed someplace but they like to stack up on the layovers. They say it saves in travel fees." I glance at her. She's looking at me and rolls her eyes. "Parents."

I smile, already liking her. "My dad does things cheap too."

"Not this though," she says, gripping the cuff of my blouse. "Brand new. You know you'd have paid a third if you'd gone second hand."

"But then we wouldn't get a couple of years out of it," I reply, giving her a wink. She laughs again.

We turn another corner before the signs on the wall start making actual sense. "Okay," Georgia says, "This is it. The school works by separating subjects to buildings. You'll start to get the hang of that as you learn your way around."

I nod, glancing down at the map and then up at the classroom numbers.

"This is you. Math 2A. I'm next door, 3B. But hey, math is math, right?"

"You'd think so."

I glance into my class. The desks inside are almost all full. I swallow, realising the teacher is already at the front of the room and the class looks like they're ready to get started. "Are we late?" I whisper to Georgia before she can reach her room.

"Almost," she whispers back with another wink. "You'll do great! See you after, or if I don't then come find me at recess and I'll show you around some more. We have third and fourth together."

A warmth fills me from the belly outward. "Thanks Georgia. It's really great to meet you."

She lifts two fingers to give me a quick salute before she pushes open her classroom door and strides inside. "Morning, plebes. Let's get this party started," she says to her classmates. Her words are greeted by a general chuckle.

SPIRIT TALKER

Before stepping into my own class, I hear her teacher say, "Just take a seat Miss Harper."

I take a breath and push open my class door. All eyes turn to me.

The teacher at the front looks like he might be in his early thirties. He's just starting to lose hair at the front, but he greets me with a smile. "Ah, here she is," he says to the whole class. "Everyone, this is our new student, Sara Brooks. Welcome to Math 2A, Sara. I'm Mr Ryan. Take a seat." He waves to one of the two remaining chairs. "Did they get you the right book?"

I sit down and tug open my backpack, digging inside for the math-book that had come in the stack Dad had ordered before we'd arrived. I lift the cover to show him.

"That's the one. Page seventy-two, everyone," he says.

Already the kids have started to turn their attention away from me as they all flip to the correct page in their books. As introductions to class go that was surprisingly smooth. I can only hope the rest of the day goes as well. And, if I can keep it together, not get shouted at by any more there-not-there nuns, and figure out where to find Georgia at lunch, I might just survive my first week at this school.

6

When the bell for recess sounds, I follow the flow of students. Many seem to be headed in the same direction and given that we share a grade it seems safe to assume they are heading either for the canteen or the quad. Because of the crush it's easier to ignore the odd face or two of my hallucinations in the crowd although, it is kind of disconcerting to see them merging and moving through real people.

The canteen proves to be way fancier than it had been in my last school. This is much more organised. They even call it a cafe rather than a canteen. A smooth flow of students moves through to order their lunches. They process a quick payment system with zero scramble for cash. That meant my jangle of coins probably wouldn't be welcome. I'd have to check in with Dad to see if he'd accounted for me ordering food from time to time. Fortunately, we'd both accounted for first day jitters and I'd brought a packed lunch.

I pull an apple out of my pack and take a bite as I move past the cafe. I try to ignore the homeless man sleeping on the steps outside. People keep walking right through him so he's not even really there. I step around him and continue to walk through the school.

The main oval takes up the largest space in the school grounds. An old ball bounces by my leg and a girl dashes over to grab it. Her ponytail is so high that the column of her hair dances from side to side as she jogs. But as I watch her, and the way she moves, I notice the blurry edges. Her shorts are bright pink instead of school standard and she's wearing a crop top that would probably get her in trouble if she were actually real.

"Ball?" she asks, pointing to it at my feet as if expecting me to pick it up and give it to her.

I glance around me. No one is paying any attention, but I still feel too self-conscious to actually do it. After all, if it's crazy to talk to your hallucinations then it's probably crazy to pick up their ball for them. I turn away, hating the thud in my gut of feeling like I'd snubbed someone. If she'd been real, then I'd probably have made an enemy for life and that's not the way I wanted to start the school year. But she wasn't real.

I continue walking along the pathways through the school, hoping to see Georgia's face, or at least catch her hair, among the crowds of kids. I don't make it more than halfway through the school before I start to think more about getting to my next class, but I begin to notice patterns in the way they've arrange the buildings. Subjects are centralised in buildings, just as Georgia had said. I feel a sense of relief. It might not be as difficult as I'd first imagined when it comes to finding my way.

The warning bell sounds and I glance down at my watch. I'd spent the whole break wandering around trying to figure out my way through this maze of a school. Instead of looking for Georgia, I check my map and head for the Mills Building. The map marks it as art, home ec. and languages. I figure it's probably a safe bet that my next class, Japanese, would be one of the rooms there. The second bell sounds just as I find a beautiful, terraced garden. A sign shows the Mills Building is just beyond.

Sadly, I glance at the garden, wishing I had more time to explore, but languages wait for no man, or woman, and I am already late for class. I rush up the steps, find my room, and manage to slide into an empty seat just as the teacher walks into the classroom.

I hadn't even taken note of the students as I'd come in, so I'm surprised when I feel a light jab in my shoulder. "Sara!" a voice hisses over my shoulder in a half whisper.

The teacher's head snaps up. I glance back to see Georgia's warm smile and the soft end of her pencil poking me. I throw her a quick wave but turn my attention back to the front of the room. The teacher is already addressing the class in an animated, fluent flow of Japanese.

"Pair with me," Georgia whispers behind me. I'd only just started to figure out what the teacher is saying so I'm grateful to be pulled into Georgia's circle as everyone pairs up. I'd done a year of Japanese at my old school which is why my Dad had selected it when choosing my classes, but I still felt leagues behind the others who seem to understand every word of the directives our teacher is giving.

Students pair up by skirting their chairs around the room. Georgia grabs hers and drags it forward so that she can sit beside me at my desk.

"I didn't see you at recess," she says.

"I took a walk around the school," I reply, "but I couldn't find you."

"We usually hang out in the Agora." She waves her hand at the window which overlooks the terraced garden I'd crossed to reach the Mills Building.

"I must have just missed you. I crossed it to get here."

She nods.

"*Nihonjin, redīsu,*" our teacher says behind us, reminding us to speak Japanese. I jump in my seat, and glance over my shoulder. I hadn't noticed her walking through the aisles.

"*Gomen'nasai,*" I apologise. I tuck my head and flip pages in the textbook in front of me to look busy until she walks away. Then, I glance at Georgia and whisper, "What are we supposed to be doing?" Georgia helps me find my page in the textbook and we start practising verses of conversation about choosing flowers in a flower market. I have no idea why that might ever be practical, but I don't want to assume it won't be on the test at the end of term.

By the end of the class I realise I'm not as far behind as I'd thought. There are sections of the textbook I haven't covered, but with a little help I can catch up. Georgia seems particularly fluent compared to our peers. As we pack our things into our bags, ready to head to our next class, she smiles and hands me my pen.

"You did well today," she says.

I tug the folded page of my timetable out of my pocket as I reply, "Not as well as you. I'd almost think Japanese is your first language."

She laughs and tosses her hair off her shoulder before pulling the strap of her backpack over it. "Might as well be," she says, "the airport I'm most familiar with is Narita International in Tokyo. My mother travels there for work."

"Tokyo? As in Japan?"

Georgia waves to some of the other students as we head out of the classroom. She leads the way and I remember she'd said we shared third and fourth period, so I fall into step beside her, trusting she knows the way. "Yeah," she says, "but like I said, my only claim to fame is the airports."

"But you've been to Japan!"

"Sure, and the Narita looks like pretty much every other airport in the world. If you've seen chrome and concrete in Sydney, then you've seen it pretty much everywhere."

I shake my head. "Trust me, I've seen chrome and concrete in almost every airport in Australia, but I'd give all four of my wisdom teeth to see even just that in any other country in the world."

"Come on, let's get to music before I tell you how boring every airport in every country is," she says, shaking her head. We walk together down a covered walkway to the Beasley building and I'm glad Georgia and I share the next class too.

We both find a place toward the back of the room and I manage to go another hour without becoming the centre of attention. I have to concentrate to ignore the droning soprano vocal stylings of a woman with a poodle-perm bleached white. She wears a frothy pink, off-the-shoulder dress with a giant bow and matching slippers. She also sings at the top of her lungs, for pretty much the full hour, and she glares at the rest of us, particularly me.

Given that our vocal coach, and the rest of the class, seem completely oblivious of her I put her in the 'not really there' category and try to pretend I can't hear her, but it gets harder and harder as time passes. When the bell sounds for lunch I sigh in relief. More than once I'd been sorely tempted to tell the soprano to shut up, but I'd held the crazy at bay. At least enough that I wasn't outing it in front of my classmates. I dart out of the door before Georgia even has a chance to grab her bag. I try to put some distance between myself and the still droning caterwaul.

SPIRIT TALKER

"Hey, Sara! Wait up," Georgia calls from the door. I rest my back on the wall outside, tipping my head back. "Not a fan of choir practice?" she asks.

I take a breath and adjust the straps of my backpack. "If music weren't a staple of this school, I'd have dropped it completely," I admit. I rub my temple with two fingers and then pinch the bridge of my nose. "Can an hour off-key give you a migraine?"

She chuckles. "Miss Carnelian can give even the most dedicated student a migraine. She's so exacting. But you didn't suck, so you have that going for you." I blink open my eyes and she winks at me. "Come on, let's get some food in you. You'll feel better after you've eaten."

Georgia leads the way back to the Agora and crosses to a section of the terrace where a couple of other girls are already unpacking sushi and panini from their café orders.

"Here we are," she says, waving me toward them. "Sara, I'd like you to meet my friends, Synthe and Jenn."

Synthe, a tall redhead with a scatter of freckles, glances up from her sushi and fixes me with a blue-green gaze. She lifts an eyebrow. "New?" she asks, as if it isn't obvious. I nod.

The other girl, Jenn, dark haired and dark skinned, almost drops her panini as she dances up and moves in for a hug. She keeps hold of the food in one hand as she wraps her other around me. I awkwardly return the motion and try to remember that normal people do this. Not me, but normal people.

"Hi, Sara!" Jenn says. She's a bubble of energy. "Welcome to Perth Modern. How's your first day going?"

Before I can answer Georgia waves me to a spot on the wall beside them and answers for me. "We just got done with music. She's not a fan."

Synthe snorts but Jenn smiles. "I wasn't a fan at first either, but you know vocal can be pretty fun if you let it. Miss Carnelian is a bit of a nightmare, but she knows how to get the most out of every voice in the room."

"You would say that," Georgia says, "you're one of her star pupils."

Jenn pouts. "I'm not a teacher's pet if that's what you're implying."

Georgia raises her hands, balancing her lunch bag on her lap. "Not at all, just that some students are actually here for the music program. You're one of them."

With a smile, Jenn nods. "Yeah, I guess. Although I never really took it seriously until I got here. There's just something magical about being part of a group, you know?"

"But you can be part of a group in pretty much anything, can't you?" I ask.

A wave of emotion hits me from Synthe's direction and I glance at her, noticing an odd look on her face. I'm not sure what I'm sensing but I can't help feeling the girl wants to say something derogatory. Georgia jumps in before she can, "Well, there are all kinds of groups but in this school being part of music is part of belonging to the school culture."

"So, you all love music?" I ask.

Georgia shakes her head. "Oh no, that's just Jenn. The rest of us are rebels." She winks at Synthe who lifts a shoulder. I can't tell if her reaction is resignation or resentment. Maybe both.

She swallows the bite of sushi and says, "We each have our own thing."

I pull my lunch out of my backpack and rest my bag against the wall. "What's your thing?" I ask, curious but also hoping I might break down the other girl's walls. She has what seems like an amazing perimeter defence system, but I'm a disarming kind of person. At least I had been before the crazy. Maybe I still could be. Hopefully, I can get her on my side.

She glances at me, expertly lifts another segment of sushi to her lips with her chopsticks and chews carefully before replying. "Drama." Of course.

"Synthe is Perth's next Heath Ledger."

Synthe shakes her head. "If I follow in anyone's footsteps it's Isla Fisher. I'm not doing the whole 'tragic end' thing."

"Yeah," Jenn says, "Synthe has her whole path laid out. All the way to L.A."

"From Home and Away to Hollywood then on to international stardom," Georgia adds. Synthe glares at them both but says nothing.

I turn to Georgia. "What about you?"

She looks at me, playing with the crust of her sandwich. "What about me?" she asks.

"Well, everyone has their thing, right? Jenn is here for the music. Synthe for drama. What brings you to Perth Modern?"

"Oh!" Georgia says, "I do a little of everything."

Jenn nods. "Georgia is the ultimate all-rounder. She's literally good at absolutely everything."

Georgia flushes. "Well, I didn't say I was good at it all. Just that I don't like to settle into any one thing. I dabble."

"But you are good at everything," Jenn repeats. She takes a bite of her panini. Georgia lifts a shoulder in a carefree shrug. Jenn swallows, then adds, "Although, if any one thing was your thing then it's that thing they don't even do here."

"What thing?" I ask, curious. This school did pretty much everything so I couldn't imagine what it might be missing.

Georgia drops her chin, for the first time looking almost embarrassed. Jenn leans forward, answering for her. "Georgia is a figure skater."

A flush of excitement bubbles through me. "Oh wow, you're not serious!" I swear my voice rises an octave with each word.

Georgia looks up at me. Maybe she's trying to judge exactly what my excitement is about. Synthe looks at me too, her gaze narrowed as she tries to figure out if I'm making fun of her friend. Georgia nods. "Yeah, I guess I like to skate."

"Roller or ice?" I ask.

Synthe snorts. "As if ice skating is even a real sport in Australia. Who the hell would want to freeze their asses off for fun?"

Georgia chuckles. She's got a point. "Yeah, roller-skating. It's epic. I love it."

"Me too!"

Georgia's face brightens and around the mouthful of sandwich she'd started chewing, she grins.

"Really?" she says. Her mouth is still kind of full, so it comes out in an odd slur. She chuckles, focuses on chewing, and swallows before adding, "You have to come with us on Saturday. We all do it."

I look at Jenn and Synthe. Jenn nods with enthusiasm but Synthe doesn't seem that keen. I can't help wondering what that girl's problem is.

"My dad and I were trying to decide between Morley or O'Connor. They're both about the same distance from our new house," I explain.

"We skate at Rolloways in O'Connor," Jenn says. "Georgia lives closer to Freo anyway and sometimes we skate down South Street from her house."

"You mean up and down. The hills, they are real," Synthe says with a groan.

Georgia laughs. "Calves and quads, Synthe. Calves and quads are what those hills are all about."

"We need them for a decent shooting duck," Synthe replies. She grins and for the first time since I'd joined them, I see a warmth under the iron-cold armour.

"Calves and quads are what skating is all about," I add, hoping maybe through this at least I'd find a way to connect with Synthe. Georgia was the epitome of warmth, Jenn was full of effervescent energy like champagne bubbles, and, if I could get through to Synthe maybe I'd be making the new friend trifecta on my first day. It was a start.

Today I'd done a great job at pretending I was normal. I was even doing a very good impression of being completely oblivious of the guy in leopard print leggings who was riding a unicycle through the planters. I'm keeping my crazy firmly in check.

7

After recess on Tuesday, Georgia points me back to the Mills Building for my first art class. I'd been looking forward to it since I'd seen my class schedule the day before. They'd scheduled me for a double session on Tuesday, so I have just shy of two blissful hours of creative work today. And after the lazy drone of my new history teacher and the brain-numbing bio class, I am more than ready to let go of the academics.

The classroom is bright and airy. Its windows look out over the covered walkway and the main oval beyond. The teacher, an elderly woman with a frizz of purple hair, wears a paint-stained apron and splattered tennis shoes. "Sara Brooks?" she asks, fixing me with slightly misty hawk-eyes. "You must be Sara Brooks. My goodness dear, come in, come in. I've so looked forward to meeting you, young lady."

"You have?" I ask, curious as she takes my arm.

"Yes, yes. I'm not one for school transcripts. It is the arts you see. So, when I saw your name joining my class list, I got in touch with your last teacher who sent over some photographs of your work, oh and that lovely article from the Herald. So prestigious."

I flush at the gush of admiration in her words. This teacher really had done her digging. How embarrassing. The article, with a quarter spread photograph of my painting, had been for the landscape I'd painted over a year ago. It had won best of show in the junior category. Mum and Dad had both been over the moon. A pang of pain washes over me as I remember.

"Oh dear, please don't blush like that. Learn to accept the acknowledgement. Your artwork truly shines, dear. I'm delighted to be able to guide you further in your journey. You have true talent and a wonderful eye for detail. I suppose that comes from your family."

I dip my head. "I suppose it does. My father is an architect and my aunt, Tara, is a photojournalist. They both have fantastic eyes for detail." I can hear the suffusion of pride in my own voice.

"And your mother dear?"

I glance at the floor, taking a breath. "She was a social historian. She liked to study mythology."

I can't help noticing how our conversation is catching the gaze of some of my fellow students. They look curious rather than envious or resentful. Most collect a small stash of art supplies, brushes, jars, and paints, before finding their way to seats in front of easels. Some settle right back into their work as if they hadn't left it. Clearly, they'd all been working on something long before I'd arrived at the school.

"Ah, yes, yes. The subject matter of the soul that work is. Not so direct a creative outlet as art, design, or photography but full of imagination and wonder, just the same." She guides me toward the back of the room. "Now, let me get you settled. I'm Mrs Martha, by the way." She winks at me. "I don't stand to none of this last name nonsense, but the school insists on the honorific, so I'm stuck with at least that."

I nod, letting the rush of her chatter wash over me. It was soothing in a strange way. Like watching a hummingbird. She never stopped moving and chatting. Even as we passed students she would glance at their work and pause to compliment or suggest as she went. She had a lovely energy about her. Warm, confident, and compellingly engaging. Even when she was critiquing an artwork and offering direction, she did it in a matter of fact way that left no room for hurt feelings but only a desire to grow.

We reach a long bench at the back of the room and she pushes a jar of brushes into my hand then shows me to one of the few chairs remaining near the front of the room. One chair beside mine is empty too but there's an easel and blank pad of paper set in front of it as if another student could join us at any moment.

The paper in front of my seat is blank too. Beside each easel is a small stand. I put the brushes down on it and run a finger over the blank page. It's coarse, thick, and dry. Mrs Martha smiles at me and touches my arm with her aged fingers. "Can you guess?"

I nod. "Watercolour."

She seems to beam even brighter. "Yes, yes. Now, it's not in honour of your landscape, I assure you. I set the medium when I outlined the term plans at the beginning of the year. But it is such a delight to welcome you with what I understand is your own favourite medium."

She places a jar of water on the stand next to my brushes and disappears to the back of the room again. She comes back moments later with a teak box held with cherish in her hands.

"Now," she adds, passing me the box, "we don't dictate subject matter in my class. You're welcome to paint whatever at all you like. Let your heart guide you. I'm sure it will be marvellous."

I open the small box of paints. The tubes inside are already well used, clearly by multiple hands, although not to the point of depletion. They were top of the line paints too, not the cheaper tutorial paints my old school had provided.

Before Mrs Martha fades away, she fixes me with a firm eye. "We give a lot of artistic license in this class, dear, but we do have one very strict rule." She pauses, making sure I'm paying attention.

"One rule?" I prompt.

She smiles, softening the measure of command that had come over her. "No talking." She pauses again and I nod to confirm. Then, she chatters on again, "You see, language, as wonderful as it is, is the domain of the left hemisphere." She taps her head. "To think the words to speak you let go of the free flow of your artistic, creative mind. So, while you paint in this classroom we listen to music and keep language to as bare a minimum as possible."

I smile at her and nod. "I understand. Thank you."

"I'll leave you to it then. Paint well, Sara."

She crosses to the front of the room and I notice, resting on her desk, a small record player. She draws a record out of its sleeve and sets it onto the player. A melody of soft, classical, piano fills the room. I run my fingers over the paint tubes and let my mind wander as Mrs Martha flutters through the room. She dips in and out with the other students. Even the soft lilt of her voice, speaking softly from time to time with other students, fades to the edges of my mind.

I feel a warm glow as I browse the range of colours in the paint box. My mind is already beginning to explore the potential subject matter I can paint with this array. I close my eyes and let my mind open itself to my imagination. Images flit across my thoughts. My mother's face keeps jumping to the front. I push it back, burying it with beaches, with trees, with animals, with city lights, with any host of a thousand different images that hurt less.

I startle, almost dropping the box when someone leans in close beside me and whispers in my ear. "So, what will you paint?" he asks.

I look up, then glance around the room hoping no one noticed the way I had almost jumped out of my chair. Everyone else seems to be absorbed by their work, thank goodness.

I try to pretend he isn't there but Grae swivels his long legs into the chair beside me. "You wouldn't imagine the eternity I have spent looking for you, Sara Brooks. This monstrous facility is as a maze to a rat."

I flick my gaze to him, then instantly return it to my blank page. A big part of me is suddenly tempted to paint him. He had the kind of features that lend themselves to portraiture. Although if I were to paint him, I'd want to do it in acrylics. They'd let me capture the colour of his eyes better. I flush, pushing the thought out of my head and instead focus on feathering my brushes. I start with a light wash over the page, trusting the instinct deep inside me that always seems to know what to paint.

We sit together, almost companionably, as I let the thick brush do the work. Grae watches its strokes too. Rhythmic, smooth, almost effortless. I smile, smelling the paint and feeling the soft wood in my fingers. I'd missed this.

Beside me, Grae falls into easy chatter. It was different this time. Different to the way he'd talked ceaselessly of his beautiful Ella-May the

SPIRIT TALKER

first night we'd met. He wasn't crafting poetry or trying to come off as charming or even endearing. He was just talking, like a normal guy, about growing up, about his family, about normal, everyday things…

Except they were normal and every day in the 18th century. And yet, somehow, that was okay too. The more I paint and listen the more I find I enjoy hearing him talk. The soft twang of his English accent gives him an air of exotic in the most mundane of ways. Practically everyone in Australia had some connection to British descent, including me, but there was something cultured in the way he phrased his words.

"And that is when the bucket flew from the window," he says. "The whole privy, not just the slosh, which I don't suppose would have been better. But I assure you, being brained by a bucket of refuse causes one, inevitably, to be just as covered in the innings as one would had its contents been upended upon one."

I can't help snorting with laughter. My brush smears a little and I wince, quickly swiping at the stray dribble of paint before it can mar the page. I glance around, hoping no one else in the class noticed my outburst.

All I needed was for someone to notice 'the crazy girl' laughing to herself as she makes a mess of her painting. Fortunately, everyone was just as absorbed in their own work as they'd ever been. There was something restful in that. Chatter among students was strictly forbidden and that, somehow, meant everyone really zoned in on their own artwork.

I glance down the row, noticing the general high quality of the work. The girl beside me is painting a dog from a photograph. It is a Scottish terrier. The colouring will make for a challenging water colour because its fur is so dark against the blank page, but the girl seems to be layering beautifully. The character of the animal is really starting to show through in the painting.

"Tis a lovely painting. Have you decided on your own subject matter?" Grae asks. I flinch as I realise he's leaning over me to look at my neighbour's painting. I shake my head but refuse to voice an answer. Fortunately, the no talking rule made it easier to refrain from responding to my hallucination.

Mrs Martha had settled into a seat at the front of the class with her own painting before her. From time to time she glances up at her students. The soft, classical music that fills the room covers the sound of brush strokes and clatter but wouldn't mask a conversation.

SPIRIT TALKER

Grae doesn't seem affronted by my lack of verbal response. "If I could find the words to do it justice, I would describe the pond where once I picnicked with my Ella-May. So too her face. What wonder it would be if only one had thought to capture that before it was lost."

Again, he goes into raptures over his Ella-May. I roll my eyes and bite down on my urge to mutter a derogatory comment.

"I see you, Sara Brooks. You think me a witless, lovelorn fool. But had you known her sweetness you would mourn the loss of her lovely face too."

The edge of my mouth tilts up as I try to imagine mourning a lovely face. I glance at Grae's. Well, I suppose I can imagine it. And without even realising it I find I'm sketching the lines of his face on my page. I sigh, resigned. As soon as he had shown up and sat down beside me, I knew, even if I didn't want to, that I'd end up painting him.

And maybe water colours were the perfect medium after all. Because, even if they couldn't quite capture the vividness of his eyes, everything else about him was soft and subdued. Like ageing paper. And wouldn't it be a shame if no one thought to capture that before it was lost.

8

Dad pushes the glass door open to the waiting room at the psychiatrist's office. I can already feel the pit of dread in my gut.

The idea of talking about what was going on freaks me out. When it had first started, we'd been to see someone, but with Mum's death so fresh they'd assured us that it was normal to feel like I'd been feeling. Now, more than six months later, it is clear this isn't normal, but I'm not looking forward to having my unique brand of crazy confirmed.

The waiting room is lined with purple chairs. Soft lamplight gives the grey walls a yellowed hue. The reception desk is empty but there's a sign there inviting patients to take a seat if they have an appointment. Or to leave a message with a phone service if they do not.

I glance at Dad as he takes a seat, then look at the closed door. "We wait?"

He nods. "We're a little early. Your appointment is on the half hour. I'm sure the doctor will be out when it's time."

I take a seat next to him and draw my bag of gaming dice from my pocket. I fidget with the dice in my hands as we wait. They are warm. The dark green lets only a hint of light through to show off the flecks of black swirls in their pattern. Feeling them in my hands helps give me a sense of grounding so I can ignore the silence of the waiting room.

Beside me, Dad flips through something on his phone. It's probably his email. Any time there is some sort of down time, waiting time, he finds something productive to do, like work. I sigh, flipping the D20 between my fingers and letting it roll into the palm of my hand. My palm isn't a flat enough surface to do a true roll, so it ends up balancing between numbers.

About ten minutes later, the door across from us opens and an older man, perhaps in his late fifties, steps out. His hair is leaning toward ash and he's got more than a few lines of life etched on his face. One hand rests on the shoulder of a tall boy. I avert my gaze, realising the person with him is our neighbour, Will.

"You take care, Will, and I'll see you again next week. Remember what we talked about, okay?"

Will doesn't answer. Out of the corner of my eye I see him shrug off the doctor's touch. He keeps his gaze fixed on the floor as he crosses the room and slams his hands into the door. The glass shudders as the door swings open. I can't help wondering if he'd even noticed my Dad and I sitting there.

The doctor does. He smiles at me. There's a warmth in the crinkle around his eyes. I flush under his gaze, fumble my dice back into their bag, and slip them back into my pocket. "You must be Sara," he says, then looks to my father. "Mr Brooks, thank you for contacting me. I look forward to working with your daughter."

Dad shifts on his feet, looking unsure of himself. "Thank you Dr. Hymore. I appreciate you fitting us into your schedule."

"Certainly. Now, you're welcome to wait out here, but our session is for a full hour so if there is something you'd like to do you can return at five thirty and she'll be ready for you."

SPIRIT TALKER

Dad looks a little displaced at the idea of leaving me there. I'm not too thrilled about it either. "He can't stay?" I ask.

Dr Hymore looks at me. There's a well of understanding in his eyes. "If you feel you could not participate without him, Sara, then of course, he can stay. But I've found most people, especially teenagers, feel more comfortable opening up when the people they love aren't in the room. I want you to feel you can tell me everything that is happening for you and I know you might not want to reveal the all of it to your father yet."

I swallow, glance at Dad, and then nod. He's right. My Dad doesn't know the full of it and doesn't need to. As weird as the idea of going into a room with this old dude alone might feel, if it's going to work it needs to happen without my Dad.

"Is that alright with you, Sara? You know you can tell me anything and if you'd like me to stay, I'm more than ready to do that." I can tell Dad actually really wants to stay. He doesn't like the idea of me revealing things to a total stranger and him being kept out of the loop.

"I'll be okay, Dad," I tell him, hoping he'll understand. He deflates and I feel a wave of guilt.

He swallows, then nods. "Okay then. I'll be right out here if you change your mind." He smiles and I can tell by the crease around his eyes that he doesn't really feel happy. "I've got some work I can do while I wait."

I nod and turn back to Dr Hymore who waves a hand to show me through the door. His office is surprisingly modern and chic. He has a feature brick wall painted white with black and white decorative prints. The couch, soft grey suede, looks comfortable. The small glass coffee table in front of it is scattered with a range of fidget toys and a box of tissues.

Dr Hymore moves to sit in his own seat, facing the longer couch. "Please," he says, his hand inviting me to the chair opposite him. "Take a seat."

He picks up a pad of paper from the side table next to his chair and turns the page. I pull the pillow into my lap and try to avoid looking at the notepad. I hate that part. It feels like being dissected, studied. But the last psychiatrist I'd talked to had written things down too.

"I keep notes during our time together so that we can refer back to any points of interest in our sessions. It's an important way to keep track of our progress and ensure nothing is missed, forgotten, or left undone."

I nod, understanding, but not feeling any more comfortable about the idea.

SPIRIT TALKER

He smiles, another soft wattage of reassurance. "I assure you, Sara. Everything you say here is completely confidential. I'm sure you understand that doctors have a strict code of conduct. The only time information might be revealed is if I feel you or someone close to you is in immediate danger and even then, only the threat is made known, not the details behind it."

I nod again and swallow. "I'm not dangerous," I tell him. At least, I didn't feel dangerous. And the hallucinations hadn't been trying to get me to do anything dangerous. They'd just been a little scary, sometimes.

I think of Grae. And of the boy in my neighbour's yard. And of the old lady at the letter box. More and more they'd felt less scary. But even when they'd had their faces melted off like the soldier in the street, they hadn't been dangerous.

"So," Dr Hymore says, bringing me back to the room. "Tell me what brings you here, Sara."

"My Dad told you," I say.

He nods. "He did, and the referral your last psychiatrist gave included more information, but I'd like to hear from you. Sometimes the people who worry about us don't know the full story."

I take a breath; not sure I want to open up to him. Who was he really anyway?

"Sara," he says, sensing my resistance. "You'll only get out of your time here what you put in. You've been referred to me because I'm someone who can help you. But this will only work if you can be willing to do the work. You have to want to get better."

I snap my head up to him, fixing him with my gaze. "I do want to get better."

He smiles, holding his pen poised. I can't help feeling like he's trying to 'handle' me. And I resent him for it. "Well then," he says, his voice calm and carefully controlled. "Why are you here?"

I take a deep breath and let it out in a long sigh before beginning. I keep my gaze averted as I talk, which I guess doesn't matter because although he looks up at me frequently, he also looks to his notepad a lot. I'm not sure if it's better or worse when he's looking at me. Even so, I begin, because that's kind of the whole point in being here. Besides, I really do want to get better. And this is where crazy people go to get better.

"I see things," I begin, not really sure how to describe what I'd been experiencing.

Dr Hymore nods, his pen poised rather than writing. "Tell me about what you see, Sara."

"Well," I say, "It began a few months ago. After my mother died." I pause, searching for the words. "The first time was just after, in the hospital.

SPIRIT TALKER

Dad had gone to bring the car around to take me home and I was waiting just inside the lobby. A man came through the front door of the hospital. Except, the doors never opened. He just walked right through them like they weren't there." I pause, taking a ragged breath, then add, "He was broken and twisted." I swallow, trying to get the image of him out of my head. It clung there, like murky tar, creating a haze over the room. It was as if just by remembering it the memory could swallow me whole and take me back there. I remembered everything about that moment. I remembered everything about how helpless I'd felt. How horrified. How I'd wanted to scream and run, but I'd wanted to help him at the same time.

I realise I'm crying and that I'd been quiet for a long minute when Dr Hymore leans forward in his chair and reaches the box of tissues toward me. I drag a breath into my lungs and take a tissue from the box.

"Take your time, Sara. Tell me what you saw."

I shake my head. "Does it even matter what I saw? It wasn't real. He wasn't there. He couldn't have been alive. More of him was hanging out of him than was held inside. He practically tripped over his own intestines. And people can't walk right through closed doors. They can't."

Dr Hymore nods but waits patiently as I crumple the tissue between my fingers and try to wrangle my breath. I still, realising I'd been rocking in place, and force myself to pull it together. When I don't continue the doctor says, "Was there anything else you remember, Sara? You saw him, did you hear him?"

I shake my head. "No, that time I just saw it. And then Dad's car pulled up outside, so I ran past it and we went home."

"You say, 'that time'. Does that mean there have been other occasions when you did hear things?"

I fix my gaze on the rug, noticing the soft, plush fabric in blue-grey, like warm marble. It would be a pretty colour for dice.

"Sara?" Dr Hymore prompts when I don't answer right away.

Slowly, I nod. "More and more," I admit, feeling the dread of that truth hitting me in the gut. "More and more since my mother died. At first, I just saw things occasionally. But now it happens pretty much all the time. And I hear things. Sometimes I smell things." I lift my gaze to his as I say the part that had really started to scare me, "Now, they talk to me."

Dr Hymore nods, meeting my gaze for a moment before dropping it to scrawl on the notepad. He'd made notes a time or two as I described what I'd seen but now his hand moved in a rapid flow as he made paragraphs of notes. I wonder what I'd said that had triggered the flood.

Eventually, he looks up at me again. "And Sara, how do you know that what you see, what you hear and smell, how do you know those things are not really there?"

I sigh, thinking about them in a flicker of instances, remembering. "Sometimes it's because no one else sees them or hears them. Sometimes they've got fuzzy edges. Sometimes the light goes right through them." I pause, letting myself think of the little signs. "Sometimes it's harder to know. It can feel so real. But there's always something, something that's not quite right about what I'm seeing."

I sense more than see the way he nods as I speak. I keep my gaze fixed on a point in front of me rather than looking at him. "Do you ever not know?" he asks.

My chest feels tight and I don't want to answer right away. Dr Hymore seems to guess that, but he lets the silence stretch between us. Eventually, it starts to feel even more uncomfortable, so I dip my chin, twice, in a simple nod.

"Sara, what you're describing is not uncommon for those experiencing significant grief," Dr Hymore begins.

He seems like he's about to say more but I cut him off. "But it's been more than six months, doctor. And it's getting worse, not better."

"I understand that," he replies. "But I want you to understand that having these experiences doesn't mean anything is wrong with you. It's easy to think, when our minds are playing tricks on us like this, that we are broken."

"Like I'm going crazy?" I say with a wry half-smile.

He nods, his hazel eyes full of compassion, "Yes, just like that. I want you to know, there can be many reasons this is happening. I'm glad you and your father arranged for you to see me, because it must be something you're struggling with. It must make day-to-day life challenging." I nod and he continues, "We have lots of tools which will help."

"Tools?" I ask, feeling a flutter of hope. "Things that can make it all go away?"

"Maybe," he says. I can hear the hint of caution in his voice. He places his pen down on the paper and holds my gaze. "I won't make you promises I can't keep, Sara. Every case is different. We won't know immediately if any one thing is working. This will take some time. But I'm very confident that I can help you."

I take another breath, this time letting it fill me up before releasing it. My hands shake and I grip what's left of the ragged, mostly shredded tissue. "I just want to be normal," I mutter, feeling very small.

"Normal is overrated," Dr Hymore says with a grin. "I'm more focused on healthy. Because there is absolutely nothing wrong with being exceptional. Your mental health, that is what I'm focused on."

He seems to note the shreds of tissue in my hand and leans forward with another. I pluck a fresh one out of the box and blot away my tears with a watery smile. Dr Hymore picks up his pen again. He glances at his watch before making a bullet point on the page.

"I'm afraid our time is running out today, Sara, but I want to take a few minutes to talk about what you can do this week, before our next visit."

I sit up a little straighter in the chair and crush the tissues into my fist. "Proactive, I like that," I say, feeling a bubble of hope.

"Yes," Dr Hymore says with a smile. "I want you to keep a log file for me." He reaches into a draw in the side table next to his chair and pulls a small, leather-bound blank journal from inside.

"You mentioned to me that you feel like these hallucinations have been becoming more and more frequent as time passes. That may be the case, but maybe it isn't. It's possible that as you become more and more distressed about what you've been experiencing your mind has been telling you it's happening more when it isn't. So, this week, keep a log," he says, handing me the journal. "Each time you see, or hear, or smell, or experience something you don't believe is there, make a note of it. Note the date, the time of day, where you are, who is with you, and what you experience. If you can, try to also make note of how you were feeling immediately before and how what you experience makes you feel. We'll revisit the log when you come back next week." I nod and he continues, "If you keep up this log while I see you, we'll be able to see if your experiences really are increasing in quantity and if the techniques I teach you in the coming weeks help to reduce their frequency."

"So, journal it?" I ask, running a finger over the beautiful journal. There's a really nice pen with it too. I wonder how much it cost because the measure of it equated in some way to how much my Dad must be paying for my sessions with this doctor.

"Yes, exactly," he says. He makes another note on his pad of paper then places it on the table beside him and rises to his feet. He reaches a hand out to me but I ignore it and push myself up out of the chair.

"Thank you," I say. My words are polite, and in a way, I am thankful, although I'm not entirely sure why. I guess it's just because I feel like we're finally doing something. My Dad, as much as I love him, doesn't really want to face what I'm experiencing. Or maybe he just doesn't know how. Dr Hymore seems to be on my side in this. He wants me to be healthy, to be sane. I want that too.

9

A few days later, as I'm sitting with Georgia, Jenn, and Synthe for lunch, I feel a strange rush of weird. Glancing around I see a vast wave of there-not-there people. I swallow and close my eyes, trying to will them away but I can hear them and smell them. They scream in frenzied panic. Salt and sea air fill every breath. I gasp, feeling my breath tight in my lungs. I gasp, because even with air around me I suddenly feel like I'm drowning. A hand touches my leg and I flinch, pulling away.

"Sara?" Georgia's voice breaks through. "Are you okay?"

I open my eyes and force a smile to my lips. "I, I," I stutter, then draw another breath. The ocean recedes, barely. "I just realised I'd forgotten there are some books I was supposed to check out in the library." I stand, grabbing my bag so fast that my lunch almost scatters to the floor. I scramble, catching it and crumpling the wrapper around my toasted cheese sandwich as I shove it into my backpack.

Georgia's warm smile feels bright, bubbly, and totally at odds with the swamp of smelly, sea-soaked shadows that hover on the edges of my vision. "Just wait," she calls as I turn my back on her. "We'll come with you."

I turn back, shaking my head. "No," I say, probably too fast. "It won't take long. Besides we have music next and, if I'm running late, I'll need you to cover for me."

There's a hint of concern in Georgia's eyes but she doesn't pry. Instead she smiles at me again, filling me up with her light. "Deal, I'll do that. But you better not skip out on me or Miss Carnelian will be the least of your problems."

"I promise," I call back before turning away from the three of them and sprinting across the terrace.

I try not to make a thing of weaving between the strange sea of people flooding the garden, but I imagine I look pretty odd taking an indirect path when the library is basically just across from where we were sitting. Still, I'm glad it's so close because as soon as I pass through the doors of the building things get really quiet again. My breath races. I hadn't run far but my heart thinks I've run a marathon. I glance back through the glass doors behind me. The terrace is scattered with students, nothing more.

I shake my head and try to slow my breath by drawing long, deep lungs full of air. "New brand of crazy," I mutter to myself as I stride past the librarian's desk and make my way to my favourite spot. There was an out of the way isle, a self-help section of sorts, that always remained completely empty. Because, I mean, what teenage in their right mind (or even in their wrong one) would hang out in the self-help section. No one wants to admit they need help. But it felt perfect, in an ironic and twisted kind of way, to write in my journal while my back was stacked up against the latest mental health books by expert psychologists. It made me think of Dr Hymore, and of feeling normal.

Yesterday, I'd become intimately familiar with the school library. It was one of the few places a girl with a leather-bound journal doesn't look out of place. Here, when I need to make notes, I just look like a studious book worm. I'd only made the mistake of taking the journal out anywhere else once. Once was enough to realise how quickly whispers spread in this school. Even something as innocuous as someone writing in a journal sparked rumours. Fortunately, they weren't the "she's crazy" kind that I could really do without. Curiosity wasn't much fun either, but it was better than certainty.

I take a few minutes, scrawling in the journal just as Dr Hymore had requested. I take note of the time and date, the where, the what, the who. I think a little more as I try to remember how I was feeling before. I remember exactly how I felt during and after. The panic still threatens to swallow all of the air in my lungs if I let myself think about it. But before? I thought everything had been normal. I'd just been hanging out with my friends, eating my lunch, everything had been normal. Hadn't it?

"Sara Brooks!"

I smile as I hear Grae's voice greeting me in his soft, clipped, British accent. Then I feel ridiculous for smiling at another hallucination. I flip open a fresh page in my journal but my pen hovers over the paper. It was the first time I'd seen Grae since my appointment with Dr Hymore. I know I'm supposed to write about every hallucination, but I couldn't. I swallow, keeping my pen poised, while I wait for the resistance to fade.

"I have looked the world over twice and then again in search of you this day."

I lift my gaze to his but bite back the urge to ask him why. As if sensing the question on my tongue he continues.

"Did you know, there is a book in this very library called 'The Gas We Pass'," he pauses, looking me dead in the eye and I try not to smile but I can't help it. "It is about flatulence. Can you believe that? And in all measure the book does quite well."

I dip my chin and try not to laugh out loud at the stunned horror on Grae's face. "There are books on almost every subject," I say, pretending I'm talking to myself because I'm not supposed to talk to my hallucinations. I mean, Dr Hymore hadn't said that specifically, but I'm pretty sure it's a thing. Maybe I'll ask him next session.

Grae shakes his head. "Indeed, and it pains me to no end the drivel that has made it to the printed page. So much has been honoured by these archives that is worth not the ink and paper it is printed upon."

Grae lowers himself to the floor beside me. He folds his long legs underneath him and leans forward to stroke his fingers down the length of the leather binding on my journal. I let my gaze linger on the soft cuticles of his fingernails.

"That is a very fine tome, Sara Brooks. Had I its like I would pen many a poem, perhaps even a book within its pages. Is that what you do here?"

I shake my head. I feel his gaze on me and lift my chin to look at his face. His eyes fix me with the depth of an ocean. They remind me of the wave of things I'd seen outside.

Perhaps sensing my discomfort, Grae reaches a hand toward me. I flinch back. "Don't," I whisper. And this time I can't pretend I'm not talking to him.

He flushes, drawing his hand back. He places it on his knee and leans his back against the shelves opposite me. He draws a breath and smiles at me. I feel my own breath catch because even in his aged, worn, and dirty white shirt and blue breeches there's something spectacular about him. It's arresting, as if he'd been pulled perfectly from history's pages, life breathed into him.

"You, my lovely Sara Brooks, are full of so much light that it blinds my heart. I fear that were you to smile you might obliterate my memories of Ella-May."

I blush, drop my chin and gaze, and try to chase down my runaway heartbeat. Guys don't say things like that to me. Hell, guys these days don't say things like that at all.

"And there it is," he whispers. I glance up at him, trying to work out what he was talking about. "Your smile," he says, "starlight captured on a face that should be reserved for heaven." He tilts his head and his eyes wander. "If such a thing even exists."

"You don't believe in heaven?" I ask, then glance around to make sure no one is listening. The last thing I need is for someone to stumble across me sitting in the stacks asking nothing if they believe in heaven.

Opposite me, Grae sighs. "I believe in the inevitable void."

I feel a stab of pain at his simple words. I didn't want to believe in an inevitable void, because then I'd have to believe that my mother was in it. "I prefer to believe that there's something more, something bigger than all of us that we go to after we die."

He gives me a sad smile. "Would you have me go to that place?"

I avert my gaze. He'd implied before that he was dead. I didn't like to think of it but of course, if he were real and not just a hallucination, he must be dead. Or a time traveller. I shake my head and laugh off that thought.

"You find a jest in the thought?" Grae asks, his tone tinged with hurt.

"No," I start. Hurting his feelings was the last thing I wanted to do. I lean forward, reaching out as if I could put a hand on his knee but then I remember he's not really there. My hand freezes mid-air. We both look at it before I snatch it back and rest it in my lap instead. "No," I say again, more calmly, "it was another thought completely."

He seems to think about this for a moment then nods his head. "I would like to hear what errant thought brought you mirth in the midst of such dreary subject matter." His gaze lingers on me. I want to resist answering but something about the waiting expectancy in his expression makes it hard to refuse engaging with him.

"Time travel," I admit.

His lips quirk in his own amusement. He raises an eyebrow. "You think me a time traveller?"

I lift a shoulder in a half shrug. "Well, no, I guess not. You're a hallucination."

He sighs. "Oh, my sweet Sara Brooks. How your mind tries to make sense of everything. It is any wonder that you are not stark raving mad."

"Am I not?" I whisper.

He fixes me with a look. There's something deep in his expression but I can't even begin to guess what he's thinking. Eventually, he sighs, then shakes his head. "I am suddenly craving a return to speaking of flatulence and the idiocy of twenty-first century writers," he says.

I laugh, this time really feeling the warmth of it. It makes me wonder how much I'd really laughed since Mum. "Don't," I say, trying to shake off the way he looks at me. Even when he is joking there is something deep and penetrating in his gaze. It's like he is waiting for me to make sense of something. It's as if he clings to a secret.

Just then, a movement on the periphery of my vision catches both our attention. Simultaneously we glance up and I flush, feeling crimson fill my cheeks.

It's one thing to laugh quietly with a figment of your imagination when no one is watching, but in Will's dark gaze I feel like a moth pinned under a microscope. I wonder how long he's been standing there and I'm about to ask him when he turns and walks away.

He didn't even say anything. Not a wave. Nothing.

What a jerk.

Grae doesn't say anything either. And, as I stare after Will's back, I can't help feeling torn between two worlds. A big part of me wanted to chase after Will. To ask him, well, anything at all. Instead, I glance at Grae, my heart full of confusion.

SPIRIT TALKER

Then I grip my pen in my fingers and begin to write. The date, the time, the location, and the hallucination. Because this wasn't normal, and I do want to get better.

10

y Saturday, Dad had finally hung some curtains around the house, but I still rose with the sun on my face. As my mind wakes to the day, I feel an awakening excitement. It had been months since I'd last skated. Dad had tried to keep up with things while Mum was sick but, after she died, we both kind of let it fade. My heart hadn't been able to find the same joy as before.

A bubble of worry rises within me as I think about it, but I push it aside. No, I'm determined to make things work here. I have to. For Dad.

So, even with doubt gnawing at my stomach, I climb out of bed, shower, dress, and make my way downstairs. Dad is already there with a light fruit muesli breakfast. Energy that doesn't weigh me down.

"Excited?" Dad asks as I drop my skate bag at my feet, sit down at the breakfast counter, and take a bite of the muesli.

I chew on the mouthful before replying. "My new friends from school should be there." It's not really a confirmation of excitement because I'm not really sure if excitement is the right word. But there was at least that to look forward to.

Dad smiles. "Just remember to take it easy today. It's been a while."

"Right," I say, my own smile wry. "Conditioning. These flabby muscles are out of shape." I lift my arm and poke my bicep.

Dad laughs. "Well I wouldn't go that far. But I know you. Once you're there you'll want to stay all day. So, what I'm saying is pace yourself. You want to still be able to stand tomorrow."

I roll my eyes. "Geeze, Dad. I'm not old like you. I'll be fine."

He raises a hand to his heart. "Ouch! Wounded! My own daughter," he says, dramatically.

I shake my head. "You started it."

As we eat together, I keep glancing at my watch. "It's okay, we have plenty of time," Dad says, finishing his food. He starts rinsing his plate.

I hurry to finish too and pass him my bowl the moment it's empty.

Even before he's finished rinsing the dishes I stand and pick up my skates. "But we don't want to be late. It's still a drive away."

Dad shakes his head, but he puts the bowls on the drying rack and picks up the tea towel to dry his hands. "Let's go then."

The drive to the rink doesn't take as long as I expected. It's pretty much straight down the freeway and traffic, headed south on an early Saturday morning, flows smoothly. Outside the rink, several girls queue up next to the door. Georgia, Jenn, and Synthe already have their skates on and instead of queueing they're skating on the smoothest section of the car park near the entrance to the rink. Georgia waves at me and I wave back. I snatch up my skate bag and head in their direction. I completely forget my dad.

"Hey!" he calls behind me. "Aren't you forgetting something?"

I turn back, flushing with guilt. He raises a folded twenty dollar note between two fingers. "Sorry Dad," I say, rushing back to him to take the money. "Thanks for the lift. I'll see you later." There's a moment of hesitation between us. A hint of the awkwardness that had been between us since Mum got sick. It is the pause in our breath that exists where a goodbye hug should be. But instead of stepping forward, I step back. And I hate myself a little on the inside because Dad can't hide the flash of pain that crosses his face.

The look is gone almost instantly, but it was there. Still, he doesn't push, instead he smiles. It's not a full smile, because even with the hurt hidden it's still a gaping wound between us. His voice, a little raspy, says, "Give me a call when you're ready to wrap up."

I swallow, pushing the pit of guilt down into my gut as I nod. "I will," I say. I turn my back on him, but I can feel his eyes on me as I cross the parking lot to join my friends.

"Sara! You made it," Georgia says when I reach them.

"You're skating already?" I ask.

She nods. "We always put our skates on before they open the doors. It means we get to be first on the rink."

"Besides," Jenn says skating up to us both as I take a seat and pull my figure skates out of the bag. "Sometimes we've skated here."

I look at the smooth bitumen. "Are you sure it's good for your skates?"

"Well the hills probably aren't, but we don't wear our figure skates for those. This bit though is pretty smooth," Jenn says.

Synthe glides over to us too and with a perfect t-stop pulls up next to Jenn. She glances over her shoulder, flicking her chin in the direction of my Dad. "That your Dad?" she asks, as if it isn't obvious.

"Yeah," I say, watching him climb into the car. His shoulders are slumped a little. As he starts the engine, he glances at me again and gives me a last smile and wave. I lift my hand in a brief wave back as he drives away.

"It's a nice truck," Synthe says. I'm not sure if she's being serious or sarcastic.

"Thanks," I say, deciding to assume true compliment if only because I want her to be my friend. They say you win more friends with honey so even if Synthe wasn't my greatest fan it made more sense to act as if she liked me. "It's for his work," I tell her.

She nods but I can tell she doesn't really care. I tug on my laces, strapping them up the boot with tight tugs. I knot them off at the top before pulling my boot cover down to my toe stop. I stomp the skate slightly on the ground, feeling the snug fit around my ankle. It felt good, like the best pair of shoes I own. Somehow right.

"These are nice skates," Jenn says, lifting my other boot and admiring it. She flicks a wheel and it spins smoothly on its ball bearings. The leather is still clean and fresh despite being more than a year old. They hadn't seen anywhere near as much wear and tear as my last pair of skates which I'd worn until the heels started rubbing from being a size too small.

"Thanks. Mum and Dad gave them to me for Christmas. I'd desperately needed a new pair. I was rubbing my ankles raw when I outgrew my last pair."

Georgia nods. "You wouldn't believe how many skates I've gone through over the years. My parents swear that if my feet don't stop growing soon, they'll be broke."

I laugh. "Same," I say. It was one of those little white lies that don't mean anything, I tell myself as I say it. Even so, maybe Georgia senses it because she gives me a strange glance. I take the skate from Jenn's hands and push my sock-covered foot inside. I tug the laces tight, tug down the boot cover, and rise to my feet just as the double doors of the rink swing open.

"Come on," Synthe says, darting to the back of the line which is already rapidly moving inside. Most people check in quickly, dropping their lesson fee, accepting their stamp, and heading to the seats or skate counter. Some of the little girls seem to bubble with excitement. Their parents either share it or look in equal parts exhausted or resigned.

Georgia, Jenn, and Synthe go before me, nudging their way through the turnstile and heading straight to the entrance of the rink. The white floor is brightly lit by strong overhead lights. I slip Dad's money across the counter, collect my change and stamp, and skate over to join them. They drop their stuff on a round carpet-covered bench and almost in unison head out onto the smooth, painted concrete.

I take a moment longer. Although it had been months since I'd skated it feels natural to have wheels on my feet again. Even so, I take a moment to tuck Dad's money into my wallet and bury that in the bottom of my bag.

I pull out my water bottle and stand at the edge of the rink as I take a sip. Georgia, Jenn, and Synthe laugh together with an older large-bodied lady. She must be our instructor. Even given her size she moves with grace and precision on her skates. She seems to have true energy and life. As if being there is everything that matters in the world. She talks easily with Georgia. I'm too far away to hear what they're saying but their animated conversation helps to relax my nerves.

I take one last sip then leave the bottle propped next to my bag and glide over to join the others at the far corner of the rink. They're stretching and warming up against the rail.

"Michelle," Georgia says to the woman, "this is the girl I was telling you about, Sara."

I skate up to them, doing a gentle t-stop. I can feel Michelle's eyes watching the way I move. "Sara," she says, "good to meet you. I can tell you've skated before, why don't you give me a brief rundown of your history before we get started so I have an idea of where to place you."

I flush, wishing I could let my skating speak for me. "Four years of five stars," I tell her, then bite my lip. I sigh before continuing. "I wasn't far off the fifth. I'm wrong footed on my spins and my last instructor was trying to correct it. My spread-eagle needs work and I was working on squats off the rink so that I have a smoother rise out of the shooting duck. But it's been a few months since I last skated so I'm probably really rusty."

She nods. "The rust will fall of pretty quick, I'm sure. Just take it easy today." She pauses as other girls skate over the rink toward us. There are a range of ages and a range of skates. I go to move away to give others a chance to come up and greet their instructor but Michelle calls to me, "Sara?" I turn back to her. "We'll talk about the wrong footed. To be honest, I am too, but it doesn't have to get in the way of competing."

I smile, feeling warm to her already. As much as I'd loved my last instructor, she'd been exacting, demanding, and very certain of everything I did wrong. I liked my spins. And while I agree that it's important to learn to spin in competition approved ways, I'd rather be able to learn to spin in both directions than to sacrifice the way my body naturally wanted to do it in favour of the other which is what my last instructor had wanted.

Georgia smiles at me as I join her at the bar. "I'm impressed," she says.

I shrug. "We'll see how quickly the rust falls off," I say with a wry smile as I start to warm up.

11

ichelle does a wonderful job leading the various stars through their practice exercises. Three helpers join her on the rink. One takes the very beginner beginners to the far wall where they practice simple glides and t-stops. Another works with the level twos on shooting duck. The third works with level three. Michelle works with level four and five combined.

Although it had been so long since I'd last skated, she'd kept me with her and my friends. Georgia, Jenn, and Synthe were all very good but there was something special about the way Georgia did everything so effortlessly. Over the course of the session I keep catching myself watching her when I am supposed to be focused on limbering up, finding my balance, and testing my moves.

By the time we start to cool down I'd found the rust really did fall off pretty quick. There's definitely something to be said for four years of muscle memory. Before we finished Michelle even asked me to show her a spin. It was a wobbly mess, my balance a bit all over the place, but I smoothed out and achieved a reasonable speed and a smooth finish, so I felt pretty good about it.

"Wow," Jenn said as I straighten out. "You're really good."

I smile at her. "Thanks."

"No," she says, "I mean really. I don't think I'll ever get the hang of it. I've been practising so much that sometimes I feel sick to my stomach just thinking about spinning."

"Well, it shouldn't make you dizzy."

She laughs. "Well it does. And I wobble all over the place."

"We can work on it together if you like."

"Really?" she seems thrilled and I enjoy feeling like I've made her day as the two of us rejoin Georgia and Synthe who had dropped to their butts on the rink to stretch out their legs. Synthe easily reached down to her toe-stop with her hand and drew the tips of her toes toward her chest. I groaned, copying the motion with significantly less flexibility.

"Gonna be sore tomorrow?" she asks with a smirk.

I sigh. "Maybe, but it'll be worth it."

"Are you done already, Sara?" Georgia asks me. "You know there's a free skate session a little later. After the speed skate."

"I saw that." I'd seen their schedule posted to the counter as I'd come in. "Do you guys stay for that?"

She nods. "Sometimes. We're staying today, aren't we?" she asks the others.

Jenn sighs and shakes her head. "I can't. My stupid brother is competing today. Dad insists the whole family has to be there to support him."

"Little league. The death of true creative spirit," Synthe snorts but she sighs too. "I can't stay. Mum's picking me up right after."

"Your Mum?" Georgia seems curious.

Synthe groans then says, "Don't ask. She's trying and I guess that's something."

The tone suggests that Synthe and her mother don't get on. I don't want to pry, and I can't help the pain of resentment. At least she still has a mother. I bite my tongue so that I don't say the words out loud.

The overhead lights flash and the DJ's voice comes over the sound system. "Thank you to our wonderful figure skaters. Next up we have the speediest skaters on the rink, Rolloways Racers, riding on out. Just remember guys, keep that speed down until the figure skaters have cleared the rink."

"That's our queue," Georgia says, pushing herself back up to her feet. She reaches a hand down to help me up. I take it, brace my foot, and push up.

"Thanks."

With smooth glides, skating directly across the rink instead of around it, we head for the left exit. Georgia, Jenn, and Synthe glide through barely stopping but just as I grip the rail to help catch me on the exit someone steps in front of me. My fingers clutch the rail to stop me sprawling backwards. A hand comes up, catching my hip. There's a little weight in the grip so I suspect I held him up more than he saved me.

"Sorry," I say, when I'm sure my skates are staying underneath me. I glance up, catching the icicles in his gaze. His lips are tight. I feel the bottom drop out of my stomach. "Sorry," I say again, unable to help myself when I realise I'd crashed into my neighbour, Will.

His gaze drops to my mouth. "I have a habit of knocking you on your butt."

I shake my head. "No way, I'm still standing this time. Besides, it was your dog, not you."

He smiles. "Right."

His hand drops away from my hip and I feel a sudden chill. Will raises his hand to his forehead in a salute. He steps around me, and glides backwards onto the rink. "Take it easy, Little Brooks," he says, turning expertly and skating away.

I have no idea where the nickname came from and I immediately squashed the flutter it causes. None of that nonsense. There was no way I was letting myself fall for the dark and broody boy next door.

12

I step off the rink as Will loops around for another lap. His gaze had turned to the rink in front of him as his speed increased. My eyes linger on him as I skim over the carpet and join Georgia, Jenn, and Synthe. Jenn is tugging off her skates. Synthe, skateless already, is tying the laces of her black boots.

"Do you really have to go?" Georgia asks.

"Really do, Georgia," Jenn says. "You know my family."

Synthe shoves her skates into her skate bag and snorts. "It's not like they ever come watch you."

Jenn seems to deflate a little further. Synthe doesn't know how to keep the nasty stuff on the tip of her tongue. I grab my water bottle and take a sip. My gaze darts back to the rink, and Will, but I force myself to look at Jenn when she speaks again.

"It's not that they don't. Well, I mean they don't, but they would. If I ever competed. But skating is just for fun."

Georgia puts a hand on Jenn's arm. "It's good that your family is so close. As much as you complain we know you love your little brother. Go, enjoy his game. We'll see you tomorrow, right?"

Jenn brightens. "Yeah, tomorrow! Did you invite Sara yet?"

That catches my attention. "Invite me? To what?"

Georgia smiles. Synthe stands, pulling her bag over her shoulder. "I gotta go," she says. I can't help feeling like it's another snub. She's less than thrilled that I'm getting invited to whatever is happening, but I try to push the assumption aside. She's probably just thinking about her Mum.

"See ya, Synthe," Georgia says.

Synthe and Jenn walk together as they head for the exit. As they reach the door Jenn turns back and calls, "Ask her, Georgia. It'll be fun."

Georgia chuckles. "I'm asking, Jenn. I'm asking."

When the two are gone Georgia turns to me and waves a hand to the wall beside the rink. We skate over together and stand, watching the speed skaters as they do warm up laps. "So, we're having a picnic. Wanna come?"

"A picnic?" I ask, turning to her.

She nods. "At the beach."

"That sounds really nice. I'd love to come but I'll have to check with my Dad. I don't really know how to get around by myself yet."

"No, that's the thing. The beach is right near your house. Jenn lives in South Perth, right on the water really. Well, across from it anyway. Her family are pretty well off. She mentioned seeing you there the other week."

I think back to the week before and my visit to the beach. It was pretty fresh in my mind because of my collision with Will. I flush, remembering. I guess I'd been pretty vocal. It probably caught some attention. I wonder what they'd said about me when they realised I was the crazy girl from the beach.

"You guys saw me?"

Georgia nods. "We didn't realise it was you until the other day when you were walking across the garden."

"Oh." I drop my gaze to my hands. They grip the wood banister that hooded the half wall. I flinch when I feel Georgia's hand on my arm.

"Hey, it's okay. I would have been mad too. That dog was a total mess."

I laugh. "Nothing like designer jeans full of salt and sand."

"Even wet you looked awesome. That shirt, vintage. Even Synthe envied it and that girl doesn't do anything that isn't three figure shopping." Georgia tucks a strand of her hair behind her ear. "So, picnic at the beach, tomorrow. You coming?"

I smile at her. "Yeah, okay. But let's avoid the dogs."

"Deal," she says. Her gaze wanders to the rink. "Although," she says, and I can tell she's watching Will, "it's not the worst way to meet a cute guy." She nudges me in the arm. "Right?"

I shake my head. "I have no idea what you mean."

Except I do of course. And while I hadn't thought of it when I was busy yelling at him about his stupid dog, and I'd tried not to notice when he was in my house, there was something about Will. A dark and brooding something sometimes, but in his less guarded moments there were hints of light. I remember seeing him come out of Dr

Hymore's office and wonder again what sends him there.

Beside me, Georgia has already moved on to other topics. She doesn't seem to need me to participate in the conversation, able to hold it all herself, so I only half listen as I watch Will skate around. He's actually really good. He keeps his gaze fixed in the direction he's headed and as he speeds up on the straights, he has long strides. His crossovers on the bends are quick slices that incrementally increase his speed further. I feel the brush of air as he skims close to the wall in front of us before carving into the next bend.

Man, I missed that. I had speed skates too, not just my figure ones. They had laces longer than my arms that strapped around the arch of my foot in red and white candy stripes. I couldn't move as fast as Will, something always held me back from really getting that speed up so fast, but even so, having the air rush through my hair, feeling it move over my skin, and feeling the wheels under my feet. It's a rush, and I miss it.

A flicker at the corner of my vision reminds me why I can't. Why I hadn't in months. I turn my chin slightly to see it more clearly. A boy stands in the shadow at the corner of the room. There's a spot at the banister that's more hidden than visible. It would be a good place to hang out and watch. And that's what this kid is doing. Except, he's not watching all of the skaters, like most of the spectators at the bar are doing. His gaze is fixed, like mine had been, on Will. Through the gloom I realise I recognise him from the swing in Will's back yard.

I'd already known he was a hallucination, not real. There was something about the tingle on my skin when I'd noticed him there. It felt as if the hairs on my arms prickled. Hallucinations are exactly why I don't speed skate.

I remember the last time, the first since my mother's death.

The rink at home, back in Sydney I mean, is pretty popular. Our figure skating classes were broken up into individual star groups because so many, mostly girls, attended. Just like here, the speed skating session immediately followed and was equally overpopulated by boys. I'd always stayed for both.

There's a degree of respect you earn by being a regular of either. The instructors are usually really passionate about skating and they like it when they can tell you're just as devoted. So, I'd gained a fair bit of kudos for being one of the few figure girls who would give speed skating a go. Triple the respect because I had my own speed skates.

But that day, I'd wrecked because of the damn hallucination.

One minute I'd been gaining speed on a straight and coming up to the inside curve for the turn. Normally I take the curves a little wide because I'm slower than most of the guys and there's just something in the pit of my gut that turns chicken shit if I approach the bend too fast. But this time I'd been kind of hating the world. We'd been to Mum's funeral the weekend before so losing her was fresh and painful. She wasn't at the rail.

Mum hadn't always stayed to watch me skate, so it wasn't unusual for her not to be there. Especially after she got sick. But I felt it ten-fold that day because it wasn't that she wasn't there, it was that she never would be again. And it hurt. I hurt again, thinking about it.

I'd skated harder than ever and was letting some of the anger out by punishing myself to keep up my speed. I cut the corner tight but as I straightened on the last cross, I slightly hooked the front of my skate. It was the kind of thing that you can recover from, but, because I'd thrown off my balance, when some strange freak, a guy in an old stanza hat wearing flats and strumming a guitar, stepped in front of me I couldn't dodge. Of course, he wasn't really there so I hadn't actually needed to dodge but trying to on my off foot while I was still trying to correct my earlier mistake meant I'd ended up just tripping over my own damn skates. I'd slammed into the floor pretty hard. Fortunately, I'd been able to roll rather than toss out my hands to stop me, so I hadn't broken anything, but the bruise on my hip had hurt for over a week after.

I realised then that the things I see could hurt me. I hadn't skated since, not even figure skating, until today. Slim lining around the edges or hugging close to the wall at 30 kilometres an hour wearing nothing but a pair of skates, jeans, and a tank top was dangerous enough. It could be deadly when hallucinations jump out at you at any moment.

I sigh, resigning myself to sticking with the figure skates. It's definitely not a good idea to try speed skating again until I get this brain thing under control.

The guys continue for several more laps. Michelle, our figure skating instructor, soon joins them on the rink. She keeps up with the best of them which is pretty impressive. I admired her all the more, especially for the pitch-black speed skates she was wearing.

After their warmup the DJ calls them to line up for the first of two races. Will and Michelle are both really good. Michelle was just a head of the mid-line and Will slightly closer the front as the pack fell into their standard places. Although it was technically a race, I could see that most of the skaters were focused more on their own technique and their personal best skating rather than actively trying to beat each other. The best of the best skaters easily lapped the back of the pack.

Eventually, they started winding down and the DJ came back over the speakers. "Okay, time to bring down that speed," he said. Once the highest speed racers had dropped to a more controlled pace, the house lights dimmed, and coloured lights started dancing across the rink and walls. "We're getting into our general skate session now. General skaters to the rink. Speed skaters, remember to keep those speeds down during the general skate sessions, for the safety of everyone. I promise we'll have another race later in the session so you can test your mettle one more time today."

"Come on," Georgia says, nudging me in the side. I stood between her and the entrance to the rink. I glance at her and grin, stepping sideways to the rail. I take one last sip from my water bottle and toss it over to my bag.

Just as I'm about to step onto the rink again Will glides past us. There's a sheen of sweat that glistens in the trails of coloured light across his skin. I freeze in place, but he doesn't actually get close enough to collide into me. He skates with practised timing over the slight lip at the edge of the rink and he glides through the gap to the table and chairs on the other side.

"Come on," Georgia urges again. I step onto the rink and push off into the flow of skaters. Georgia sets the pace beside me and we skate a couple of laps. Each time we round the far end my gaze searches for Will again.

He grabs a towel off the back of a chair, slings it over his shoulders, then heads up the stairs to the kiosk. On the next lap he's standing at the banister with a frosted bottle of water. He takes a long sip, his Adam's apple bobbing as he swallows.

Georgia keeps up a healthy casual speed. We weave around the inexperienced skaters. Most of the beginners hug the edges, staying close to the railings, but a young couple of wobbly-feeters flail their arms. Georgia and I have to split up to dart around them. She passes on the inside and I pass on the outside. As we step into the next curve, I do a short inside turn and start skating backwards. I lose sight of Will, which is probably a good thing because I'd been obsessing over him long enough.

With my chin twisted slightly to look over my right shoulder, I let my skates scissor as I skate the straight edge at the far wall. The crossovers while I'm skating backward feel so smooth and natural. I'd missed this. The lovely play of motion that flows from the wheels up my legs. The rest of my body seems to follow on from the movement of my feet. The muscles in my thighs burn just a little. Conditioning, I remind myself.

I pace a few laps, keeping my motion smooth and focusing on the music and the weave of people. Georgia's found her own pace and as she passes me, I see she's chatting with another skater, a dark-haired guy about our age. I chuckle. Good on her. She lifts a hand and waves at me as they pass. I smile and wave back, giving her a sly wink.

With each lap I edge a little closer to the centre of the rink. There's a solid line that demarks the general skating lane and most of the skaters respect it, leaving the absolute centre of the rink clear. At my old rink a bunch of us would have camped out in the centre, practising our figure skating moves. It surprised me that others didn't do that here. Maybe not as many of the figure skaters stayed for the general skate session.

Above the centre of the rink, a disco ball spins. It creates a sparkle of glittery light that rains down and out in a scatter across the floor. I turn the inside curve just inside the line and rotate back to a forward skate to do two more ever-tightening laps before pulling up with a t-stop directly under the ball.

I try to pretend there's no one else around. When I was surrounded by my old friends all practising their moves it felt natural to do it with them. But here, I'm pretty sure I'll stand out. Still, I want to shake off a bit more rust before I call it quits for the week. Besides, the burn in my upper thighs needs some calf action for balance. I chuckle to myself as I position my feet and shift the weight. Heel and toe. I flick my hands out just a little for balance. Heel and toe.

Eventually, when I feel confident the motion is smooth, I add the shoulder rotation that turns it into a spin. I focus my line of sight and keep my arms wide to hold the speed down. Muscle wise, the only thing I really want working for me right now is my feet. I keep the heel/toe combination tight and let the wheels do the work.

The spin is a little wobbly. Keeping it slow means it takes more effort to keep it balanced. I feel the slight cramp in my toes and sigh as I let my heel drop slightly and turn my skate to circle out of the spin into a lazy spread eagle.

"That's pretty good," someone says from just inside the inner edge of the rink's centre. I glance up, then flush, realising Will is standing there, watching me. Of course, I was asking for it. He probably thought I was trying to show off. Except that spin sucked so maybe not.

"Thanks," I say, "just trying to shake some of the rust off. It's been a few months since I last skated."

"If this is you rusty you must have been phenomenal a few months ago." He falls into an easy spread eagle that hugs the inside line of the rink. He's actually got a pretty good turnout for a speed skater.

I shake my head and turn slowly so that I stay facing him as he circles around me. "Not particularly. My instructor hates that I'm goofy footed."

He chuckles. "Goofy footed?" he asks.

"It means that I spin in the wrong direction. Clockwise when I should be counter."

He drags his skates together to stop in front of me. "Does that matter?"

I lift a shoulder. "At competition level it can."

"And that spin you just did? Clockwise or counter-clockwise?"

I think back. I hadn't really been focusing on doing it 'right'. But just doing it. I sigh. "Clockwise." I shift my feet, alternating the heel and toe in the other direction. "The other direction is harder."

"Can you show me?"

SPIRIT TALKER

He glides over to stand beside me and looks down at what I'm doing with my feet. "Have you ever figure skated before?" I ask.

He waves his hand at the rim of the inner circle where he'd just been skating. "A few basic things, spread-eagle, shooting duck. I've got a pretty impressive flamingo."

I laugh. "Flamingo? I don't think that one's counted."

"Well it should be, do you realise how hard it is to stay on one foot and keep moving?"

I nod. "Actually, I do, mine is pretty impressive too." I glance over to him. His eyes meet mine. There's a sparkle in them that glimmer through the haunted look, but the haunting is there in the background. "So," I say, trying to put aside the niggle of pain I feel when I see it. It's like he has an aura of it that cloaks him. "With a spin on roller skates you want to have one foot to your toes and the other to your heel. In figure skates you have to get the angle just right so that you're balanced upright enough but don't accidentally skim the toe-stop on the ground." I glance at his skates, speed skates, "I guess you don't have to worry about the toe stop."

He nods. "Heel, toe," he repeats, copying the motion with his feet. I make sure I focus on the right combination for a counter-clockwise spin and he copies. He wobbles as he lifts to toe on one foot and tips to heel on the other.

"Put your hands out a little to help you balance."

He nods as we both put our hands out a little and then do the foot motion again.

"Okay, to get the spin happening, you rotate hip and shoulder with your arms." I try to explain it but it's easier just to show him what I mean. This time, I pull my arms up, and then as the spin begins to rotate, I pull my hands closer to my chest so that I have a little more speed.

The spin is just as wobbly as the slow turn I'd done in the other direction. It takes more effort to hold my feet in place and keep the toe-stop up off the floor. Eventually, after about three turns, I feel it snag so I let my other leg go out wide and use the toe-stop to end the turn. It's lazy, and clumsy, and a bit of a mess.

Still, I let myself come full circle so that I'm watching Will. "Think you can try it?"

He nods, dancing the toe-heel again with a little bounce. "Toe, heel, and spin, right?"

I smile. "Right. And breathe."

He swings his arms and his whole body wobbles like a teetering bowling pin. "Whoa," he says, throwing his arms out wide. Still, he manages two full circles. His feet keep growing wider and wider apart and his hands flail a bit. He drops his heel and drags his wheels a bit before he comes to a stop. He shakes his head. "That was terrible."

"No," I tell him, "That's good. You managed full rotations on your first spin, and you didn't end up on your butt. I call that a serious win." I grin at him. "You should come for the 7am session next week."

He raises an eyebrow. "Figure skating? With the girls?"

"They're not all girls. Guys figure skate too you know. There's even pairs skating."

"There's no street cred. in pairs skating, Sara." I flush a little, liking the sound of my name in his mouth.

"And it's all about the street cred. is it?" I ask, trying not to notice the heat on my skin and so glad that the coloured lights on the rink hide it. "I'm surprised you don't play roller hockey then."

He grins. "Who says I don't?"

That catches my attention. "Do you?" I ask.

He shakes his head. "No, but you didn't know that. I might have." He circles a lazy loop doing a backward turn and keeping one foot firmly in place. It's actually a really graceful motion. He could probably pick up most of the figure skating moves pretty easy if he'd really wanted to. "Nope.

I feel the need, the need for speed," he says, full on Tom Cruise impersonation.

"You did not just quote Top Gun. Who are you, my father?"

He gasps. "You wound me," he says, raising a hand to his heart. "Top Gun is a classic."

I can't help but smile. My Dad loves that movie and I have to admit, at least to myself, that I don't hate it.

"Sorry about the other day, by the way," I look up at him and he must catch the confusion on my face because he adds, "with my dog?"

"Oh," I say, dropping my chin. "It's okay."

"He really didn't mean any harm. I hope your outfit survived."

"Nothing the washing machine couldn't set to rights." I don't really want to talk about the other day. I feel stupid enough as it is for overreacting. Should I say that to him? I decide not to. No point compounding how stupid I feel by admitting to it. "So," I say instead, "how's your footwork?"

I skim a little to the longest edge of the inner circle and face the DJ's side of the rink. The music had picked up pace. It had a good beat to it. I was out of practice but there was something I loved to do because not many people could do it.

Will looks at me, his chin tilted. I wave him out of the way and he moves aside. Keeping time with the beat of the song, I criss-cross my skates in a Riverdance-like sidestep. There's a pattern and coordination to it that takes quite a lot of practice to master. It's a cross between tap dancing, line dancing, and Russian foot kick dancing although with less kick and less squat. I chuckle a little as I do it because there's an energy in it that I'd really, really missed.

Fortunately, even as rusty as I am, something in my muscles must remember because I manage the full length of the inner circle before dropping into a backwards turn and gliding back to the other side.

Will looks pretty impressed and I'm pretty impressed with myself too. It doesn't always go so smoothly. From the edge of the rink a third pair of skates does a scissor stop beside me. "Wow, Sara, that was awesome," Georgia says.

The boy beside her lets the wheels of his right skate drag in a grinding stop beside her. He flicks his hair out if his face. "Very cool."

"You have got to show us how to do that," Will says. He pushes off and does a sharp scissor stop in front of me. Georgia and her friend space out around me too.

I chuckle. "It takes some practice, but I'll show you."

For the rest of the session the four of us mess around with stuff in the centre of the rink. Occasionally we break out for a bit to do a few laps, both forwards and backwards, weaving around the other skaters. From time to time the DJ wrangles people into a game. Will takes part in everything but Georgia and Blake sit out with me to watch.

And, through it all, I catch glimpses of the boy in the corner. A quiet smile lifts his lips. I can't help feeling like he is happy with the way Will hangs out with us. It's weird, but since he isn't stepping into my path and causing me to face plant into the concrete, I try my best to just ignore him. Who the hell knows what that hallucination is about? I'll have to add it to my journal later. Since it isn't messing with me, I'm not about to try messing with it. Let sitting hallucinations sit. I'd rather be skating.

13

Jenn comes by my house the next morning. She's dressed in a really pretty cotton outfit with bright pink and yellow frangipanis all over. Her dark hair is pulled back in a high ponytail and the shoestring straps of the dress rest on her brown shoulders.

"Wow, your place is really nice," she says, complimenting the house when I open the door.

"Thanks," I say with a smile. I tug my backpack over my shoulder and pull down on the edge of my shorts. I'd bought them online and they were just that inch or two shorter than I would have preferred. Especially since normally I wouldn't have anywhere near this much leg showing.

Noticing the way I fuss with my clothes, Jenn grabs my hand. "Enough, you look great."

I shake my head and chuckle but trust her judgement. "Come on then." I draw the door closed and we start walking down the street toward the foreshore. "Georgia says you live around here?"

Jenn nods. "A few blocks over. Our apartment overlooks the water. Everyone comes over for the Skyworks."

"The Skyworks?" I ask, not sure what that is.

"Yeah, every year the city puts on a big Australia Day celebration, with fireworks over the river. It lights up the city. The view is pretty spectacular. It's actually the reason my parents chose our place."

"Your folks are big on Australia Day?" I'm surprised because I'd assumed she was aboriginal.

She lifts a shoulder and the strap of her dress lifts with it. "It's a little controversial, I guess. Definitely not the greatest historical association, but we try to focus on the positive. We love our country and want to celebrate it. And honestly, what better way to acknowledge and raise awareness of the amends still needed then to highlight it on Australia Day?"

"I guess it's a really big topic. I hadn't thought much about it before."

She smiles, tilting her face up to the sun as we walk. "Most don't," she says, "Except when it hits the news in January every year. That's why it's worth it, I think. It makes people talk about it."

I nod, understanding in some small way although I imagine I'd never really understand the full of it. That sort of thing hit me in a different way. My own family heritage was deeply rooted in different traditions. We love our country too, but more like people settling into a new home rather than people who had built the home from the ground up.

Our conversation dips to less loaded chatter as we round the corner. The green grass and white sand of the South Perth foreshore comes into view. Jenn points to a cluster of kids settled in the sun. "There they are."

Georgia waves to us as we approach. "You made it!" she shouts as our feet sink into the sand.

"You starting without us?" Jenn calls back. Georgia tucks a plastic container full of strawberries back under a towel. She quickly sucks the tips of her fingers.

"Not guilty," Georgia says with a wink, clearly guilty. She motions to the sand beside her. "Come, settle in."

We lay out our towels alongside Georgia's and sit down.

"Where's Synthe?" Jenn asks.

Georgia sighs. "Turns out her Mum wanted to see her again today. Apparently there's some new drama going on." Georgia glances at me, then gives Jenn a pointed look. "She doesn't really want to talk about it."

I don't know the full story there. I'm guessing, by the look Georgia gave Jenn, that Synthe doesn't want me to know the full story. Odds are Georgia and Jenn would talk about it if I wasn't there. That is fair, we still barely know each other and it's clear Synthe's not my greatest fan. Still, I hate feeling like I'm cut out from something rather than really belonging in their group.

Georgia changes the conversation pretty quickly, clearly heading off any awkwardness. "We have some good eye candy again today," she says, turning her gaze out over the water. A group of young guys were out on their boards again. It got me thinking that this was probably a weekend tradition among both groups. Especially with the way the guys kept glancing our way and showing off over the water.

"Any of them yours?"

Georgia shakes her head. "No way!"

"What about Blake?" I ask and nudge her in the arm. "You two seemed to be getting pretty cosy yesterday."

"No!" Jenn gasps. "You did not!"

Georgia flushes. Her smile is shy which is something I hadn't really ever associated with Georgia before. I mean, I hadn't known her long, but she always seemed too upfront and outgoing. In a way it felt normalising to realise she had at least one shy bone in her body.

"It's really nothing," she says. The blush over her cheeks is definitely not sunburn.

"Oh, there's something," I tell her. "With him too. I could tell."

She meets my eyes, hers full of hope. "Really? You think so?"

I fan myself with my hand and an air of dramatics. "Sparks, I tell you."

She sighs. "We're just friends. He goes to Penrhos."

Jenn smiles, reaching past Georgia to pull the container of strawberries out from under the towel. "It's not like that's an ocean away or anything, Georgia. It's closer to where we are right now than our own school is."

"I know." Georgia doesn't look or sound convinced. She gazes out over the water at the other guys doing their antics on boogey boards as if they're surf boards. My gaze wanders in the same direction, but instead of the group of guys, I notice a lone figure off to the side of them. I'd already started to recognise his shape. It was Will.

I notice that from time to time the group of guys glance over at him. It makes the way he sits on his board, a lonely figure floating over the water, even more pronounced. He seems practically oblivious to them. Oblivious to all of us.

"Fate will guide you," Jenn says, bringing my attention back to the girls and to Georgia's love life. Not that Will was anything to do with my own. Jenn attaches some amazing load to the word 'fate', like somehow its hand is in everything. Which, I guess if you believe in that kind of thing, is exactly what it means. She pops a strawberry in her mouth and waves the container toward me. I take one, pluck off the green stem and leaves, and bite down on the red, juicy tip. It's fresh, and sweet, and warm.

As the three of us look out over the water. The sun beams down, warming our skin. A prickle of sensation tingles over my arms again. I don't want to look because I know the beach is populated not only with real people but the there-not-there people that seem to plague my waking moments. I don't want to see them, but I can't help it.

I keep my view fixed ahead and ignore the long dark legs that stand, feet in the water, just at the edge of my gaze. It was ironic, given what Jenn and I had talked about, that this would be an aboriginal elder in full ceremonial garb. Even down to the long-carved stick in his hand. Except I wasn't noticing him. I'm normal. I chant it over and over in my own head. Nothing to see here.

Instead, I focus on what Georgia is saying. She and Jenn had started talking about an upcoming Cheer event. "Do we have to go to those?" I ask. In the two weeks since I'd started at my new school, I'd had to endure three excruciating sessions of fitness and cheer. Sports was not my thing.

Georgia shrugs but it's Jenn that answers, "It's not mandatory," she admits, "but it's a lot of fun, Sara. You should come. I swear you'll enjoy it."

I shake my head and take another strawberry from the container. "I doubt that."

Georgia grins. She and Jenn had both seen my ineptitude because we shared the class. "You don't have to join the cheer if you don't want, Sara. Just come and watch."

"But the cheer is so fun!" Jenn exclaims. "You should join us."

"Maybe I'll come watch," I reason. Belonging was important, but not quite enough to justify making a fool of myself with flailing limbs and total lack of coordination.

"How can you be so good on skates but be terrified of doing the same things without the wheels?" Georgia asks.

I fix her with a look. "It is so not the same thing."

A movement over her shoulder catches my eye and I gasp as I see a small child, alone, standing deep to his chin in the water.

"What?" Georgia asks, glancing over her shoulder. A wave comes over the boy's head. He disappears beneath the water. I hold my breath, waiting for him to surface but he doesn't.

"That boy," I cry, and before I realise what I'm doing I'm sprinting across the sand. I kick off my shoes as I run and pull my shirt over my head, thankful that I'd pulled my bathers on under my clothes that morning. I dive into the water and, with strong strokes, swim out. From the beach I can hear Georgia and Jenn shout out to me. When I reach the point where the boy had disappeared, I dive under, searching the murky, sand-swirled shallow for him.

His little body drifts in the water. His eyes are closed and his skin looks pale and grey. I grip his arm, pulling him up. I reach an arm around him, holding his back to my chest as we break the surface. We both gasp for air when our faces touch the sky.

I pause there a moment, just holding him up and kicking to keep us both above the bobbing water. I'm suddenly really glad that the river doesn't have the same crash of waves as a real beach. I fill my lungs then start swimming with one-handed strokes back to shore. I hold the boy with my other arm and pull us both up the sand.

It's not until I reach the beach that I realise Georgia, Jenn, Will, and the others, guys and girls, are all standing there gaping at me. I glance at the boy who lies on his back in the sand. He stares at me too.

I notice the slight blur to his edges. I notice the way the water doesn't seem to flow around him like it does me. I notice the way his body doesn't sink into the sand like mine. Suddenly, I realise he's a hallucination. No one else can see him. I must look like a total idiot.

My breath, already ragged from the run and swim, suddenly feels tight in my chest. My eyes sting. It's not from the saltwater. I blink back my tears.

"What on earth, Sara?" Georgia asks me as Jenn runs back down the beach to grab my towel.

I shake my head. Trying to bring reality into alignment. The boy wasn't real, but I'd felt him in my arms. So now not only could I see, and hear, and smell, but I could touch my hallucinations?

I reach over, just to see, but the boy pulls his arm away. His gaze is sharp, penetrating, as if even he doesn't quite understand what just happened. Then he's gone, just completely disappeared, as if he was never there.

I blink, trying to understand it but it doesn't make any sense. I can almost imagine the odd look on my face. Will has an odd look on his face too. The underlying spectre of sadness seems stark. His face is pale and his lips open. I can tell he's trying to make sense of what he just saw too but there seems to be something more in it. I can't explain it to him. I don't think I can explain it to anyone.

When Jenn hands me my towel I take it and wrap it around my shoulders. I push myself back to my feet and brush the sand off my legs. "Just wanted a swim," I say, as if that could possibly be a reasonable excuse to just suddenly sprint at the ocean and throw myself in. Will shakes his head. Instead of saying anything he goes back to the water and pulls his board up to the beach.

The others shake their heads. They're laughing at me as if I'm the biggest idiot in the world. I'm definitely not making any fans there. Georgia and Jenn both sigh as the guys return to the water and carve their way back to their boards too. A group of girls whisper to each other as they turn their backs on us. They head back to their towels and sunning themselves on the sand.

Georgia and Jenn both stay with me as we walk back across the sand. I stoop to pick up my shirt and shoes. When we get back to our towels, I shove my stuff into my backpack.

The girls settle back down on their towels and Jenn pulls a bottle of sun lotion out of her bag. I glance down, but I can't get what just happened out of my head. It was hard enough trying to be normal. I was glad they weren't treating me like a freak, but I couldn't help feeling utterly ridiculous.

"I'm going to get going," I say, my voice quiet. Georgia glances up at me.

"Are you sure you're okay?" There's real concern there, but I can't let myself feel her pity.

"I think I'm just really tired. Too much skating yesterday." She nods but I can tell she doesn't really believe me. "Thanks for inviting me out. See you tomorrow?"

She nods again. "Yeah, see you at school."

I give one last glance at Will's retreating back. He's dog-less today. He's not headed home, instead, he walks up the beach along the water. In a way I'm glad because it means I can walk home without looking like I'm following him.

The warm sun on my back feels strange because there's a chill lingering on my skin. It's not really from the cold water. It's from the pit in my gut. The thing that sits there, reminding me that I'm not normal. And maybe I never would be ever again.

14

In a school that should have been full of students there was a strange mixture of hallucinations in the hallways. I think it was the odd looks the other kids kept giving me that made them seem to accumulate over time. I'd begun to notice that the more I stressed the less control I had over what I could see. As if just being worried made them appear. Maybe that's how mental illness worked.

This time it felt like even my hallucinations were in on the rumour mill. Word had definitely spread about the freaky girl on the beach. I tried to reassure myself that there really wasn't anything to it. What had people actually seen, after all. A girl dive into the water, swim awkwardly back to the shore with one arm, and then collapse on the beach.

It's not like I tried to give my hallucination mouth to mouth or something equally weird.

I'd thought about it most of the night and decided that if anyone asked, I'd tell them I was practising for Malibu Rescue Junior Life Saver. At my local swim club back in Sydney we'd been shown a series of rescue strokes. It wasn't impossible to believe. Hell, I could even pretend I'd been part of Bondi Rescue. The people here didn't know me well enough to not believe me.

Except there was a difference between pretending something and outright lying. Wasn't there? And it's too easy a thing to do to send the gossip rounds hurtling in a direction I don't want to go. I definitely don't want to be landed with the label of 'pathological liar'. It's hard enough accepting the labels that are true. Freak, weirdo, crazy girl. Better stick with avoidance, or when that's not possible, honesty.

Thankfully, no one asks me until recess when I join Georgia, Jenn, and Synthe in the terraced gardens. Even then, Georgia introduces it as a quiet sideline to me, "What was that about yesterday?"

I don't want to lie but I can't force the truth out of my lips either. I decide the make believe will do as an excuse. I lift a shoulder, trying to pretend there's nothing really in it. "Practising for Malibu Rescue Junior Life Saver."

Georgia fixes me with a look. I can tell she doesn't quite buy it. But Jenn bubbles, turning toward us. "I love that show!"

Synthe gives me an odd look too. Hers is more assessing than Georgia's. It's like she's trying to figure out exactly what kind of bug I am. I'm suddenly glad she doesn't have a pin to stick me with. I can imagine her doing it.

I smile at Jenn and ignore the looks Georgia and Synthe are giving me. "Me too," I tell her. "My old swim club taught us about survival swim and how to pull someone out of the water. It was really cool."

Synthe rests what's left of her vegan wrap on the brick wall. "I heard you looked like a crazy person, rescuing no one."

Ouch. That hurt. Mostly because it was true. Synthe hadn't been there so it's not really fair for her to judge.

"Synthe," Georgia says, a tone of censure in her voice.

"What?" she asks. "That's what I heard. Half the school saw you," she says to me.

I shake my head. "Half the school was not on that beach yesterday. I bet half the kids that were don't even go to our school. We were in South Perth and the kids here come from all over."

Synthe shrugs, picking up her wrap again. "That's just what I heard," she says before taking a bite.

Georgia leans forward and puts a hand on my shoulder. "Everyone will have forgotten all about it by tomorrow."

I hope so, but I try to pretend I don't care. "I'm not worried," I lie. That kind of lie, the little white kind, was okay, I reassure myself. Everyone lies like that sometimes.

A group of people a few planters down breaks into laughter. The three of us glance in their direction. I shrink a little, realising they're looking at me. Okay, maybe not by tomorrow.

I resign myself to being the talk of the school for a while. Or, if I'm lucky maybe it's just our grade.

I reach down to my own lunch which I'd left on the wall beside me. My hand brushes something warm and I flinch away. It had been a fleeting touch and I can't even be sure it really was a touch when I realise what I'd touched had been another hand. A there-not-there hand. Grae's hand.

His blue eyes grip and hold mine. I desperately want to ask him if he'd felt that, but

SPIRIT TALKER

Jenn, Synthe, and Georgia are already looking at me strangely.

"Are you going to eat that ghastly thing?" Grae asks, pointing to the cheesy mite scroll I'd been reaching for.

In my head I answer him, 'of course,' but I glance at my friends and instead choose to say nothing. I shake my chin, just a little, which might be entirely the wrong message. I mean it as a kind of 'go away, leave me alone,' kind of shake but when I pick up the scroll and take a bite he tilts his head in confusion and I realised he probably thought I'd meant that I wasn't going to eat it.

He sighs. "Revolting thing. I will never understand the human need to mix filthy foods together."

I so wish I could answer him. Instead, I keep my gaze averted and focus on biting, chewing, and swallowing. If I keep my mouth full then maybe I won't be tempted to hold a conversation with my hallucination while my barely-on-the-brink-of-friendship friends are watching.

The others fall into conversation again. I can't bring myself to talk to them either though. So, I just listen, and pretend I'm part of their group. If I pretend it long and hard enough maybe it'll become true.

15

*T*uesday morning, as I walk into Art for first session, I am kind of sad that my B week schedule doesn't give me a double session of Art today like A week does. Still, at least I'll have some quiet time if Mrs Martha's silence rule is carefully applied.

I gather art supplies from the back of the room and make my way back to the chair I'd been assigned last week. My painting, more sketch than anything at this point, was already positioned on the easel. The soft wash of background colour had yellowed nicely. On its surface, Grae's handsome face, in sketched pencil, looked like a lost soul from a different era.

I sit in my chair and arrange the paints on the stand. I position my jar of water and stroke the bristles of one of my brushes to remove a trace of dried paint. Thinking of Grae, I glance at his chair beside me but it's empty.

My partner on the other side, the one with the beautiful dog, smiles at me. "Hey," she says.

"Hi," I reply. "Your dog is beautiful," I tell her, gesturing with my brush toward her painting.

She smiles, gazing at her dog. There's a hint of sadness in her features. The smile doesn't quite reach her eyes. "Thanks," she says, her voice soft.

"Is he yours?" I ask, probing just a little to see if she'll talk.

"He was."

I take a breath, realising my mistake and feel the sudden wash of her pain come over me. That was something new too. I mean, technically it must just be one of those hallucination things. Do you get feelings that are real? It's weird. But more and more I'd felt emotions that I'm pretty sure aren't mine. This felt like her sadness not my sadness. It wasn't like I'd ever had a dog that died. Just a mother, the vicious stab of that inner thought bit back.

"I'm sorry," I say. My voice is tight with the emotional pain. Not just the hallucination pain, but my own too.

She looks over at me. She doesn't seem to care about the tear at the corner of her eyes.

"Thanks," she says. She looks back at her painting, tilting her head at it. "I wanted to remember, you know? I don't want to forget him."

I nod, because I do know. The thing is, she's braver than me. I'd thought about painting my mother, but I hadn't been able to convince myself to do it. I wasn't ready yet. It made me wonder how long it takes for things like that to hurt less. How long would it be before my mother's face reminded me of the happy times more than the pain?

"He's beautiful," I tell her again.

"He's not so bad either," she says, setting her sadness aside. This time her smile is deeper and she lifts her chin to gesture toward my sketch. "Boyfriend?"

I can't help laughing, because it's ridiculous. I turn toward her and raise an eyebrow. "You think my boyfriend is an eighteenth-century poet?"

She lifts her hand, raising the brush she's holding in one. "Hey, I'm not judging. Maybe he's into cosplay or something. I could totally picture him with a lute." I laugh even harder at that. She might be able to picture it, but I can't.

"Strictly a quill and ink kind of guy. If he were real."

"So, imagination, inspiration, or history?"

SPIRIT TALKER

I sigh, gazing at Grae's face in my sketch. "I have no idea," I say, then realise that's strange. How can I have no idea what I'm painting? Still, my neighbour doesn't seem to catch on to my confusion.

"I'm Rhea, by the way."

"Sara," I tell her.

Just then, Mrs Martha stands up at the front of the room. She claps her hands together to draw our attention. "Welcome back, everyone. Now remember, what is our number one rule in this class?"

Rather than answering her, everyone else raises a finger to their lips. I copy the action, realising how literal she makes the silence rule. I grin, feeling a little silly but since everyone else is doing it I hope I don't look as ridiculous as I feel.

"Exactly," Mrs Martha says, rubbing her hands together. "Please, begin."

Some of the others had already started so they got right back into it. One or two finish gathering their things. Within minutes the whole class has settled into quiet, contemplative motion. Each of us focuses on our individual project.

I stare at Grae's face in the pencil lines in front of me and wonder how to start. I could picture him in my mind as if he were really here. I glance at the empty chair and wonder where he is.

Great, now I'm wishing for hallucinations? My brain really is breaking.

I push the thought out and pick up the paints instead. I mix my colours and focus on placing the strokes on the page. The page is real, the paint is real, the picture is real. That's what I need to focus on.

About twenty minutes into our painting session I'm sitting, waiting for a section of the painting to dry, and rinsing my brush.

"Is that me?"

I drop the brush and it clatters in a wet slap on the floor. I grimace, bending down to pick it up. I damp the wet bristles dry on a rag and turn to glare at Grae. I should have known he'd turn up. I'd practically willed it on myself.

He's not looking at me. His gaze is firmly fixed on my painting. The sketch was still there but the paint had begun to add definition to his features. It did so in an odd, jigsaw puzzle kind of way because with watercolour you only put paint on when you're making sections of the image darker. So, there were parts of his face I hadn't even started to paint yet.

"I see myself in your painting, Sara Brooks," he says. He reaches a hand out tracing the lines without touching the page. "You have a fair eye.

SPIRIT TALKER

Will it be as a mirror glass reflection when it is completed?"

His fingers are long. I remember how warm they'd felt yesterday when I'd brushed against him. Except of course I hadn't. Because that's just crazy. I try to pretend he isn't there. Because he's not.

I mix a new colour and carefully paint into sections of the page that are dry. Grayson's face is definitely starting to come out of the page. I shouldn't have painted him. Acknowledging my hallucination like this is just going to keep it firmly fixed in my mind. How am I supposed to stop hallucinating him if I keep making him more and more real in my head?

"You pulled a boy from the water on Sunday."

I gasp at Grae's words. My brush flickers, splatting a dab of paint in the wrong place. I quickly dab the paint with a tissue and try to mop it clean, semi-successfully.

What is Grae is even talking about? He wasn't there. He can't have seen me. Besides, no one saw the boy. He was a hallucination. But I can't say that because then I'd be talking to a hallucination. Besides, Mrs Martha had her silence rule. I press my lips together and draw a breath through my nostrils.

"There is a great deal of talk about you today, Sara Brooks. Your peers have even created a new name for you but it has none of the kindness of any name I'd give you so I will refrain from repeating it." Grae lifts his boot to his lap and starts toying with the laces. He keeps his gaze on the sole and avoids looking at me or his painting. I can't help feeling like he feels guilty for the name the other kids are calling me. Maybe he feels guilty for knowing it. I wonder what it is, but I can't ask.

"As for myself, I would call you hero, or miracle girl. Were he not already dead you would indeed have saved that boy's life and you thought nothing of your own when you did it. Why did you do it?"

I shake my head.

"The others say you looked ridiculous. I suppose you must have. To them you would have looked like a soggy fish that flailed ineffectively amongst the salty strands and undulated your way onto the sands." He chuckles, picturing it himself. The image he describes flashes in my own mind, but I banish it, refusing to let it take hold.

Even so, the idea of it sunk its claws into me a little. No wonder they were whispering about me behind my back. I probably looked like a complete loon. I could lie to my friends about pretending I was practising being a life saver but that didn't make what I'd done any less ridiculous. No one would believe I'd been trying to save a boy's life. No one could see him. Except, maybe, Grae?

I glance at Mrs Martha. She's absorbed in her own painting at the front of the room, having recently sat down after another lap around the class. Today's record plays the soft strains of a piano and violin duet. I lean toward Grae, inching a little closer to his chair. "You could see him?" I whisper.

Grae leans close to me. "Why are we whispering? Are we in each other's confidences?"

I gesture to the room around me. He looks around. I wonder what he sees when he looks at the others. If they can't see him, does that mean he can't see them? I have no idea how hallucinations work.

"Ah, your peers." So, he can see them. He glances over at the teacher. "And the endearing Madam Martha's rule." I nod.

"Could you see him?" I ask again, keeping my voice low. Rhea glances at me, her gaze narrowed. I flush, "Sorry," I whisper. She gives me a shy smile, then returns her attention to her own painting. She's putting the finishing touches on her dog.

Grae leans back in his chair. "Of course, I could see him. I can see them just as you do."

"You can?" I say, then glance around as I realise I'd said it much louder than I should have. Mrs Martha's gaze snaps to me but I pretend I'm painting and act as if I had been all along. She can't really be sure it was me. Besides, the music was loud enough that she can't have known what I said.

Beside me, Grae chuckles. "Be careful, Sara Brooks. Madam Martha is very firm in her rule. She may very well banish you from her class for the rest of the day if she catches us conversing."

"We aren't conversing," I hiss at him, pitching my voice very low. Behind me, one of the other students cough. I'm clearly not pulling off this silence thing very well and they're letting me know it. "Did you see him?" I demand, one last time.

I feel a prickle on the back of my neck and wonder how many of the others are looking at me. I drop my head, looking down at the brush in my hands. I stroke the bristles dry and press my lips together.

"I saw the boy, Sara Brooks. You were a valiant goddess. It touched my heart that you would risk yourself for one of us. I've not seen the like of it before."

SPIRIT TALKER

I can't figure out what he means by that. Risk myself for a hallucination? Of course no one does that. It's crazy. I hadn't really risked myself anyway. It's not like the water was deep. Besides, I couldn't just let the kid drown.

"That boy and his brother," Grae says, pausing as he considers his words, "there is a bond between them. I have sensed their united sadness. It holds the boy to the world. And the boy holds his brother to it. I suppose that, at least, is one benefit of the dead."

That confuses me even more. It wasn't the first time Grae had implied, or perhaps even stated, that what I was seeing was dead. He'd said the same about himself. But he talked about the boy as if he'd been a real person. As if he had a real brother.

I swallow, letting his words percolate in my brain. If my hallucinations were developing back-stories, I might be in real trouble. I wanted to write about it in my journal, but I'd have to wait for recess. I wanted to ask Dr Hymore about it. He would probably have some ideas.

Grae seems to fall into his own thoughts and the rest of the class passes with silence between us. I think about his words but can't really put a line on exactly what they mean. I do, however, decide to talk to Dr Hymore about it when I see him this afternoon. It had been a strange week for hallucinations. I needed some answers if I was ever going to unravel the mess my brain had become.

16

It's a little weird to be here, at my psychiatrist's office, by myself. Still, since our sessions are private it doesn't make sense for Dad to wait around and driving in and out of the city is a bit of a nightmare. Besides, he had other things he'd needed to get done so we'd agreed I could get myself here straight from school. If I needed help at any stage, I can call him. It's not like the place is hard to find.

I pull open the front door. The waiting room is otherwise empty. I tug on the strap of my satchel. My fingers stray to the bag of dice in my pocket. Restlessly, I pace the room rather than sit down. I take a few minutes to browse the paintings on the walls but keep checking my watch. Almost to the dot of time, the door behind me opens. I pull my hand free from my pocket, then clench my fingers not really sure what to do with them.

I wanted to wave, as Will and I pass each other again between sessions. It's ridiculous. This time Will dips his head acknowledging me as he passes, but he still says nothing.

I flush when I realise Dr Hymore is watching me gaze after the boy like a lovesick puppy. That's not what is going on here.

"Good afternoon, Sara. Come on in," he says.

I hurry past him and take my place on the long couch opposite his chair. I pull my satchel into my lap and dig into it for my journal. Dr Hymore smiles at me as he takes a seat.

"Did your homework?"

I nod. "Yeah. There's a lot here," I say with a frown.

"That's okay," Dr Hymore says, his voice soft and gentle. It's reassuring, but it doesn't really make me feel better. Because, as I flip through the pages of my journal, I realise there really is a lot. Some days have several entries. And some entries are really long.

Dr Hymore watches me flip through the pages. He lets me scan them for a couple of minutes before clearing his throat. "May I see?" I grip the pages more tightly suddenly afraid to give them up. He leans forward slightly in his chair. "It's okay if you don't want me to read the entries, Sara. These are a baseline for you. I'm not going to grade you on them. And I don't need to read what you've written. Perhaps, instead, we could just talk about one or two of the situations you faced this week."

I lift my head to meet his gaze, still clutching the pages. "I did want to ask you a few things. Is that okay?"

He sits back in his chair and adjusts the notepad on his knee. "Of course, what would you like to know?"

I swallow, trying to decide which question to ask first.

"Can you," I pause, suddenly really nervous, "I mean, does anyone ever talk about actually feeling their hallucinations? Like they're really touching them?"

Dr Hymore nods slowly. "You're talking about experiencing the physical, tactile, sense of contact."

I nod. "Yes."

"It does happen," Dr Hymore explains. "It is something that is usually more common with a more pronounced experience. I do feel you might be one of those so you may find your hallucinations are experienced from several, perhaps even all of your senses."

I shake my head. "I don't like it."

"How does it feel?"

I swallow again, wishing the lump in my throat would go away. I'm not sure if there's a frog in there or if I just want to cry. The doctor waits patiently, his pen poised above the page of paper.

"Take your time," he says.

I take a deep breath. It helps me shove down some of what I'm feeling so that I can talk. "Sometimes it just feels so real, you know? One time it was just the brush of a hand against mine. Warm."

"But there's something else?"

I nod. "I pulled a boy out of the water. It was so real, like I was really saving him. Everyone was watching. But when we got back to the sand, I realised he wasn't real, and everyone was laughing at me."

The doctor's brow furrows. "Can you tell me more?"

So, I explain it all to him. About how I'd been hanging out with my friends at the beach when I'd seen the boy go under. How I'd run into the water and pulled him out. All of it. The more I talk about it the easier it gets to talk about. I glance up at the doctor again but there's a line of worry on his brow.

"Did you ever feel you were in danger?" he asks.

I shake my head. "No." I pause, thinking back. "Well, I mean I guess it can be dangerous to rescue people. When we were taught about it we were told we have to be careful because a drowning person might not understand you're helping them. In survival mode they could be just as likely to pull you under as to let you pull them up."

He nods. "You said you felt the boy as if he were really there. Could his weight have pulled you under?" Dr Hymore's voice was full of clear concern.

I frown. "I guess. But what does that matter? He was drowning."

"I understand that," he says. I can tell he's smoothing out his own thoughts. It's kind of weird to watch him because there's a murky quality to the emotions that cross his face. As if his personal and professional self are at odds with each other. Eventually, the professional wins and he smiles at me. "Sara, you're a remarkable person to act as you did."

There's so much compassion in Dr Hymore's hazel eyes that I can't hold his gaze. I shrink a little, wishing he'd stop looking at me. When I glance up again he's averted his gaze and scrawls another note on the notepad.

When he lifts his head again I avert my gaze, but his words are warm. He uses that soothing voice that I bet has calmed down a lot of patients. Right now it makes me feel he's treating me like a toddler. "I'm sure the way the others reacted was very difficult for you, Sara."

I don't want to answer him because it's a stupid question. Of course it's difficult. I'd discovered at lunch today exactly what word the other kids had been using to describe me that Grae had been too gentleman to repeat. It wasn't nice.

"Sara," Dr Hymore says now, his voice still treating me like a little kid, "I want you to know that it's natural to feel as you do."

"You don't know what I'm feeling," I tell him, and then feel petty because odds are, he probably did. After all, isn't that what his job is?

"I can guess. Among your peers you must have felt embarrassed to be the centre of their amusement. Perhaps a little disconnected. Uncomfortable."

"Unnatural?" I add, then wish I hadn't.

He nods slowly. "Perhaps." He pauses. I can tell he's staring at me, but I refuse to look at him. "Sara, have you heard of a condition known as schizophrenia?"

I lift a shoulder. "I guess."

"What do you know about it?"

I feel anger rising inside of me. I don't like the word. The label. Because it's one for the crazy people instead of the sick people. I bite my lip and shake my head. I can't say that.

Dr Hymore watches it all across my face. He puts his pen down and leans forward in his chair. "Sara?" he asks. I can tell he's probing because he wants to understand my reaction before telling me I'm crazy.

I shake my head again. "I'm not crazy," I tell him. I mean I must be, that's the whole point, isn't it? And he's a doctor who treats crazy people. He'd know if that's what I am or not.

He sighs. "Sara, that's not what I'm saying. Nobody is crazy. It's just sometimes the chemicals in our brains do odd things. People with schizophrenia experience disconnection from reality."

"But I don't," I jump in. "I know what's real and what isn't." My breath is fast, and I try to catch it. "It's never not real." I try to explain.

The doctor picks up his pen again and writes a note. I wonder which part of what I'd just said was the crazy part he needed to write down.

"I mean," I add, "I know that I'm seeing things that aren't really there." He nods so I continue. "But I'm never not also in the real world. I'm never disconnected from reality. It's always there too."

He's still scrawling on the page, but I wait for him to finish. When he does, he looks up at me and says, "I understand what you are saying, Sara. I know it can be difficult to accept. But what you experience, the things you see and hear and smell and feel that aren't really there, those are a disconnection from reality. Your mind creates them."

I look down at the grey carpet and realise I hate the colour. When I'd first seen it the tones had been neutral in a comforting way. Now they just felt like they defined a very boxed in sense of normal. There was no vibrancy in it. A world without Grae would be grey, like that.

I take a breath, letting my thoughts sort themselves out as I try to work out what I should say. Instead, Dr Hymore continues, "Sara, the point I'm trying to make is that you can experience a normal life. There are medications that can help."

I lift my chin. "Medications?"

"Yes. You see," he begins. He flips a page in the notebook and leans forward to place the pad on the coffee table between us. "Your mind has various channels that fire information to create what you see and experience." On the pad of paper he draws a series of lines, representing the neurological system and the reception system that feeds that information. "It's controlled by a selection of chemicals and when those chemicals are out of balance you can experience inconsistencies. There are medications that have been formulated to correct these chemical imbalances."

I nod. The drawing makes sense and there's reassuring logic in what he says. "So, I'm not really crazy, just that some of my chemistry is a bit out of whack." I cling to that. "Medication can fix me?"

His shoulders drop a little and he sits back in his chair. He takes the notepad with him. "Well, Sara, it's a little more complicated than that, but in your case, I do think medication will help you in your day-to-day living. It will help prevent the hallucinations from disrupting your schooling or getting in the way of your making friends. It will help prevent outbursts that make you stand out among your peers."

I nod again. It would help me not act like a freak in front of other people. I can get on board with that. "Okay," I say, cautiously because I'm on board with not acting like a freak but I'm still not sure I one hundred percent love this idea.

He makes another note on the notepad, then fixes me with a look. "I'd like to check you into my in-patient clinic," he says, holding my gaze. "It's the safest and fastest way to get your medication situation sorted out because you can be monitored day and night. We can adjust your doses or change your medications on the fly and keep you safe if there are any complications with your symptoms or the side effects."

The instant he said the word 'in-patient' I pictured white padded walls and steel bars. "You want to put me in a mental institute," I say, my voice flat. "I'm not dangerous." I suddenly wish my Dad were here. Dr Hymore felt dangerous. I pull my feet up, wrap my arms around my legs.

"Sara," Dr Hymore says. His voice seems far away. "An in-patient clinic is a very comfortable place. It's not a prison. You'd be there voluntarily and can leave at any time. It makes sense to have you in a safe place because medical adjustments can be difficult."

I lift my chin and fix him with a glare. "You said medication would help."

"In most cases it does," he explains. "But it's not a simple thing of taking a pill and suddenly you're fixed."

SPIRIT TALKER

I wanted it to be. Why couldn't it be that simple. If a chemical imbalance makes my brain not work properly then a pill should fix it.

"Sara, the human body, the human mind, is more complicated than that."

I wonder if he was reading my thoughts. He probably just reads my expressions. I'm like an insect pinned for examination under a microscope. Clinical, detached. He doesn't even know me.

"I don't want to." I'm not exactly sure what I don't want. Definitely not the padded cell. It's hard enough being around my own crazy but psychiatric wards were full of everyone else's crazy too. Besides, there's no way everyone at school wouldn't hear about it and then I really would be what they called me.

"It's not-" the doctor begins but I cut him off.

"No," I shout. I wince, realising how loud I'd let my voice get. "No," I say again, regulating my volume. "I want to stay with my Dad. He'll help me. He can monitor the side effects. I'll take the medication exactly as directed. But I'm not going to a mental institute."

Dr Hymore releases a tight breath. He grips the pen in his hand like a vice but draws another breath and forces his shoulders to drop as he exhales. "Sara," he says again, his voice still tight.

"If you want to help me, then help me," I say, holding his gaze.

He nods, a short single dip of his chin, then draws a different pad of paper out of the draw of his side table. He scrawls a short note on it then signs his name and rips the page off the pad. He hands it to me. "Exactly as directed and every single day this week. I want to see you here again next week. If you have any interactions that are concerning book in early. Don't wait to see me."

I take the note, nodding the whole time. I don't understand his anger, but I try not to let myself become afraid of him. We hadn't known each other long but he's supposed to be on my side. He wants me to get better too. I have to remind myself of that because the scowl on his face makes me wonder.

"And keep tracking your experiences in your journal, Sara. That's important too."

We wrap up the rest of the session just talking about the side effects I could expect and how it may take time for me to feel the medication's effects. I'd wanted to ask him about how hallucinations are made. Where they come from. Why my brain creates poets and boys and crazy old ladies. But I wasn't sure I wanted to hear his answers anymore. Besides, if medication could stop it all, if it could make me normal, then it didn't really matter. Did it?

174

could stop it all, if it could make me normal, then it didn't really matter. Did it?

17

’ve followed the doctor's directions and taken the medication exactly as prescribed for the past three evenings. I want to believe it is helping. Maybe it is. Grae hasn't come to hang out writing poetry for his lost Ella-May and the old lady at the letter box hasn't been there the past two days either. But there were other things.

Still, I haven't needed to sneak into the library to scrawl in my journal today so there is definitely something happening. Maybe. This time I am here because I have a real reason; books.

After my visit to Dr Hymore, I want to learn more about chemical imbalance and the medication he prescribed me. I know there are some books on psychology in the library stacks. I had leaned against them several times over the past couple of weeks. So that's where I am heading before fifth period.

A few people are settled into various parts of the library. Friday seems to be the busiest day for extra study sessions. Some students have a free period after lunch, but I was looking forward to finishing the week with art.

My eyes found Will the moment I stepped into the room, but I try to ignore him as I walk past the row of desks where he sits. Books are scattered around him. I keep my eye averted, and almost yelp when a book skims across the desk and lands with a heavy thud at my feet.

"Oh, shit. Sorry," Will says. He's immediately up from the table and standing at my side before I even have a chance to bend down to pick up the book. We both bend, each taking the book in one hand. Our fingers touch. I flush, letting my hand drop away as we stand. Will puts the book on the table. I can't resist checking the cover. It surprises me and my gaze scans the covers and spines of the other books he had collected. They all dealt in death, the afterlife, reincarnation, and ghosts. I feel a shiver across my skin. He'd lost someone too. Maybe his Mum since I still hadn't seen her. It was just him and his dad.

"Pet project?" I ask. Will drops his gaze and lifts a shoulder. He weaves back around to the other side of the desk and sits down.

I notice then the boy in the chair beside him. He was the same boy. The one from Will's back yard and the beach. I swallow, pretending I can't see him, because the medication is supposed to be working. Instead, I pull out a seat and sit across from Will.

He probably doesn't want to talk to me but maybe he needs someone to talk to. "Want to talk about it?" I ask, then quickly add, "It's okay if you don't. I mean, I never want to talk about my Mum either, so I get it. Just that, if you did want to talk," I glance down at the table, "I'm here, you know?"

I can tell he's looking at me. There's a prickle across my skin whenever he looks at me. The silence between us stretches for at least a minute, maybe two. When I risk glancing up at him his gaze is fixed on the desk in front of him. His fists are clenched and the muscles around his jaw are tight. He clearly doesn't want to talk.

I push back in my chair. "Don't worry about it," I say, about to rise to my feet.

"Wait." He reaches a hand toward me but the desk between us prevents him from actually being able to grip onto my arm. Even so, I feel arrested in place. I let myself sink back into my chair.

More time passes. I'm not sure if I should get up or not. He wants me to wait but he still doesn't seem to want to talk to me. I sit, wondering about how I'd felt shortly after my mother died. My friend, Erica, had tried to get me to talk but I didn't want to. So, Erica just sat with me, and that was enough. I decided to do the same for Will. Even if he can't talk, I can sit with him.

Just sitting is comforting in a way, even for me. We settle into a calm, quiet silence, so when he does eventually speak, I'm almost startled by it. "It was my brother," he says, his voice almost a whisper.

I glance at the boy beside him. He mirrors the grief on Will's face.

I want to give Will a chance to open up, so I just stay in my silence and wait. Eventually it begins to pour out of him. But he's strong, he talks about it but doesn't cry, doesn't shake, his whole body sits with it in a strange tightness. I wonder if he's holding on for my benefit, or if he knows that letting go even just a little will bring the whole dam down.

"Bobby was seven. We were at the beach. I was supposed to be watching him, but I got distracted with my mates," he pauses, letting his breath catch up with him. "He went under."

I nod and wish I could reach out to hold his hand, which is weird because it's Will and we weren't even that close. But as he described what happened on the beach, I watched him, and the boy beside him, and remembered them both from just days before when it had happened again. Bobby had gone under and it was too late to save him, even if I did, Will couldn't.

"I was too late to save him," Will says now and the silence falls between us again.

I don't know what to say. My mind searches for the words. I wonder what would have helped me when Mum died. But there are no words.

Eventually, Will speaks again, "Do you ever wonder what happens to them, after?"

Do I wonder? I think about my mother.

Dad and I aren't particularly religious. Dad had travelled the world and studied religion all over the place. He believed in something after death. A greater consciousness, reincarnation, peace. I sort of believed too but I don't know.

"Dad doesn't believe," Will says. "Back to the worms I guess."

I try to let that sit with me, but it doesn't. I shake my head. "Does it bring you comfort to believe that about your brother?" I ask Will, but before he can answer I add, "I want to believe there's something more than that because it hurts too much to think that's all there is for my mother."

Will nods. "Yeah." The single word is quiet, reflective, and full of pain.

"What do you think happens?"

He thinks for a moment before replying, "I don't really know. But sometimes I feel like he's still here, you know? Like he's still close. Like, if I just closed my eyes, I'd be able to see him and feel him. Like it's not too late."

Beside him, the boy puts his hand on Will's arm, but Will doesn't seem to feel anything at all. There's raw pain in both their faces.

"Would it help? If you knew he was here with you?"

Will's penetrating blue eyes rise to look right at me and for the first time it feels like he's really seeing me. "I don't know," he says, and there's a rawness to his voice. "It depends how it all works. I mean, I wouldn't want him trapped here." He pulls one of the books out of the stack. "When they talk about ghosts they talk about unfinished business and haunting. I don't want that for my brother. That's not peace."

I nod. I wouldn't want that for my mother either. "So, what then?"

"I guess I want both."

I smile, it's the kind of smile that acknowledges how impossible it is to want everything at once. "I don't know if we get both." Even admitting that means maybe we at least get one or the other, but I don't know if that is true either.

"Then I guess I just want to know that he's okay, you know?"

That I did know. I nod. "Yeah, I know."

The companionable silence falls between us again. This time Will starts flicking through the book about ghosts again. I pull another toward me and we both browse. I guess we're both searching for that sense of peace or knowing. My father would have said we needed to draw on faith, not knowing. After Mum had died, he'd said she'd found peace and was no longer in pain. I'd clung to that because it felt good to believe it. But I didn't know, and it wasn't easy to just let myself believe it without knowing now that Will had questioned it. Besides, Will needed to know too. Maybe something here would tell us both.

18

The weeks kind of blend into each other. It had become almost natural to down a tablet with a glass of water before bed each night. At first, Dad had been reminding me but now it was as routine as brushing my teeth and changing into my pyjamas. There was a new normal. And maybe it was helping.

It had been a while since I'd freaked out in front of other people. The kids at school had moved on to gossip about the guy who had shut down the school cafe. He'd made a report that there were rats in the storeroom. We're pretty sure there aren't, although there were several days when kids swore they were sick from contaminated cookies.

Georgia, Jenn, Synthe, and I had made do with packed lunches the past few days. Synthe was furious, especially on sushi days, but her parents had found a place around the corner that did a decent California roll. I've been getting by on peanut butter with strawberry jam. Dad didn't seem to care at all.

Still, after a few days of PB&J I was looking forward to ordering nachos at skating. Grease and cheese were just what I needed.

Focusing on food probably wasn't the best way to spend the morning session. Michelle kept having to remind me to concentrate as over and over my spins had been a sloppy mess. At least I was spinning in the right direction and getting pretty good at doing both directions consistently.

"Sara, concentrate," Michelle says again as my foot wobbles. I tighten the hold on the heel, toe combination and feel my balance solidify. "Good," she says. I turn out and she moves her focus to another student.

"What's with you today?" Synthe asks. She'd become a little less bitchy as I'd spent more time with her and the others. I was nowhere near being on her list of favourite people, but she at least greeted me warmly and spoke more than grunts to me.

I lift a shoulder. "I'm hungry."

Jenn laughs. "Seriously? This is all about your stomach?"

"Hey, it's been a rough week, okay?"

"For you maybe," Synthe says, with that snide aside I'd come to accept was just part of her natural charm.

"Not all of us have our school lunches catered for us, Synthe," I snipe back. "I'm hanging out for cheese and grease."

"You know what would be awesome? Cheesy crust pizza," Georgia says. I can picture it instantly. So soft and rich with cheese that it's practically dripping. The ham, cheese, and pineapple practically slide off the dough. I moan, thinking about it.

Jenn sighs. "They don't do that here."

"No," I agree, "but you know what they do? Nachos."

As we talk, Michelle winds up the session with the other students. "Make sure you practice," she calls out as the lights flash over our heads. Before she can even finish, I glide across the rink to the exit. I almost crash into Will because I'm so preoccupied with getting out of there.

"Hey there, where's the fire?" he asks.

"Nachos," I say, as if that's any explanation at all. The look of confusion on his face has me and the others chuckling as we all skate past him and head straight for the stairs up to the kiosk. Synthe and Jenn head for the table with the best view while Georgia and I put in an order for all of us.

I tap my card on the eftpos machine and call out to Greg who was the regular behind the counter. "Taking our seat!"

"I'll call you when it's up, Sara," he replies. It felt good to be one of the regulars. There was a cool sense of belonging when even the staff know your name.

"You know," I tell the others as I sit down, "we could do the cheesy crust too if you want."

"What did you have in mind?" Georgia asks.

"Well, Dad has been on me about inviting people over. We've got a six-man tent that hasn't been used in ages. Maybe it's time for a slumber party?"

Synthe rolls her eyes. I want to roll mine back but try to ignore the way she tends to get on my nerves. "A slumber party?" she drones, "Like little kids?"

"It could be fun, Synthe," Jenn says, ever the optimist. "And it has been ages since we did anything like that."

"What about a real party?"

I shake my head. "My dad would never go for that. But just the four of us? That could be fun."

SPIRIT TALKER

I can tell Synthe still isn't convinced. Georgia smiles. "That sounds like fun." She fixes Synthe with a glare. "Come on Synthe, even your parents wouldn't be cool with a full on party. Last time we stayed at your place they'd barely left us alone to talk and they kept checking the liquor cabinet as if they were afraid we'd raided it the second they turned their back."

Synthe's sullen look confirms this. Clearly this had been before my time which just goes to show how long ago it had been since they'd gotten together like that, picnics at the beach aside.

"So, should I ask my dad?"

Georgia and Jenn both nod. Synthe shrugs a shoulder. "Whatever," she says, which from her is probably as ringing an endorsement of the idea as I'd ever get. I smile at her and then the others.

"Okay then."

When the order comes up, I glide over to the counter. We'd all become pretty pro at carrying several drinks and trays of food across the carpet even on our wheels. I bring our food back to the table and the girls and I all dive in on it. It isn't until we are scraping the bottom of the nacho tray that my gaze starts to stray to more important things. Like Will.

The speed skaters are on their final race with the house lights fully up. The song on the stereo system has a strong beat and fast pace that matches their strides. Will has found a good groove in step not far from the lead of the pack. He calls out something to a guy next to him. It is Georgia's friend, Blake. I can't tell what he says, but he must have been egging Blake on because they both add a burst of speed as the finish line looms ahead of them. Will pushes hard and his friend does too. Blake nudges him in the arm but Will keeps solid and inches over the line ahead. They are both laughing as they drop their pace and circle the rink a few more times to cool down.

My belly complains a little as I push myself to my feet. I toss the empty nacho box in the bin and make my way back to the wall. "I'm going to regret that," I say to Jenn who comes up beside me.

"I'm already regretting it," she says with a groan. "Maybe I'll sit out the first few minutes."

I grin at her. "The pain is worth it."

"So worth it," she agrees. The rink begins to clear of speed skaters. The DJ announces the start of the general session and the moment the house lights drop to mood lighting I step out onto the rink. Georgia falls into step beside me for the first few laps.

"No Synthe?" I ask.

She shakes her head. "Her Dad came early to pick her up."

"Everything okay?"

Georgia doesn't look too sure, but she smiles anyway. "Sure. I bet it's all fine. You know what her folks are like."

I really don't. It is hard enough getting to know Synthe, but I have the impression that things are a little rocky in her family. When either of her parents tell her to jump she is quick to act. There is a strange insecurity in that. I feel a little sorry for her.

"Just us then. Jenn is still recovering from nacho-regret."

"No regrets here," Georgia says with another grin. "Race you?"

I shake my head. "Nope, my regrets are real. Besides," I say, stepping backwards and gliding in front of her, "I have to practice my spins. Michelle will be on my case if I don't have them nailed next week."

Georgia nods, her gaze skims the rink and I can tell she's looking for someone.

"He and Will were racing earlier," I say, giving her a knowing look. She blushes but doesn't say anything. Instead, she settles into her own pace and watches the entrance where Will and

Blake are chatting while they sip at their bottles of water.

I fall back, circling slowly to the centre of the rink.

Despite how unfocused I'd been earlier, I'd listened carefully to Michelle over the past few weeks. She shared some really valuable tips that had upped the quality of my spins already.

I find the centre of the rink and take my place under the disco ball that marked the most central point. I don't need to be in the centre of the rink to perform, but I like the balance and symmetry of this spot. Somewhere inside me is a bit of irresistible showmanship. Some might say a showoff, but I push that thought aside and focus instead on style and effect. I'm not doing this for anyone but myself. I glance to the edge of the rink. Georgia has pulled up at the rail and is talking to Will and Blake. So, maybe I can admit there's just a little bit for someone else's benefit. But mostly it's for me.

I focus on my feet again. There are two vital parts to maintaining perfect balance for a spin. The feet and aerodynamics. Feet, hips, chest, arms, head; everything in alignment. Well fed, and with the nachos finding a spot deep enough in my stomach to no longer be a flight risk, I find a level of focus for the first time in days.

SPIRIT TALKER

Heel, toe, spin. Everything else, even Georgia, Jenn, Blake, and Will fall away in the motion. Instead, my mind narrows on the movement. Flex, lift, turn. Arms out, pull tight, twirl. Breathe.

My eyes trace the walls of the rink. There are people skating but they're more like shifts of colour in the backdrop of the general impression of the rink. They're like the changes in light. In this movement there is just me and the turning of the world.

And then it isn't just me. A face, suddenly so close that if I'd reached out I'd hit them, interrupts the flow of the world around me. I gasp and feel my foot wobble. The back wheels of my toe skate hit the ground and my foot yanks with it. My balance collapses completely. I go to brace myself, hands dropping to my hips. Even as I do it, I know it is the worst possible way to prepare for a fall.

A pair of strong hands catch me from behind. I slam into something still hot, and warm, and a little damp. My breath, suddenly fast, is full of him. I glance up, expecting one face but seeing another.

"Will?" I ask. His hands steady me on my feet. My ankle pinches slightly but holds my weight.

"You okay?" Will asks. I glance over his shoulder. Grae stands there, looking very sorry for himself and for me.

I reach up and tuck my fringe back behind my ear. "Uh, yeah," I say, searching for a way to explain what had happened. "Just lost my balance."

He nods. "Almost got intimate with the concrete."

"Yeah," I say again. "Thanks, you know, for saving me."

Behind his shoulder Grae tries to get my attention. Frustration bubbles inside of me. Why am I still seeing him? Grae was one of those constant things. Even after being on medication for weeks he makes regular appearances.

He almost always shows up for art class. There I could reason it off as my conjuring him because of the painting. But he showed up in my room more often than I was willing to admit. I wasn't even always writing it down in my journal anymore. Sometimes he'd just hang out, writing poetry, and talking about his life. In a way, we'd become friends, and it was hard to let him go. I liked having him around. Mostly. But even so I pretended more often than not that he didn't exist because if I pretended hard enough then maybe the medication would actually start working.

SPIRIT TALKER

It wasn't. Not really. I'd just gotten very good at pretending.

19

I think Dad is more excited about the slumber party than my friends and I are. Well, I'm pretty excited too but all last night my dreams had kept replaying my last sleepover on eternal loop. My best friend, Erica, had come over and we camped out in the back yard. The house in Sydney didn't really have much of a yard but we managed to make do with the little scrap of space that fit a two-man tent, mostly.

It hadn't been long after Mum died. Dad wanted things to feel normal, so he'd arranged with Erica's parents for her to come over. I wasn't sure about it because I'd already noticed some of the strange stuff. Erica seemed a little uncomfortable about it too, but she focused on making me laugh and it was always good to have her around. We could sit quietly together, and we did for some of it. But she also tells the best jokes so as the moon rose above us and I tossed and turned unable to sleep she'd sat up and we'd let another couple of hours pass just messing around and having fun.

Eventually though, it was really late, so we'd settled into our sleeping bags. I remember wishing I could fall asleep, and then being asleep. I don't know how long I'd been sleeping when they came upon me, but I'd definitely been asleep.

I remember the jolt of awareness like waking up from a dream, except when I opened my eyes they were still there. Faces, dozens of them, looming over Erica and me. I'd seen things before, but this was the first time they'd felt almost real. It was the first time they'd seemed scary, like they could be violent. The whole experience had been visceral, tangible. It made me wonder if what I was seeing might really be there.

Even thinking back on it I can see them clearly as if they could step right out of my mind. I drag a breath into my chest to push it back. I didn't want to conjure them. I don't know how my hallucinations work but I don't want to ruin this slumber party before it even begins.

I push back the zombie faces and the blood-stained uniforms of the soldiers. I push back the sense of their hands passing over and through me. I push back my own screams, and Erica's. Instead, I focus on the glass of water I am filling at the sink. I focus on the little sheet of pills in my hand.

I pop one of the pills and swallow it. I take a breath and catch a reflection in the glass of the kitchen window. It's Synthe who must have just arrived when my Dad answered the door. She gives me a look. I try to convince myself that it's curiosity not judgement. She snorts as she drops a small stack of pizza boxes on the counter.

"Pizza's here," she says. She doesn't wait for a response, just stomps out the sliding door into the back yard where Jenn and Georgia have pulled garden chairs around our fire pit.

Dad comes in too, carrying soft drinks. He pulls some glasses down from the cabinet and sets them on the counter. "I'll make sure the slices are cut up properly. Do you think they'll want plates?"

I glance at my friends through the glass. I can already feel a welling of doubt in my stomach. I'm not sure I'll be able to eat the pizza. I glance down at the pack of pills in my hand and snap another one into my palm. I down it with the water and then tuck the tablets into their slot on a high kitchen shelf.

"Sara?" Dad asks. I realise I didn't answer his question.

"Uh, yeah, probably. Do we have any paper plates and plastic cups?"

He frowns. "I hadn't really thought that far ahead."

I roll my eyes. He'd made us wait a whole week for this anyway because he'd wanted to make it a real party, but he'd forgotten one of the most basic things. Still, pizza and Pepsi were at least a step in the right direction. "Plates are good, Dad."

I grab the glasses and one of the bottles of Pepsi and head outside.

"No vodka?" Synthe asks as I set the glasses down on the outdoor table. It's impossible to know when Synthe is joking because she always delivers things in a flat, blunt way that seems completely serious.

"Not this side of midnight," I say, trying to keep it light and assume she was joking. Jenn laughs so at least it had hit the mark with someone.

"My dad would never let us anywhere near a liquor cabinet," Jenn says.

"I don't think my dad even has a liquor cabinet," I tell her. "Don't worry, it's strictly caffeine and cheese tonight."

"Now the cheese I can get in on," Georgia says. She jumps to her feet as my Dad comes out balancing a stack of plates and pizza boxes. She takes the boxes from him and flips the top lid the instant she puts them down on the table. She pulls up a slice and has already eaten half of it before Dad waves a plate in her direction. She flushes, glances at her half-devoured slice, and sheepishly takes the plate. "Sorry."

"Hungry?" I ask.

She grins at me. "What can I say, we worked up an appetite."

"Only because we avoided the nachos this week," Jenn says, taking a couple of slices and putting them on her plate. She pours a drink and takes her plate and glass back to her chair.

The fire pit is just a small half barbecue. The flames create an orange glow on the charcoal. The whole thing is more for atmosphere than warmth. It doesn't make sense to have a real fire at this time of year but it's not really camping without something. I'll have to get the marshmallows out later just to justify the little flicker of flames.

Each of us settle in around the fire with our plates of pizza and glasses of Pepsi. Dad glances at us and shifts on his feet. I decide to put him out of his misery because he's clearly uncomfortable. "Thanks Dad," I say.

"You all set?" he asks.

"Sure, you can leave us to it. I know you want to go watch Castle."

There's a wash of relief over his face.

"Thanks for the food," I call as he retreats inside. He slides the glass door mostly shut. I'm not sure if the crack is so we can come in easily if we want to or if he's leaving it open so he can keep an ear on us. Once he settles in with his show it won't matter either way. I swear he's not deaf but for some reason he has to have the television cranked up several decibels beyond deafening.

I take a bite of pizza. Normally I'd be drooling over this. Cheesy crust Hawaiian is my favourite, but tonight it feels like cardboard in my mouth. This was clearly a bad idea. I watch the others as they chat together. They, at least, seem comfortable and content. So maybe my dread is all in my head.

"You and Blake were getting cosy," Jenn says to Georgia with a cheeky smile.

Georgia, plate balanced on her lap, raises her hands in defence. "There's nothing going on."

Synthe rolls her eyes. There were volumes of language in that movement and she'd mastered having whole conversations with it.

I smile, unable to resist joining their teasing. "Oh, trust me, there's definitely something, at least for him."

Georgia shakes her head. "You're imagining things. We're just friends."

"If he's too chicken to ask you out then you have to ask him," Synthe says. She's the last person you'd think would have good relationship advice, but I have to agree with her.

"You can talk!" Georgia says, her voice a pitch too high.

"I don't know what you mean."

"You and Jordan?"

Synthe snorts. "He's practically my brother."

"He is not!"

I place my plate to one side and lean forward in my seat. "Who's Jordan?"

Synthe glances at me and I feel like maybe she won't tell me. We hadn't exactly become besties in the weeks since I'd started hanging out with them. But I hoped I'd at least started bringing down her barriers. Georgia and Jenn give her a pointed look and she sighs.

"He's the brother of my sister's boyfriend," she admits.

I raise an eyebrow. "Cute, I take it?" The barest hint of a blush flushes her cheeks. I'm almost shocked because it's the first time I'd seen any real vulnerability show through her armour. "Very," I say with a grin.

She lifts a shoulder and lets it drop. "I guess. But like I said," she glares at Georgia, "he's practically my brother."

"It's not like you're blood," Georgia says.

"It would be awkward. If Taryne and Jeff get married, then he'll be there for every family gathering for the rest of our lives."

"A match made in heaven," Jenn says. There's a soft glow about her. She could light up the darkness with her optimism. "Like fate."

Synthe stares at her and shakes her head. "You have no idea what you're talking about."

"I get it," I say. "It's scary. If things don't work out, you'd have to see him and pretend nothing happened."

Synthe nods. "Exactly."

Jenn sighs. "Why do you always think the worst will happen?"

"Because it always does," Synthe says bluntly. I hate the little voice inside of me that agrees with her. I wanted to believe I could be optimistic, like Jenn, but realism is safer.

Jenn takes a bite of pizza and gazes into the pit. I feel bad, like we snuffed out one of the sparks that keeps her lit up. I search for a way to reignite the light. "What about you Jenn? Any prospects?" I ask, then take a sip of Pepsi from my glass.

She looks at me and shakes her head with a sad smile. "Nope. I just live vicariously through your love life."

I snort and Pepsi flies everywhere. The others all pull back away from me.

"Gross," Synthe says. She picks up a napkin and makes a show of wiping herself down. Which was a little insulting because I definitely hadn't actually hit her with the spray of sacrificed black liquid.

"Sorry," I say.

"Hit a nerve?" Synthe asks. There is amusement in her gaze, and I feel another spark of surprise. Maybe I had started to open the door to her heart.

"Of course not."

Georgia and Jenn both look at me as if my nose were ten inches long. Georgia grins. "Oh please, you can't pretend."

I glance at the wooden pickets of my back fence. Then give the girls a pointed look.

"Oh, I forgot," Georgia says. "Sorry."

"What?" Jenn asks.

Georgia leans over and whispers in her ear. "Neighbour?" Jenn gasps. I glare at her and she flushes, then whispers, "Sorry!"

"There's nothing going on there anyway," I say, although even I'd started to wonder, in that little secret part of my heart that's allowed to wonder such things, if maybe something could be. After the time we'd spent chatting in the library I'd started to feel like I could get to know him. We greeted each other when we passed in school. He'd even sat next to me once for history although that could have been a coincidence of seating rather than a conscious choice. Still, he'd been warmer than when we'd first met. Capable of speech, even occasionally a smile, but we weren't dating.

"But there could be," Georgia says, echoing my earlier thought.

I shake my head and shrug. It's non-committal, but the best I can manage in way of denial. "There's too much other stuff going on there."

"Other stuff?" Synthe asks.

I glance at the fence again, then sigh. "I can't get into it, but let's just say that I'm not in the right frame of mind to be dating. I've just moved here."

"That was weeks ago!" Georgia swipes another slice of pizza and takes a bite before saying around her mouthful, "You should go for it, Sara." Except it's full of pizza goop so comes out a little strange. Synthe and Jenn both groan.

Synthe raises her hand to shield her eyes. "Geez, Georgia. Eat with your mouth closed, would you?"

"I was talking!"

"Well talk with your mouth empty."

I chuckle. There was something about Synthe that I was really starting to like. Yes, she's prickly, but she can be funny as hell too. Not in a deliberate way, either, but in a wry way that I really click with.

"Let's just change the topic huh?" I suggest, picking up my glass. My mind is still on Will and the way we'd connected over death and the afterlife. Before taking a sip, I add, "Anyone know a good ghost story?"

Surprisingly, Jenn was the first to jump in. "I love ghost stories. Oh my God, you wouldn't believe the one I heard about Fremantle's old power station."

I raise an eyebrow. "Fremantle has an old power station?"

"Yeah, it's mostly run down and in ruins now. It was abandoned decades ago. Sometimes kids go there to tag it with graffiti or take some really cool photographs. It's right by the beach. Actually, we should go sometime!"

"But it's haunted." Synthe stands up from her chair and crosses to the brand new six-man tent Dad had set up for us. I feel like she's about to grab her stuff and ditch us. "Come on, guys! You've eaten, and ghost stories are better told in the dark."

I can't help the little bubbles of thrill that shiver through me at her words. Who would have thought Synthe of all people would really get into this, even leading the way? She unzips the tent and starts tossing blankets and pillows around the place to make it cosier inside.

I shove aside the abandoned pizza box and finish my glass of soda then follow her.

Georgia grabs one last slice and picks up the boxes. "I'll be right back," she says, carrying the boxes back inside the house.

Jenn, Synthe, and I settle onto the air mattresses. I pull a blanket around me. The outside lights flick off. Then Georgia makes her way back. She holds a torch which shines a white beam of light across the backyard. She lifts it to her chin as she steps over the lip of the tent. "Who wants a ghost story?"

Synthe reaches behind her to zip the tent up. "Jenn is going first," she says.

"Ah, but I'm going second. I thought of a good one."

"Fine, but then me because I've got a good one too." Synthe says as Georgia stumbles over the air mattresses to reach the farthest one. She drops the torch and it scatters light around us. There's just enough moonlight shining on the tent to create a grey glow everywhere the torchlight doesn't reach.

I scoot forward on my own bed and we circle around sitting cross-legged and facing each other and the middle of the tent. Jenn reaches forward and picks up the torch. "So, me first?" she asks. In the grey I can see the others nod and lean closer.

I don't really have a ghost story to share but if everyone is taking turns then I better start thinking of something. I feel a shiver as the last of the backyard disappears and it's just me, three girls, and a strange, wet, old woman, sitting inside our tent.

20

A long minute passes in silence. Jenn holds the torch to her chin. It casts deep sunken eye shadows and creates an odd red glow as the light passes through layers of skin. As the silence lingers Synthe shifts in her spot. I pull the blankets a little tighter around me.

Georgia seems most uncomfortable. She leans forward, clutching her fingers in her lap. Eventually she gasps out, "Jenn! Just start!"

Jenn just looks at her. She gives her a dead stare. Then, suddenly, her eyes roll back and we can see the whites. Georgia screams and Jenn cracks up laughing. She looks at each of us in turn, then begins.

"It was a dark night and the coastal winds had picked up. They howled along the sand dunes and whipped up the sand until it stung on the skin of three young boys," she began. "Now, when I say young, I mean our age. And they probably shouldn't have been out as late as they were because they had school the next day. Maybe karma has something to say for what happened to them."

Synthe snorts. "Karma?"

Jenn fixes her with a look.

Georgia leans forward. "Don't interrupt."

"As I was saying, three boys ventured along that beach one dark night."

"How is this related to the old power station?" Synthe asks, interrupting Jenn again.

Jenn grimaces. "I'm getting to that, if you would just be quiet. So, where was I? Yes, the three boys, spray cans stashed in their backpacks, were heading along the sand dunes to the old power station. It loomed ahead of them, dark and foreboding. Their torchlight cast a beam upon the crumbling walls and shattered windows."

Jenn waves the torch around the tent. It creates an atmospheric simile that helps add foreboding. "But they weren't alone," she continues. "They couldn't see him, but the old duty manager still patrols the old power station. The boys ventured inside, shouting and laughing to each other as they painted the walls in their latest tags."

"Hey you!" Synthe shouts, her voice deep and menacing. We all jump, even Jenn.

"Synthe, would you stop?" Georgia glares at her.

Synthe lifts her shoulder. "Nothing wrong with the occasional jump scare." She tries to look innocent. I wonder if there's a hint of her own fear there. Sometimes people do stuff like that just to make themselves feel less afraid, but Synthe looked more bored than bothered by Jenn's story.

Georgia rolls her eyes at Synthe. "Can you let Jenn tell the story?"

Synthe sighs. "Fine." She lays down on her stomach and props her head on her palm. "Tell the story."

Jenn smiles and puts her feet on the floor, leaning forward as she sits. "The boys had been there perhaps an hour when things started to get strange. At first, they thought it was just the wind. It creaked and groaned through the old bones of the building." Jenn added sound effects for the creaking and groaning. She was really making a production of this. I'd have to up my game if I want to compete on their story telling level.

She continues, "And sparkles of light danced over the walls." She twinkled and flashed the torch. "The boys, a little spooked, stayed close to each other. They weren't little kids, so they weren't afraid of the dark, not really, but there was more than darkness inside the old power station."

She fixes us with a look again, one that said, the story is really about to begin. "Now, there was a really awesome section of wall that the boys wanted to leave their mark on. There had been rumours all around school that only the bravest kids ventured to that point. It involved a little parkour and a lot of luck. But, boys being boys, they weren't afraid to give it a go. Except, the old duty manager wouldn't have it. The first boy made the leap just fine, but just as the second tried, the old duty manager reached out his ghostly hand and grabbed the boy's leg. As they touched the boy felt the grip and stumbled. He glanced down, and just the hand on his leg appeared in the world."

Georgia and Synthe both watch in silence. They're attention fixed on Jenn as she tells her story. I listen, trying to imagine it too. I have no idea what the old power station actually looks like, but I picture crumbling concrete, shadows, and boys like Will and Blake.

"'Dylan?'" Jenn cries, her voice husky as she tries to affect a boy's voice. I jump, startled by her raised voice. "'Dylan!'" she cries again. "But the boy wouldn't answer. He'd fallen down an old elevator shaft. The jump hadn't even been a big one, but he hadn't made it. His friends, one either side of the shaft, peered down to his crumpled body several stories down."

"Stories? Elevator shaft? He died?" I was totally lost. Because in my mind the boys had been on the ground floor. Kind of. Maybe not knowing what this building looked like made it harder to follow the story.

"Of course he died," Synthe says with one of her classic eye-rolls. "It's a ghost story. People have to die for there to be ghosts."

I fix her with a look. "But the duty manager had already died. Obviously. He's the ghost. You can't just go killing kids for kicks in your stories."

Jenn shakes her head. "I'm just telling it like it was told to me."

"Except you're not," Synthe says. "Cause when I told it to you I did it way better."

"Well you do better then," Jenn snaps at her. "It's not my fault you already knew the story. Besides, you ruined it by interrupting. I was gonna tell it right."

Georgia reaches forward and places a hand on Jenn's leg. "It's okay Jenn. It was a good story."

"Yeah," I agree, "It really was. I'm just sorry I didn't quite follow along. I don't know what the old power station looks like, so it was hard to imagine."

"Whatever," Synthe says. Sometimes she could be a real bitch and I didn't like her at all at those times. "My turn," she says, taking the torch from Jenn. Even when I don't like Synthe, I can't resist another ghost story, so I don't kick her out of the tent.

Jenn settles back, wiggling around in place until Georgia waves to her. "Come sit with me." The two huddle close, leaning on each other as Synthe begins her story.

Synthe and Georgia both had similar stories to tell. Each about some dark and stormy night in the middle of nowhere and some kids getting into trouble they shouldn't be. Synthe set a dark mood with a grisly poltergeist murderer who stalked the Esplanade hotel killing guests. Georgia told a beautiful but tormenting story about the Russian ballerina who haunted the stage of the old Edgley Entertainment Centre. When they'd both finished, four sets of eyes turn on me.

I shift on my spot. The strangest set of eyes are those of the old woman. "Tell them," she croaks, her voice a hissing wisp of sound that sends a shiver over my skin. I try to pretend I don't see her. I don't hear her. My meds are working.

SPIRIT TALKER

Instead, I focus on my friends. "I don't really know any ghost stories."

"Tell them," the old woman says again, louder this time. "Tell them about the pool that lies buried beneath your beds. Tell them, about Theadora. Tell them about me."

I don't want to, because listening to her, telling her story, is like believing in ghosts. And believing in ghosts is just as crazy as starting to think you might be seeing them. A hallucination is a hallucination. Brain misfire. Not real.

Georgia gives me an encouraging smile. "You can make something up if you like. It doesn't have to be good, but please, will you try?"

I glance at the old woman. It was just a story. And if it's a hallucination then I guess I did make it up, right? I swallow, not really sure.

I take a breath, then begin, "I guess there is one."

Jenn and Synthe both shift in place, giving me even more of their attention. Georgia strokes a hand down Jenn's hair. I take a moment to grab a bottle of water from the corner then settle back down in my place. I crack the lid and take a sip before continuing.

"Long before my Dad and I moved here, this house belonged to an old woman, named Theadora," I glance to the side where Thea sits.

She smiles at me and gives me a short nod. And, as she tells me her story, I tell it to the others.

"She was a lovely old woman and she enjoyed helping teach the young people to swim in her backyard swimming pool. In those days, a backyard pool was a rare thing and children from all over would come to Thea, visit her pool for fun or to learn." I swallow, feeling the dread building as Thea builds up to it. If she was a ghost then she'd died, somehow. I didn't think she was leading me toward a death by natural causes.

"But as the city grew, a new public swimming pool was being built by a fancy developer. He was a rude and brutish man who turned Cheeto orange when challenged and wore a suit that should have been finely tailored except it looked like something scraped together because he couldn't stand still long enough for even his tailor to get his gargantuan measurements correct."

Even Synthe seems entranced, and so am I. I add my own embellishments to the story Thea recounts, but the more I recite what she tells me the more I feel like I am almost having a conversation with her.

"The man wanted everyone to swim at the pool he was building but the neighbourhood had come to love Thea and her little backyard pool.

SPIRIT TALKER

They didn't mind that it didn't have several lanes or wasn't competition length. It was fun, and cool, and inviting. Plus, she made scones and biscuits that no public pool snack bar could mimic at any dollar.

"The pool opened to no public fanfare and as the days, and soon weeks, passed the man grew increasingly desperate. He issued notices and threats. He even tried to get the council to force Thea to stop using her pool. But Thea was a gumptious woman. She had guts and she wouldn't let some inflated balloon of a man tell her what to do. Instead, she threw a party and invited everyone.

"The old man came. He was full of bluster and everyone disliked him, especially Thea." I smile as she tells me the name she'd giving him. "Really?" I ask her, forgetting that I'm supposed to be telling her story to the others, not talking to her.

Georgia shifts and I glance at her, realising my mistake. She glances at the corner of the tent where Thea sits and swallows. Can she see her?

"Really what?" Synthe asks me. She glances at the corner too, then back at me, clearly seeing nothing out of the ordinary in the tent.

"Nothing," I say, perhaps a little too quickly. "At the party, Thea and the developer had dark words. He threatened to end her if she didn't close down. The townspeople defended her, telling him to go. And he did. He left the party in a huff and the squeal of his Mercedes tires.

"That night, as Thea cleaned up the back yard by the light of a gone-midnight moon, a shadow crept through the side gate. It squeaked a little on its hinges. She'd been meaning to get those oiled. Perhaps, if she had, she would have had no warning at all. But even so-"

I pause, my own breath caught. "He killed you?" I ask, putting it all together myself with a sudden dip of utter dread.

This time Synthe, Georgia, and even Jenn glance at the corner of the tent. The masks of their confusion confirm that they can't actually see her. But I have to know. I'd come too far in this story.

Thea gives me a sad smile. "Of course, dear," she says, her voice gentle. "You knew at the beginning. This is a ghost story after all."

"But it's not fair!"

"Sara?" Georgia asks, her voice quiet and hesitant.

"Did he get in trouble? Did he get arrested?"

Thea smiles sadly and shakes her head. "His swimming pool was never successful. Even after my death, those I'd taught became a little afraid of the water because I'd drowned. The rumour spread that it was an accident. People just stayed away from pools for a while and his closed down because of it."

"And him?"

"Sara." I jump as Georgia's hand touches my leg. My whole body is shaking. I glance at the others. Jenn is shaking too. Her face is sheet-white. Even Synthe looks a little shocked. I glance between them and Thea.

"I have to know," I whisper. I'm not sure if I'm telling Georgia or Thea.

"Know what?" Georgia asks.

"If he paid for it. For murdering her."

Georgia bends down, dropping to her knees beside me. She takes the torch from my hands and fixes me with a firm look. I want to glance away, to look at Thea again, but Georgia grips my chin. "Sara," she says again, this time firm, "It's just a story. There's nobody there."

I shake my head, and she drops her hand away. "But she is there. That's just it. I see her. She's real."

I don't know when I'd started to believe that. There was something about letting myself hear her story. It wasn't mine. I couldn't be that creative. That was real. She was real. Did that mean all of my hallucinations were?

I swallow. "She's real," I say again.

Beside me, Jenn pushes herself up. She's slightly crouched in the tent as she crosses to the door and unzips it. "I think I better get your Dad," she says. I'm not sure if she's just too freaked out and wants an excuse to leave or if she's actually worried about me.

"I'm not dangerous. She's not dangerous." I try to tell her. She shakes her head.

"Is that what the meds are for?" Synthe asks. She stands up too. "You really are crazy."

I swallow again. "I hate that word," I snarl at her back as she steps out into the moonlight. I really did hate it. The word felt wrong, and bad, and mean. "I'm really not," I whisper not really sure who I'm saying it for.

"I know," Georgia says softly. She pats my arm. "But I think the slumber party is over."

Dad gives me a questioning look as even Georgia goes to join him. He stands with Jenn and Synthe at the back door. I shake my head and he turns to the girls. I can tell he's apologising. "I'll call your parents," he says.

They go back inside, but I sit there a while longer, in the dark. Even Thea has fallen silent, although I still see just the hint of her lingering on the edges of my fuzzy sight. I swipe at my eyes and realise I'm crying.

"It's not fair," I tell her again. She nods her head.

"Life, and death, rarely is."

21

I feel a little wrecked when I wake with the sun on Sunday. My own bed feels strangely alien. I think it's because I'd been expecting to sleep out in the tent. After the others had left my Dad had come out to talk with me. I tried to explain. He'd said he'd get on the phone with Dr Hymore and arrange an emergency session, but I didn't feel like it was an emergency.

"That was quite the spectacle last night," a voice says from the seat at my desk. I push the blanket back and sit up. Grayson sits there, his feet propped on my desk. I can't help feeling a wave of comfort seeing him. It had been almost a week and I was starting to worry he wouldn't come back. Then I remember I'm not supposed to want to see him, so I scowl at him instead.

"You saw that?" I ask, then add, "What are you doing here?"

He looks hurt at my snappish tone. He fixes his gaze on the quill pen that he twirls between his fingers. Ink splatters from the nib onto my carpet but when I glance down there's no stain.

"You seemed troubled last night. I didn't wish for you to be alone, Sara Brooks."

"Well I was alone. I couldn't see you. Unless," I pause wondering how this whole 'ghost' thing works. If he's not a hallucination, did that mean there are times when I can't see him even when he is there? "Am I never alone?"

He smiles at me. "The other is a strange thing, Sara Brooks. I couldn't begin to explain it to you. But you are both alone when you will it, and never alone, at the same time."

"That doesn't make any sense."

"Think of it like the air around you." He stops, frowns, then shakes his head. "No, perhaps not. It's pervasive like that I suppose. It is always there. You see it in the gust of wind but even when it does not bluster it surrounds you. The other is like that. So yes, in that way it is the air."

"So, when I go to the bathroom there are ghosts around me?"

He chuckles. "One would not impose on your privacy. It is not the done thing."

"Ghosts respect boundaries?"

He tilts his head, then places the pen on the edge of my desk as he rises to his feet. "We," he begins. A look of confusion fills his features. "It is a difficult thing, Sara Brooks. You see, there is the here that is now, and the not here that is before or after. There is all time and all the world, beyond even if one were to venture there. You are but one small part of it. Minuscule, although I must admit you are the brightness in my day of late. I do so enjoy talking with the living and I have little occasion to," he diverged.

"But minuscule?" I say, prompting him to finish what he was explaining.

He smiles. "Yes, what I mean to come to about it is that as delightful as I am sure it might be to watch you shower," his eyes sparkle with mischief, "there is more to the world, to the universe, that makes such things trivial. That is to say, the other would have better things to do than to stalk you on your trips to the bathroom. Your privacy is more or less assured."

I smile, unable to resist it. "More or less?" I ask, raising an eyebrow.

He swallows and I see the bob of his Adam's apple and the flush on his skin. "More or less," he says again. He turns away and tilts his head as if he's listening to something, but he gazes out at the early morning sun.

I join him by the window. From here we can just see the hint of blue from the river and the rising city beyond it. "Beautiful day, isn't it? I can't get over this view. Sydney always seemed so drab."

Grae glances at me. "I would venture that it is a beautiful day for a walk. Would you agree?"

I meet his gaze. There's something in it, a knowing. "What are you getting at?"

He shrugs his shoulders and shakes his head. "I do not meddle. I simply thought you might like a walk along the beach. It is Sunday, after all."

"I don't always go to the beach on Sunday," I say, but realise I had kind of made a habit of it. Not intentionally, just that the weekends here were always so beautiful that I couldn't resist. I turn back to the window. It does look inviting out there. I sigh. "Okay, I guess I do agree." I chuckle as I turn and head for my closet. "Are you coming?"

I glance back at him as I open the doors of my cupboard. He shakes his head. "No," he says with a smile. "Minuscule, remember? I've other things to do." And then he's gone, disappeared, moved on to other things I guess.

I chuckle. "Damn ghost has a better social life than me," I mutter as I head for the bathroom to change.

The walk to the beach is relatively peaceful. I don't walk alone. People walk the paths nearby. There are real people, and there are the ones who exist in the world in a strange there-not-there way. Even they disturb me less than they had before. Some move in loops as if stuck in time. Others roam but take little to no notice of the living. They just exist.

As I walk, I start to filter them out. It's as if I can selectively see. There was an odd sense of control in that. It makes it easier to walk knowing that they are there but that they are also outside of where I am. I don't think I understand it at all, but maybe I would, one day.

The beach is relatively quiet. It's still fairly early so I guess I'm beating the normal weekend crowd. The sand crumbles under my shoes, slipping through the gaps in my sandals. I kick them off my feet and reach down to pick them up. I'd opted for shorts, a light summer singlet, and had even slipped my bathers on underneath so that if I decided to take a swim I could.

Down by the water I see a familiar golden-haired dog. It sits beside a boy, one who had also become relatively familiar in the past few weeks. Will. They both look out across the water.

I pause, uncertain. Should I go up to him? Would he want me to?

Instead, I head down the beach, walking in the water and feeling the sand squelch between my toes. I walk that way for about ten minutes before turning back. They're still there, sitting together, by the water. I go to walk past them as if I don't see them, but Will calls out to me.

"Sara!"

I feel a bubble of thrill and turn an extra high-watt smile on him as I feign surprise at seeing him. I love that he called out to me and I feel a bit silly for it. We're nothing, not really, despite what my friends had said last night.

"Hey Will, didn't see you there," I lie. I can't help flushing a little because of it. I pretend it's just the sun and bend down to pet his dog to cover it. "Hey there, Nikki. No ball today?" I stroke the soft golden fur. It's still damp from the water.

Will grins, then says, "Nope, you're safe from a soggy butt." He pats the sand beside him. "Wanna sit with me?" I glance at the spot next to him but the bubbles in my belly won't let me sit there. Instead I sit next to Nikki and run her fur through my fingers.

Nikki nudges my hand with her snout, so I rub her ears. "Do you always come out here on Sundays?" I ask Will, curious if it was part of his routine too.

I watch him over Nikki's head. He lifts a shoulder. "I guess," he says, "most weeks anyway. What else is there to do?"

"Well, we're pretty close to the city. It's just a ferry ride away."

He glances past me down the foreshore to the Mends Street Jetty where the ferries pick up passengers from South Perth for trips to Elizabeth Quay. "I guess." He doesn't sound particularly keen on the idea. "I haven't really felt like doing much. Not since," he pauses, then shifts on the sand and glances at me. I wonder if there's guilt in that. There seems to be something but I'm not sure what it is.

I'm torn for a moment, wanting to pry but not sure I want to ask directly. Instead I look for the work around and realise there was something we had in common that could get me there. "Is that why you see Dr Hymore?" I ask. His gaze snaps to me. There's darkness in it and I wonder if I overstepped. "I mean, for not wanting to do stuff." I shrug, not really sure I'm explaining what I mean at all. "People do that right? See a psychiatrist because they can't find any motivation?" Like depression, I think but don't say.

He swallows and turns his gaze back out over the water. He takes a breath then lets it out in the long sigh. "I guess," he says. I'm actually surprised he opened up, even that much.

"Because of your brother?" I probe a little deeper, tentatively.

Will is quiet for a long minute but eventually says, his voice quiet, "Yeah, because of Bobby." His voice cracks a little on his brother's name. "It was a long time ago."

"Not that long." I think about my Mum. It's still close even so many months later. There's still a sense of missing her that forgets, sometimes. Like at any moment she could come home. I wonder if that feeling will ever go away. I can't imagine what it must be like for Will, because for Will it wasn't just the hole of his brother missing from his life but the guilt of feeling like you're the reason it's there. That must be so much worse.

When Mum died there was a little release valve in the feeling too. I could almost accept it because it was better than her still hurting. The cancer had been hardest at the end. It ravaged her. Tore away at the parts of her that should have worked. In the end, she was less her and more her pain. So her death, in a way, it was better than that. We'd lost her to the cancer long before she really died.

But for Will, with Bobby so young, and fresh, and healthy. One minute he was playing, safe in the water, his whole life ahead of him. Then all of that went under. Is it worse to lose someone like that?

"You see him too," Will says. It takes me a moment to realise he was talking about Dr Hymore not Bobby.

I drop my hand to the sand and run my fingers through the warm, dry grains as I take a moment to focus. "Yeah," I admit. "But it's different."

I'm not sure I want to admit exactly why I see Dr Hymore. But I could at least talk about my mother.

"My mother died months ago too. But it was different with her. She had cancer." Even that little c word still felt hard to say out loud. Someone would probably say I should talk to someone about that too. Even when she'd been sick we, Dad and I, hadn't really talked about it. There was too much of it in the hospital that whenever we weren't there we just wanted to forget. I didn't need to tell Will that.

"You don't seem depressed," Will says. Again, his words are soft, sensitive to the topic, but there's a curious probing in it too, like he's trying to figure me out.

I shake my head. "I'm not. In a way- I mean I miss my Mum but by the end we were kind of okay with it, you know? She fought it, yeah, and there were times we thought she might beat it, but by the end it was more of a letting go. I guess we had a chance to begin grieving before she died."

I'd wandered away from Dr Hymore and really hoped I'd steered Will away from it too but apparently not. "So then, why do you see Dr Hymore?" I'm surprised by how direct the question is and glance at him. He looks angry, but sometimes it's hard to tell. Was it because I talked about my mother? Sometimes he's so hard to figure out.

"I wasn't avoiding the question. It's just different for us. That's what I was trying to say." I know my voice sounds defensive, but I can't help it. I shake my head and go to push up from the sand, but Will reaches over Nikki to grip my wrist.

"Don't go." His plea feels tormented. He swallows again, letting go of my arm. He turns back to the water. "I'm sorry, okay. I just wanted to know," he pauses, takes another breath, looks me directly in the eye, then adds, "I just want to know you."

I feel that, in the flutter of butterflies in my belly. He wants to know me. Is that like friends, or more than that? I can't take my gaze away from the sparkle of blue in his eyes. They are darker now, like deep water. I feel like my mind is running a million miles a minute asking a million questions. Can I trust him? Being deepest among them.

Maybe. A little voice inside whispers. I take a breath then say it, in little words. "I see things."

And there it is, out in the open. Except Will looks more confused than ever. "You see things?" He looks like he's trying to process that. "Of course you do, you have eyes, they work."

I shake my head. "No," I say, more defined, "I 'see' things." I emphasise the word. "Things that aren't, that can't really be there. I hallucinate. Dr Hymore says I'm schizophrenic."

Will sits with that a moment and we both fall silent. I realise it's probably actually a really big thing. I mean, if a guy, if Will told me he was certifiably insane I'd probably have reason to have serious cause for pause, if not true concern. But at least he didn't run away.

"It's not like I'm an axe murderer or anything. It's just that sometimes I see things, and hear things, and feel them too. Things that no one else can see."

Am I digging myself in deeper here or does it make more sense when I explain it like that? Does it make me less of a freak?

"Like what?" Will asks, "What things?"

I glance past him and realise for the first time that the boy was back again. Not Will, not

Grae, but the young one that seemed to shadow Will. The one I'd seen in his back yard and again in the library.

"People," I say. "People who have died."

It's the first time I'd really put that connection into words. They always were. Always dead. I wonder if I should mention that to Dr Hymore. Would it make a difference to my diagnosis?

Will seems to think on it, and I do too. Nikki nudges me in the side and I stroke my hand down her back as I think, and wonder. Eventually, Will breaks the silence between us. "You know," he says, "some people believe they really can see ghosts."

We both fall silent again but it's the kind of silence that doesn't need words. There was something in the way he said it. Something accepting, like he'd taken the whole 'she's crazy' thing and flipped it on its head. Because if people really could see ghosts then maybe I wasn't crazy. Maybe it was real. And either way he'd be okay with it. He'd be okay with me, broken or not.

We sat together for a long time on that beach. Me, Will, Nikki, and the boy, Bobby, his brother. It felt right. And eventually we talked more. Just him and me. And Bobby left us to talk. We walked along the foreshore, dropped Nikki home, and stopped for hot chocolate at a café. Then Will spent hours showing me around the animal exhibits at the zoo. The whole day passed, just him and me, together.

And it was good, probably better than any of the days had been since I'd arrived. Because it was out there, and Will was okay with it. Maybe that meant others would be too, like my Dad. Maybe. Someday.

22

y the time Will heads home, Bobby had joined us again. I watch him and his brother walk away. I don't want to intrude on that dynamic. It feels strange, as if Bobby, or maybe Will, has something sacred there when the two of them were together. So, rather than walk back to our houses together, I stay sitting on the beach and watch as the water changes colour with the setting sun.

Although we are more inland and the river runs in from the ocean to the west, I can imagine how it must look to see the sun set over the sea. It is an odd feeling because in Sydney the sun rises over it instead. Here, as the sun sets, the city lights up and the changing orange to purple to black of the sky casts a cascade of colour over the lightly chopping water.

With the disappearing sun comes a cool stillness in the air. The foreshore empties of people and the sand chills beside me.

I could stare out over the water for ages. And maybe I had.

When someone comes to stand beside me, I almost don't even stir. His energy is warm and safe and just as calm as the water and the breeze and the growing night.

He flicks a shell from his hand and it spins in slow twirls toward the water. I expect it to plonk under the surface, but it touches the water and disappears. There's no splash, no plop, no ripple.

"Who knew even shells can be ghosts?" I say, unable to resist it. I turn to look up at Grae.

He tilts his head. "Where does spirit begin and ghost end?"

I have no idea what he means but he doesn't look like he's expecting an answer. Instead, I ask, "What is it all for?"

"For?" he asks.

I try to make sense of what I'm asking him. Seeing him, and Bobby, and even the others who had been in the there-not-there reality over the course of the day, I'd begun to wonder. "Well you're here, and Bobby, but you have all of time and space to explore. And is there something after? Why don't you go there? What are you here for? What are any of them here for?"

Grae stares out over the water so long that I don't think he's going to answer. Eventually, I stand up and turn to head home instead. "Walk with me?" he asks. I turn back. His face, lit by the lights across the water and the streetlights and the shadows from the growing night, has something else within it. Something deep, and painful, and real. And it wars with something else that doesn't want to be any of those things.

"Will you tell me if I walk with you?"

"Sara Brooks," he begins but I raise my hand.

"Don't," I say, sure he's going to try and make excuses or tell me I wouldn't understand. "I need to know. I mean, there has to be a reason. There has to be a reason I can see you and that you're here, with me. Or what is it all for?" I pause, trying to collect myself because the idea of there not being a reason is worse than even just having hallucinations. Because if I can see ghosts, and it's just because I'm crazy, then… I shake my head. "Or is it just another way for my life to get screwed? Is it just another thing to make it suck and make it hard and make it not fair?"

"Sara," Grae says, this time softer. And it's more arresting because he only used my first name. "Walk with me," he says again, "and I'll tell you."

I stare at him, trying to work him out, trying to work myself out. But it's too hard. Eventually, I just nod, and we walk in step along the edge of the water in the still wet sand where the tide had been not long ago.

We walk maybe a kilometre down the beach in silence and I start to wonder if maybe he won't tell me. But then he does. "The life I lived was a very great many years ago. It was a challenging life. A life where I existed, knowing I would never have the voice I needed to speak the things I needed to say. Or to write them. I had not that power."

I wonder how it all ties together but rather than interrupt him I listen. His breath is soft, shallow, and somehow, I have no idea how, I feel the warmth of his skin radiating against my arm. We aren't touching, but I feel the warmth of his closeness in the cool of the night.

"When I died there was much of the life I had wanted left undone. I gave it up with too much left unsaid. I left no legacy, no truth behind. I left too much of life unexperienced."

He falls silent. We walk a way more in silence. I wonder if he will continue but he doesn't.

"So that's it?" I ask, finally unable to wait for him to explain more. I could hear the hurt and anger in my voice because the way he said it made me blame him. "You gave up your life and now you stay, like this," I wave my hand to gesture at his there-not-there form, "because you couldn't finish what you should have stayed alive to finish?"

He sighs, pausing on the sand, and turns to me. I look up at him, his grey-blue eyes, his soft mop of hair, his day-old stubble. "I stay because I don't ever have to leave. I can be forever. In this way I am not forgotten. I can still be heard, albeit briefly and by few. I refuse to leave a meaningless life behind me."

"But you are forgotten." I realise how bluntly I'd said it and try to retract the words. "I mean, it's been so long, all who knew you, they're gone too. What if letting go of this, letting go of the you that you were then, what if that is your true chance at having your voice. What if letting go is what true immortality is?"

He shakes his head. "You do not understand."

"I understand that you haunt me because of your ego. You want to be heard? I hear you, but you don't have anything to say."

The little bob of his Adam's apple feels at odds with the scowl on his face. He turns his gaze back to the inky blanket of the Swan River. "I still say much," he says, but his voice is small. "But perhaps I'll say nothing more of it to you."

The statement hurts. I didn't expect it to. I didn't even know this person, this ghost, whatever he was. It's not my problem if he wants to cling to this there-not-there existence. What did I even know about what came after?

Except, even when he seemed happy, he didn't really seem happy. He made light of things and he recited his poems for his darling Ella-May, and he talked about having all of time in his fingers, but he didn't live it. He moved through the world, through all of time and space, like a shadow. He didn't really touch anything. Even the shells he threw in the river couldn't create the ripples that it was so very clear his soul longed to make.

Grayson needed more than this. And maybe the only way he could get more, since resurrection was three hundred years too late, was in letting go of who he had been before and giving his soul a chance to become again.

23

It takes me a few moments to realise that while I'd been pondering the meaning of it all Grae had done his disappearing thing. That hurt even more. I'd wanted to comfort him, to let him know that I did like having him around, that I did enjoy his company, but he didn't give me a chance. Or maybe I didn't give him that reassurance fast enough. I was too busy unravelling it all in my own head.

I sigh, both sad and exasperated. Boys. They're impossible.

I turn back the way we'd come and begin walking back up the beach. My mind swirls with it all. I guess I'd kind of begun thinking about it when Will and I were in the library. The idea of there being an afterlife and reincarnation was comforting. The idea of my mother having a chance to go on beyond her death, it felt meaningful in a way that dying doesn't.

I don't like the idea that she might be stuck existing in the non-existence like Grayson. I wonder what life, or not-life, is really like for him. Maybe he does feel fulfilled by it.

But if he did, why would he roam? How can he be happy without really being able to connect with others? A spiritual, emotional nomad. Is there contentment in that?

All of it swirls around in my head. It weighs heavy. I try to shake it out like clearing cobwebs from a mind that didn't get enough sleep. But the pain and confusion linger. My heart aches and I don't know if it's for him, or for me, or for Mum, or for all of it.

I almost stumble when I realise that I'm not alone on this silent strip of beach. There, by the water, standing with his feet where the tide ebbs and flows, was Bobby. I wonder why he's back, why he's not with Will. He gazes at me and looks as if he's been waiting.

"You're Will's brother, aren't you?" I ask.

He nods. His eyes are deep, and dark, and sad. But the silence between us lingers when he doesn't speak.

"Do you talk?" I ask, wondering if maybe there was something more there, beneath the surface. Will hadn't really told me much about his brother.

Bobby nods again, but he seems to take a long moment to get the word, "Yeah."

"Will told me about you. About the accident."

Bobby nods. "I," he pauses again, like the words are hard. "I died."

I nod. "But you're still here." The night had grown cool. Not uncomfortably, just enough that my arms feel the chill. I tilt my head to gesture up the beach a little way. "Want to sit with me?" I ask. Bobby nods again.

He has a quiet way about him. His eyes sparkle with a knowing that seems really intelligent, wise even, but there is a strange delay in the way he seems to think and speak. He walks up the beach the way I'd indicated and sits down on the sand, again facing the water. I sit beside him and we both gaze out at the city lights and the curve of the snake-like bridge lit up over the quay.

"Will still needs me," Bobby says. And I realise he's answering my implied question. I hadn't asked him why, but he knew I was wondering.

"Does being here help him?" I ask. I'd wondered that, because I'd wondered if I should mention it to Will. As we'd spent the day together Bobby had come and gone. It was like there was always two places he wanted to be.

Will and I had talked more about ghosts, about seeing things, and about believing that something comes after. I'd wondered more than once if I should tell him about his little shadow. The boy with the big eyes.

I hadn't told him, because I didn't want to hurt him.

Would it hurt him?

For me, I'd let go of my mother. I love her. I'll always love her, but I want to know she's not stuck. I don't want her soul to be trapped to an existence watching without touching, seeing without saying. It's like always having glass between you and the people you care about. Over time, that distance must feel like a vast void of emptiness. What would that kind of anguish do to your soul over the years? And then watching as the ones you loved die? Watching their loved ones? Never really being a part of any of it. Just watching.

I don't want that for her. I wouldn't want it for me. I don't want it for Grae, or for Bobby. Poor little Bobby. Watching the pain his brother feels.

SPIRIT TALKER

Unable to help him understand that it wasn't his fault. Is there guilt when you're a ghost? Will felt it for failing to protect or to save his brother. Did Bobby feel it for the pain Will goes through now? Does he feel like it's his fault too? What would an eternity of that be like?

Surely, letting go is better.

"I can't go," Bobby says, and again I realise he's answering a question I'd asked a thousand thoughts ago. I wonder if he processes the questions slowly or if he spends his time finding his words. "I need to know he'll be okay. Dad too, but especially Will. They need to both be okay."

And I realise then that he doesn't linger to suffer for it. He's not really trying to help. He just doesn't want to let go without knowing that they will be happy again.

Which is maybe more heart breaking. It made me wonder again if my mother was still here. Did she wonder about me? Did she worry about me? Was she waiting to see if I'd be okay?

"I'll be okay," I whisper. Then, realising I'd spoken out loud, I try to change what I'd said for Bobby. I attempt a wavering smile. It's harder to smile now, but I want him to believe me, so I try, for him, anyway. "They'll be okay."

He looks down at the sand and runs his fingers through it. The sand doesn't move, and he sighs. "I can't build sandcastles anymore."

The idea of this little boy who could miss the sandcastles he used to build broke me. I wanted to reach out, to fill his hands with the sand, to build the sandcastle with him. I remember the way I'd felt Grae. The hallucinations weren't only sight or sound or smell. Sometimes, I could feel.

I turn toward him then reach my left hand over the sand, letting grains stick to the dampness of my palm, then reach for his hand. Our fingers touch. His hands are warm. He turns his head. His eyes are wider than even before.

"I can feel you," he says, his voice full of whispered awe. His whole body turns toward me. "I can't feel no body now. Not since. Not after. But I can feel you."

The rush of words is like a bubbling brook. Like they're bursting from him without the pause for thought. Like just the sensation of someone's hand in his, of his hand held in someone's, was the most important thing in his world in that moment. It had been months, I realised, since he'd felt someone's touch. How simple a thing, and how important, how vital.

"I can feel you too," I say, simply and softly.

SPIRIT TALKER

A tear falls from Bobby's eye and trails down his cheek. I lift my other hand to brush it away then rest that hand in my lap. "They will be okay, Bobby. You can trust that. You don't have to stay."

He looks down at my resting hand. I can tell he's thinking about what I've said. Silently, I urge him to believe me. Because maybe this was the point. Maybe I can see him because I'm supposed to help him let go. What other reason could there be.

My heart sinks again when he shakes his head. There's a deep crease of worry on his face, like he's remembering something more. "No," he says, and he feels very certain. "Will needs me. I can't go yet."

"But he really will be okay," I say, this time more determined to make him believe me. I don't know how. I don't know how he'll ever be okay with the idea that he killed his brother. I mean he didn't. But I could tell that Will felt that. He felt that in failing to protect his little brother, in failing to save him, he'd killed him. And how could anyone ever really be okay with that.

I look over at Bobby again. The little boy sits quietly, gazing at his hand in mine. Maybe Bobby was the answer. He wouldn't leave without knowing his brother was okay. Maybe knowing his brother is okay would make Will feel better too.

"Are you okay, Bobby?" I ask him. He lifts his gaze to mine. The depth of his grey-blue eyes sparkles in the flicker of light that glows along the foreshore.

"What do you mean?"

I think about it a moment before answering. "Well, you want Will to be okay about you being gone, right?"

Bobby nods but there's reserve and hesitation in his expression. He's not sure where I'm going with this. I'm not really sure either but I have to do something.

"Well, maybe that's what Will needs too? Maybe Will needs to know that you're okay. That you're not hurting, you're not suffering, that there's something more for you." I pause, realising maybe there's something even more that Will needs that only Bobby can give him. "Maybe he needs to know that you don't blame him."

"It's not his fault," Bobby says, really fast, in the way that is deeply knowing and that objects to even the idea that he, or anyone else, might blame his brother.

"I know. But he doesn't believe that, Bobby. Does he?"

Bobby shakes his head. "He thinks it's all his fault. I didn't mean to."

I nod. "I know. It was an accident. It wasn't anyone's fault. But maybe knowing it would help Will. Maybe knowing that you believe that will help him."

Bobby thinks on this for a long moment, then shakes his head. "But Will doesn't hear me." There's a desperate longing in those few words. "I tried when I first came. I shouted so loud. But he never hears me."

I squeeze Bobby's hand and he lifts his gaze to mine again. "But I hear you," I tell him. And a little spark of hope lights up his face. "I can tell him for you."

24

Hand in hand, Bobby and I walk back across the sand and grass to the street that leads us home. He swings our arms as if enjoying the tactile touch and momentum of having that contact between us. The streetlights cast my shadow down on the pavement and I can see the way my arm swings with the nothingness. Bobby doesn't cast any shadows.

Despite it feeling like the sun had gone down hours ago, it's not really all that late. Still, I realise my Dad had probably started to wonder when I'd be home. I glance, guiltily at the light streaming through our kitchen window. He was probably already making dinner.

SPIRIT TALKER

I glance down at Bobby whose own gaze was fixed on his front door. He'd grown still. "It's going to be okay, Bobby," I tell him. "But I have to duck home and see my dad first."

Bobby looks up at me, wide eyed. "But you said we'd talk to Will. You promised."

"We'll talk to him. I do promise. But I don't want my Dad to worry about me."

I catch a glimpse of him through the window. Bobby does too. He sighs and drops his hand away from mine. "Okay, I guess. But you won't be long, right? I want to talk to Will."

He'd become kind of excited about the idea since I'd mentioned it. I realised he probably had so much to say. I thought about how much I'd want to tell my mother if I could talk to her. It made me wonder why I hadn't seen her. I hoped it was because she wasn't stuck here, worrying, like Bobby. Or with things left undone and unsaid, like Grae.

"I'll be quick," I tell him, and cross to the front door.

Dad must hear the door as I nudge it closed behind me. "That you, Sara?" he calls. As if it would be anyone else coming into our house.

"Yeah, Dad. Sorry I'm so late."

I head for the kitchen and see him straining the spaghetti. He's preoccupied with that so doesn't see I'm standing in the room when he calls back as if he's trying to be heard across the whole house. "Was about to send out the cavalry. Saw Will get home about an hour ago."

"What makes you think I was with Will?" I ask. Dad jumps, not realising I am standing so close. I reach past him to grab two glasses out of the overhead cabinet. I put them on the counter behind us then reach into the cabinet underneath for two dinner plates.

Dad finishes straining and turns to serve the pasta onto the plates. I head for the fridge and our grated cheese. Spaghetti Bolognese, especially my dad's spag bog is nothing without a whole heap of cheese. As I turn back from the fridge, I catch Dad's raised eyebrow.

"What?" I ask, aiming for a completely innocent look. "We were at the beach."

"Ah huh." He turns back to the stove where the sauce is simmering. He turns off the burner and stirs the sauce with a spoon.

"Actually," I say, "I was thinking of going over there after dinner."

He turns with the hot pot in his hand and fixes me with a look. "You want to go over to a boy's house at night?"

"Dad," I say. Even I can hear the whine in my voice. "He's our neighbour."

"Oh, trust me, Sare-bear. Many a girl's head has been turned by the boy next door." He grins, teasing me.

"It's not like that." Although I'm pretty sure it maybe could be. Maybe. But not tonight.

Dad glances at the clock, then starts spooning the sauce over our pasta. "You can go but I want you home by nine, okay?"

I glance at the clock too. It was only just gone seven. I wonder how long it takes to tell someone their dead loved one wants to have words. How much time does one need for a conversation like that?

"Ten?" I counter. When Dad looks like he's about to argue I add, "We're right next door! If you start to worry you can just knock on the door and I'll come out. Besides, Rich will be home and it's not like there's anything going on between us. I just want to hang out and chat for a bit. He's a good friend."

I knew the word 'friend' was probably the crux word there. After what had happened with the sleep over the night before he knew how hard I was having it making friends. I had no idea how Georgia, Synthe, and Jenn were after it all. I feel a flush of guilt realising I probably should have called at least Georgia today to find out. But then maybe she should have called me.

I scatter cheese over the top of our spaghetti while I let Dad decide. "Okay, ten o'clock. But not a second later, Sara. Or I will come knocking on that door and embarrass you so completely you won't want to show your face anywhere near that boy again."

I believe him. He's pretty good at being entirely too embarrassing.

We eat together at the table. It was something I'd always loved about our family. We came together for meals. It had been different since Mum died. Quieter, more of a gentle, sometimes silent, companionship. But it was a touchstone. It made me feel like there was a place where I'd always belong. Here, at our table, at dinner time.

But I was also keen to get outside and go talk to Will, so I powered through the spaghetti pretty quick. Dad hadn't even finished half of his by the time I downed my glass of juice and rose to my feet.

I'm about to abandon my dishes but Dad shakes his head. "No way, dishes first." My shoulders sag and I roll my eyes at him. Deliberately I pick up the knife and fork, the plate, the glass, and stack them neatly in the dishwasher.

"Can I go now?"

SPIRIT TALKER

He chuckles and shakes his head which is really a yes, not a no. It's a yes with a side of how ridiculously obvious I was being about how much I wanted to talk to Will.

For Bobby, not for me, I tell myself. But it's not entirely true.

25

Bobby is sitting on the Saint-James's front step when I come out of the house. He looks really sad. He glances up as I step over the row of plants that line the edge of our front yards. He brightens as I come over.

"You came!" he says.

"Did you think I wouldn't?"

He drops his chin. "Well, maybe. I don't know you very good. I don't know why you want to help me."

I put a hand on his shoulder. I feel the lightness of him, as if my hand could pass right through, but I fix my thought on the touch and he becomes more solid under my fingers. "I like you, Bobby. And Will, and your Dad. I don't want you all to keep hurting so much. I want to help."

SPIRIT TALKER

Tears stain the rim of his eyes. He blinks, trying to clear his vision and nods his head, snuffling his nose a little.

He really had been worried I wouldn't come.

"Let's go talk to your brother."

Bobby wipes his sleeve across his nose and stands up. We both approach the door, side by side. I knock, and wait, then ring the doorbell for extra measure. The bell peals with a long strain of music that echoes through the house. From deep inside I hear a dog begin to bark. The barks get louder as the dog gets closer to the door. Interspersing the barks, I hear her snuffling under the rim of the door.

"Dad!" Will shouts as the dog continues barking. He must be somewhere upstairs. I glance up but I can't see him.

"I'm writing," Rich shouts back.

"Dad, the door," Will shouts. I shake my head. It seems really ridiculous. Families are strange. Everyone seems to have different ways of doing things. At home, if the doorbell rang, we'd just answer it, not argue about who would answer it.

I wonder if I should ring the bell again but don't. Nikki's ongoing barks make it clear there's still someone at the door. They know I'm here and they must know that I know they're home.

A door slams upstairs and not long after the front door finally swings open. Will stands there with one hand on Nikki's collar. He looks pretty pissed off, but he brightens when he sees me which gives me another of those strange belly flutters.

Nikki strains against his hold. Her snout snuffles at me and she jumps at me, but Will holds her back.

"Sara," he says, with a smile, then tugs back on Nikki again, "Down girl." She whimpers but settles. Her gaze seems to flick between me and Bobby. It gets me wondering if maybe she can see him too. Deep in her throat she makes an odd whining sound.

I turn my gaze back to Will. "Hi," I say, suddenly really shy and not at all sure I should be here. How the hell do you tell the boy you're kind of falling for that his dead brother wants to talk to him?

I stand there, looking stupid and awkward long enough to realise I probably look stupid and awkward. "Can we talk?" I say, just because I have no idea how else to start.

"Yeah, sure." He steps back, tugging Nikki with him and giving me space to come inside. "Want to go to my room?"

I glance at the stairs. Did I? I mean hell yeah… But this was going to be awkward enough. Besides, I wondered if they still had Bobby's room up there. I glance at him. He looks uncomfortable too. Like the idea of going up there makes him feel a bit sick. Too close for comfort.

"Can we go out the back?" I counter. I'd seen their yard. It was nice. And Bobby liked it out there. I'd seen him on the swing and playing his guitar.

Will closes the front door behind us and lets Nikki sniff at me a moment before letting her go. She's much calmer now and after checking me out she turns her attention to Bobby, sticking close to his side. He drops his hand as if to stroke her fur. I wonder if he can actually feel her or if she can feel him.

"Sure," Will says, responding to my question. He doesn't seem to notice the way Nikki hovers. Bobby and the dog are already leading the way, so I follow them. I can feel Will's eyes on my back and realise I'm doing a weird thing. Wandering through a stranger's house and knowing exactly where to go. Oops. I pause and let him show me the way.

Outside, the stars are on fire. The beautiful day we'd had together opened on an enchantingly, cloudless night. I look around their tidy yard. It's understated, with a quiet beauty. Their house has an elegant, modern feel to it. Pristinely kept. And the yard too, was clipped, and neat, and orderly. It seemed so at odds with the turmoil of emotions that seems to churn through the people who live here.

Will reaches the steps that lead down off the porch to the grass below. He sits down and leans his back against the railing, then gestures to the opposite side of the step. I take a seat, then glance again at Bobby.

Bobby looks suddenly scared. I can feel what he's feeling as if it's my own fear. And maybe some of it is. This wasn't going to be easy and a part of me regrets making the offer. But I had promised him. I couldn't break that.

"Ready?" I ask. Bobby shakes his head.

"Not yet."

"Okay," I say. Bobby crosses the yard. He sits in the swing and I watch as he pushes his legs back and forth. I wonder what it must look like for Will as the swing starts to sway back and forth. But when I turn to Will he's too busy looking at me to notice.

"You okay?" he asks, and there's a knowing smile. "Company?"

And suddenly it is okay. It's all okay. Because in the space of the hours we'd spent together today he really did understand. When I did weird things, when I spoke to people who aren't really there, or who are but that he can't see, he didn't feel strange about it at all.

I smile at him. "Yeah, I'm great."

"Today was good," he says. I can tell he's remembering the beach. Had we really spent hours, the whole day, just hanging out? Wandering the foreshore, the cafe, the zoo. I guess we had. And it hadn't felt strange at all.

"Yeah," I say again. I think I'm getting too dependent on that word. But it encompasses so much more than a simple affirmative. It is like saying 'it was amazing' with four little letters.

As we start to talk about the day we'd had, I relax. My back leans against the wooden railing. My leg is so close to his that we're almost touching, but not quite. We talk together for ages and it feels so easy. The moon rises higher in the sky and the stars come out in full force. Eventually, quiet lulls between us.

"I'm glad you're here," Will says, his voice deep. There's something beneath the surface but I can't tell what it is.

"You are?" Of course he is. I could tell, but it still felt strange. "Why?"

He lifts a shoulder in a careless kind of half shrug. "I don't know. I guess I like having you around."

"I like being around you too," I tell him. But I let my gaze wander away because the intensity in his is more than I can handle. He's okay with the fact that I see things. But I still don't know if he'll be okay about me talking to him about this. I watch Bobby. He's still swinging on the swing and he watches us with a thoughtful look as he does it. When I meet his eye, he gives me a curious look. I raise an eyebrow, asking without words. He nods.

I take another moment to wonder exactly how to broach the subject. "Have you ever wondered about Bobby?" I ask. The words feel hurried and awkward. I feel Will tense up beside me which is weird because I hadn't thought we were sitting so close to each other. But there's a sudden wave of tension radiating from him. A barrier that went straight up when I mentioned his brother's name.

"Sara, don't," he says. I wonder if he already knows. Maybe, somewhere within him he does. He had to wonder. Maybe he hoped. Maybe he didn't.

I turn to him. His jaw is locked, his eyes darker than ever. I want him to smile again. To relax and be that friendly guy who seemed to light up just because I rang his doorbell. I don't want to hurt him.

"I'm sorry," I say. I don't know what I'm sorry for exactly. I guess I'm sorry that it has to hurt so much.

"I don't want to talk about that."

"I know, but it's important. For both of you."

His shoulders lift a little, like he's protecting his neck. It's an odd gesture, a shrinking, pulling away, closing me out kind of move.

"You said, Will. You said that maybe what I'm seeing is real. And if it is then I need you to know. I need you to listen. Because he's hurting too. You're hurting him."

"Stop it," Will snarls, his face dark with anger. He shoves himself up off the stairs and starts to pace the yard. He shakes his head, glaring at the dirt in front of each step. "You don't know anything."

I realise that I'd stepped a little too close to his own sense of guilt and I try to peddle it backward. I walk toward him and reach out, putting my hand on his shoulder. "It's okay, Will," I say, but she shrugs me off.

"Leave me alone!"

"I just want to give you a chance to talk to him. He wants to tell you things. He needs to. He needs to know you'll be okay so that he doesn't have to stay anymore."

Will shakes his head. "You really are crazy."

"You said you believed me."

"You know, I didn't say that so that you could make fun of me. We're real people Sara. He mattered to me. Don't mess with it."

"I'm just trying to tell you, Will. He doesn't want you to blame yourself. It's not your fault."

I can tell he's not really hearing me. His whole body has walls up. I don't know if I'll ever be let inside again.

So much for being able to help people. This was a mess.

"Just go, okay," Will says, his shoulders drooping. Sadness weighs over him, washing away the anger. "Just leave me alone."

"I thought you of all people would believe me."

He shakes his head. "No, you don't even know what you're talking about." I can feel the sparks of his anger and grief and pain ricocheting through him like bolts of electricity. "Just go!" The anger flares again and he glares at me. I feel completely lost and just stand there, staring at him for so long that he shakes his head. "Fine," he snarls, "You stay, I'll go." He storms away, stomping across the porch.

SPIRIT TALKER

He slams the back door and leaves me here, alone, in the yard. The swing beside me still sways back and forth but it's empty. I gasp, trying to find my breath as a wave of pain floods through me. This time it's all mine. Because I really had thought he believed me. He didn't think I was crazy. Trusting his faith had given me my own. But maybe I really was broken, maybe none of it was real.

My legs feel week and I realise I'm shaking. I suck a breath into my lungs and try to stop freaking out. The back door creaks. I glance up, hoping it's Will, almost dreading it might be because I don't want him to call me crazy again.

Rich stands there, his hand on the door frame. "Can we talk?" he asks, quiet, concerned, and perhaps a little curious.

I don't really want to talk to him. What would I say? What did he want to say to me? Would he tell me to leave them alone, like Will had? I don't know, but I couldn't not hear him either.

Rich comes out and sits on a small garden bench. I hadn't seen it before. Behind a neatly clipped hedge, it was hidden from view of the back step and the back fence. "Come sit and talk with me, Sara. It's okay, really."

I glance at the back door, wondering if I should just go home. But there's a little voice inside me urging me to stay, to listen. There's something about the way Rich carries himself. Even the way he sits, waiting. He's not pressuring me to do anything, but I can see in him a need to put out into the world some of what he's feeling. There's too much pain left inside, and he needs a way to express some of it.

So, I do go and sit with him. It feels awkward and intrusive and kind of weird to have a guy my dad's age sitting beside me. We sit in silence for a while and I wonder if maybe I should say something, but I don't know what to say.

Eventually Rich says something first. "I appreciate what you're trying to do for Will."

I glance at him, wondering how much of what Will and I had argued about he had heard.

"Will is in a lot of pain. It's mostly my fault. When we first lost his brother, I was very angry. We all were," Rich explains.

"It wasn't Will's fault."

Rich nods his head in a single, brief affirmative. "I know that, now. But at the time I guess I blamed him too. Because blaming him was easier than blaming myself. When bad things happen, we want to believe something could have stopped it. Something should have stopped it."

I knew exactly what he meant. When Mum got sick, I'd been furious. Furious that the doctors hadn't caught it sooner. That Dad hadn't noticed how sick she was. That I hadn't. I could understand that pain.

"But you don't blame him, not anymore."

"I don't."

"Maybe you need to tell him that."

Rich sighs and the silence between us lingers again. "You're right, Sara. I should," Rich admits. "He won't want to hear me. He doesn't like to listen to me anymore."

"You have to try."

"I will." The silence descends again. I glance across the yard, seeing my own house and the window to my room. It's dark and empty. No Grayson. I hope he's okay too. Everything was just a mess. Eventually, when it seems like Will's dad doesn't have anything else to tell me I stand up.

"I should get home," I tell him. He nods.

"I'll show you out."

When we reach the front door, he pulls it open. "Sara?" he says, and I pause on the threshold, turning back to him. "Thank you. For trying with Will. I know it might seem like it isn't helping, but I think it is. He's been more himself since you came along."

A hint of a smile flickers at the corner of my mouth. It fades as fast as remembering that I might have just completely stuffed all that up by pushing

Will too hard. But I liked the idea that I brought a little light into the darkness he'd been facing since Bobby's death.

And maybe that was enough. A little light, and the chance to maybe, eventually, forgive himself. Even if we could never be friends. Even if he hated me forever. Maybe that would be enough.

26

School feels kind of empty on Monday. So much had happened, so much had changed, over the weekend that everything feels strangely ordinary. Suddenly, double math is the most mundane thing ever. Or maybe it always had been but because of how extraordinary everything had been it felt odd to sit here and learn about linear equations.

When the bell rings for recess I head for the terraced garden, and my friends, because that's what I'd done for lunch at school pretty much since I started here. Even before I reach the terrace, I feel an odd kind of tension in the air. I glance around and see some of the kids giving me strange looks. Some of the there-not-there people are too, but theirs are curious.

"Sara! Sara!" A young woman dressed in an old-fashioned nurses outfit calls out to me, rushing over. She's one of the ghosts and I can already feel too many sets of eyes on me, so I try to pretend I don't see or hear her. She tries to grab my arm and I flinch, but her fingers pass right through my skin.

Hey eyes, full of torment and longing, are so deep and dark and haunted that I want to reach out to her. But I can't. Because being the crazy girl at school would be worse than hell. I was having a hard-enough time pretending as it is. And there's something about the atmosphere now that has me worried.

It's worse when I reach the garden. Georgia, Synthe, and Jenn sit in our usual spot along the wall. They chat to a group of guys about our age. Synthe in particular seems to be loving the attention. She flicks her red hair back over her shoulder and laughs, then glances at me, leans close to the guy standing opposite her, and whispers something to him. He glances my way too, his eyes a little too wide. Synthe laughs again. And I feel my gut sink to my knees because I already know what's coming.

I try anyway though. "Hey guys, sorry about the other night."

SPIRIT TALKER

Georgia looks at me and there's regret in her eyes. I know what's coming and she knows what's coming and feels sorry for me because of it.

"You can't sit with us," Synthe says. She lifts her chin and shifts against the wall to create less room for me.

I swallow and feel the tightness in my jaw. I don't want to cry but I can feel it all sitting there on the surface, so ready to break out. If I let any of this get away from me, I'll look like a complete wreck. I swallow again and remind myself I barely knew these girls anyway.

The guys they had been talking to linger as if they're watching a spectator sport. "Is it true?" The one Synthe whispered to asks me. He raises his hands and waves them in front of him. "Wooo," he calls, in an eerie, spooky way.

Is that all they'd told him. About ghost stories? But the guy grins and lifts his hand to his head, swirling a finger, in the universal symbol for full on crazy.

"Can I talk to you guys? Alone?" I ask, my gaze fixed on Georgia. I know I'm pleading. Not in my words, but in my gaze, because I can feel desperation right to the core.

And I hate feeling so many eyes on me. It's not just Georgia, who keeps her gaze averted as much as possible, or Jenn who doesn't look at me at all, or even the glee in Synthe's taunting looks, but it feels like the whole school, or at least our whole grade, is here to see this.

"There's nothing to talk about," Synthe says, clearly the group's voice. "We don't want you to hang out with us anymore."

"Why?" I ask and fix a glare on Synthe.

She looks me dead in the eye. "You're a sheep, Sara. Trying to fit in when you don't belong."

I'm hit with several waves of emotion at once because something in what she's saying feels one-hundred percent smack on, I never really belong, but sheep? Really?

I glance at Jenn. She keeps her gaze fixed on the ground in front of her and fiddles with the sandwich between her fingers but doesn't raise it to her mouth.

I glance at Georgia. I can feel her sympathy more. There's something in her look that says I'm sorry without having the courage to actually do anything about anything. They'd made a decision about me, and maybe about their own sense of acceptance and belonging, and I didn't fit.

Beside me, the guys start baaing. And the hurt, the confusion, the wrongness of it feels like a whole sack of bullshit. What the hell did they know anyway? And I don't even need them. Except I do. Or maybe I do. I don't even know.

I glance up, something drawing my eye past Synthe and see Will. He's watching too. Of course he is, because humiliation, being outcast, and having everyone know that I'm a mental case just isn't bad enough. I want him to do something, to say something. But his face is blank, almost absent, and I think that hurts more than any of it because I suddenly realise that he's not seeing me anymore. I don't light him up anymore. I'm nothing.

I suck a shaky breath in and close my eyes for a half second, just to pull myself together. Because I can't let myself break down in front of these people. They're not worth it. Except they are, and that's why it hurts so much. But they won't fight for me. They won't protect me. They won't believe me. Not even Will.

I lift my chin and force myself to fake a defiance I don't really feel. I pull my shoulders back instead of letting them droop forward like I really want to do. I fix first Synthe, then Jenn, then Georgia with a brief stare that says more than any scathing words could.

Then, without saying anything at all, I turn my back on them and walk away. Because what can I really say anyway? I'm not a sheep. I'll never be like everyone else. But they're right, I've tried for so long to fit in and pretend I'm normal when I'm not.

So, I let their eyes follow me. I let the there-not-there people look on with their curiosity. I let them whisper behind my back, or not. And I head for my sanctuary. My alone place. My library, and my journal, and the stacks where my head touches the books about crazy people like me.

Because who the hell cares about any of them anyway.

Except I do. I find the darkest part of the library and settle in. I blow off Japanese and Music, then can't even look at Jenn when I finally surface, puffy eyed and pathetic for English.

And for the first time I truly feel alone. Surrounded by everyone but cast out, and different, and completely, utterly alone.

27

It's weird to be in Dr Hymore's office on a Monday. Tuesdays had just become a normal thing. He'd check in with me, tweak my medication doses, ask about how I'm feeling and if I'd been seeing things. Sometimes I'd tell the truth, sometimes I'd lie, and life had become a new kind of normal.

Today wasn't normal. School had sucked. I had no friends. And the medication didn't work anyway.

I am and always would be crazy.

Dr Hymore begins after we sit down opposite each other, "Your Dad tells me you had an episode over the weekend."

I hate that word. 'Episode'. It's dehumanising like what I experienced was an aberration, a wrongness, a disconnection from life. But Thea had been real to me. She was real. She was a real person who had experienced real pain and a real wrongness at the end of her life. Her story mattered. It wasn't just 'an episode'.

I swallow, because only a crazy person would say that to their doctor. Instead, I say, "The medication doesn't work."

"Tell me about that," he responds, pen in hand poised over the paper. Right now I hated that notebook. It turned me into something clinical, to be studied, a freak.

"About what?" I ask. I lean back in the chair, letting it envelop me. I know what he is asking but I don't want to tell him anything at all.

"How does the medication make you feel?"

I shake my head. "It doesn't work. I haven't stopped seeing things. Even when I said I did, or pretended I did, I never did. They're always there. The medication doesn't work." It was like a floodgate of frustration opened so I just keep spewing it all out. "I wanted to pretend. And it gives me fuzzy edges so I can sort of pretend that I'm seeing less. I can pretend they're not there sometimes, or even just pretend I'm imagining it because it's blurrier and it's harder to understand what they're saying. Sometimes when they talk it's just a buzz of noise because the words are harder to make out. But they're still there."

He nods in that condescending way that has always really just pissed me off. "So, you're finding the hallucinations are less distinct. The medication has some effect. Maybe we need to increase your dose again."

I fix my gaze on the coffee table between us rather than meet his eyes. I realise how much he actually probably doesn't really listen. Or maybe he hears selectively. Because the medication doesn't work. I'd told him that. Increase the dose?

"It makes me sleepy. It makes it harder to focus and to concentrate. It makes it harder to paint and to see even my own memories. It makes the whole world hazy. And it doesn't even work."

I can feel his gaze on me. Patient, nodding, his foot sways a little where it rests in the air because he's crossed one leg over his knee. "Sara," he says, and I know he's trying to draw my gaze, but I refuse to look at him. He sighs, then continues, "I'd really like you to choose a voluntary in-patient treatment."

I do glance at him then. "Why? I'm not crazy!"

The edges of patience in his features annoys me even more. So does the way he slowly explains. "What you're experiencing is not normal, Sara. And when we adjust your medication as an out-patient we have to do it very slowly and very carefully because it is difficult to monitor and control the potential side effects. But if this medication isn't working for you," he raises his hands to silence me because he knows I'm about to insist again that it doesn't. He continues, "and you're right, it's possible it isn't helping, but that just means we haven't found your right fit yet. We have other things we can try. If you were an in-patient, we could find the right solution for you much more quickly."

I grew more and more restless with every word. Feeling skittish I push myself up from the chair and pace the room a little. He watches me move while I think about what he's asking of me. Eventually, I pause and look at him. "I don't want to," I tell him. "I've got school. I've got friends," my voice cracks a little on the last word. His razor-sharp wit catches that too.

"You father tells me the incident on Saturday involved your school friends." I nod. It's not worth lying about. "These sorts of things can put a strain on relationships, especially ones that are relatively new and fragile."

"I'm fine," I tell him and return to pacing. "The hallucinations aren't even bad. And I mean, maybe they aren't even hallucinations."

"What do you mean?" The sharpness is in his voice again. There's a kind of tension, like he's not sure how close to the edge I am and he's stepping very, very carefully. I wonder if it's just part of the job to always be on edge because crazy people are dangerous. I try to pretend that must be it because it's not like he needs kid gloves for me. I'm not going to hurt myself or anyone else. He knows that, right? Maybe he doesn't.

So, I look at him, meeting his gaze, and letting him really see me when I ask, "Can't some people see ghosts?"

The look of disappointment that crosses his face disappears behind a mask so fast that I wonder if I imagined it but I'm pretty sure I didn't. "Sara," he begins, slowly again with that deliberate way he has when he feels like he needs to explain something very, very simply. "It's vitally important that you focus on keeping your objectivity. Remember, when you first came to me, you were able to see the distinction between what was real and what was hallucination. That's a very good thing, but the more this goes on in your life the harder it can be to remain objective. It's important, for your health and for the success of the work we do here, that you continue to maintain that line between what is real and what is not real. That's what we all want for you."

Was that the standard answer? That believing in ghosts is like believing in Santa or the Tooth Fairy? Like I'm giving into a fantasy instead of facing reality?

"But the people I see, they're always dead people. Some of them had whole lives. Like Grae, and Thea, and Bobby." I hate the sound of desperation in my voice.

Dr Hymore glances at his watch and sighs with frustration. "I'm sorry but we do need to wind up today. I want to take more time with this Sara, so I'll allow for a double session tomorrow. And I think we should speak to your father about this. I'm going to strongly recommend he goes forward with an in-patient option for you."

"I don't want that!" I know I'm almost shouting. And he makes me feel even more childish when he fixes me with one of those understanding, compassionate looks that I've come to believe less and less the more I know him. I put my hands on my hips and glare at him defiantly.

"Sara, I know it's difficult to understand at your age, but this is a transitional point in your life. Right now, if we approach your condition with the right care and procedures, you can live a very ordinary, normal, productive life. The outcomes are very different for those who go untreated. Schizophrenia is the kind of condition that can and will impact every aspect of your life. Your relationships, your education, your whole future. If you can't make the right decision for yourself, then your family will need to make it on your behalf."

I hate that I believe him. I hate that I can already see the way it's affecting my whole life. Does it matter if the ghosts are real or not? It makes the people around me pull away. It makes it harder to just be me.

I try to remember the girl I was before I started seeing things. Before I lost Mum. Before.

I'm not that person anymore. Life was simpler then. I never wondered if I'd be okay. I never wondered if my mind was broken. It's hard enough as it is, without being crazy.

And what did it matter anyway. If they were ghosts and I could see and talk to them, I wasn't helping them or the people I care about. My seeing Bobby wasn't helping Will. I couldn't even help Grae or Thea. And it certainly wasn't helping me.

28

Normally, the ride home on the ferry after my appointments had been relaxing. I'd sit by the window and watch the light chop of the river water beneath us. I'd look for the little brown blobs of jellyfish under the surface of the water. I'd clear my head and start to feel better.

The ferry itself was busy with people heading home after work, but it was busy in the way where everyone was real, and alive, and not part of my crazy mind making things up. It felt so normal and it helped me feel normal too.

But not today. Today, my mind kept churning. I hate the idea of going to a psychiatric institute. The centre that Dr Hymore had talked about didn't actually sound that bad, but my mind keeps conjuring locked and padded rooms full of people screaming and crying and thrashing about. I pictured getting strapped to a bed. I pictured wearing unflattering white gowns and sitting around in groups where they expect you to share with other crazy people.

Besides, right now I was just the girl who flipped out about ghosts at school. In a few days, I hoped, the rumours would die down and everyone would just go back to ignoring me. I'd be okay with that. Even if I never really made any new friends, I'd be okay just being invisible. But the girl who is out of school for days, weeks, months, because she's in a loony bin? Well she's not invisible when she comes back.

And, if I'm away, then I can't even try to fix things with Will or Georgia. They'd both know. How could they not? And who would want to be friends with the crazy loony-bin girl anyway?

And honestly, if I wanted to be real with myself, I don't even know if I want to not see Grae, and Bobby, even Thea. I wasn't even sure if I would see them again. Grae had been so angry and Bobby was hurting. I'd made things worse for both of them. But they were my friends. Sort of.

All this churned through my mind as I gazed out of the window. The trip across the Swan isn't all that long and my mind is still churning as I tag off and walk along the jetty and foreshore, heading home.

It's still warm outside, the sun heading for the horizon, but probably at least another hour, or maybe two, from setting. I try to clear my mind as I walk along the footpath that lines our street. The ghosts walk with me although because of how preoccupied I am I find it pretty easy to pretend they aren't there, and they pretend I'm not too which helps. I wonder if word had begun to spread in those circles too. Everyone wants to avoid the girl who keeps ruining people's lives. Even the lives of the dead.

If that's even what they are.

I sigh, feeling the cruel circle of it all again. Either I am crazy, or I'm not, and not knowing sucks. Maybe it would be worthwhile seeing if Dr Hymore can get me sorted out on medication.

I'm quiet, still contemplative, as I open our front door. At first, I'm not sure if Dad is home, but then I hear his voice in the kitchen. I go to call out but realise he's not alone. Our neighbour, Rich, is with him.

"Not everything that's real in the world has to make sense, Mitch," Rich says. "Believing that is the only way I can write the books I do."

"I've read your books, Rich. You're meticulous. There's no hooey fluff in your mysteries. That's what I like about them."

"Sure, I'm a man of science and I believe in research. My crime scenes are exacting. My cops are rigorously accurate. But there's always an undercurrent of the mysterious under the surface."

"You believe in ghosts then?"

I freeze with my hand on the kitchen door. Suddenly, I feel like I'm under a microscope. Are they talking about me?

I hear someone sigh and assume it's Rich. "Mitchel, look. Sometimes things happen that we just can't explain. What I'm saying is that maybe it helps Sara to feel closer to her mother."

"You think she sees Grace?"

"I don't know. Maybe she does. She definitely talked about seeing Bobby. How could she even know about my son if what she said isn't true?"

There's a clatter of dishes. I wonder if Dad is using them as a way to keep his hands busy. He does that sometimes.

"Someone would have told her about him," he finally says. "Who knows what her mind decided to do with that?" He pauses but I don't think he's expecting an answer to the question.

Instead, he says, "Maybe she thinks she can help them. Her hallucinations. Bobby. It would be so like her to want to help people."

Rich's voice is warm and compassionate. "I think she did help him." There's a shuffle of wood on the floorboards, probably Rich resettling on his seat. "I think it helps Will to believe that he can still connect with his brother. It helps Will to believe his brother doesn't blame him. Hell, it helps me to believe that."

There's a short pause. I can imagine Dad thinking and shaking his head. He's the kind of person who could never believe that. If it's not real, concrete, provable, then he won't believe it. Blind faith has never been his thing. It's why he struggled so hard to remain optimistic when Mum got sick. He knew the numbers. To him, those were what was real.

But Mum would have believed. She believed to the very end that miracles happen. To her, faith was believing that love is eternal. It's why letting her go wasn't as hard. She'd honestly believed that even if she didn't survive, she'd never leave us.

Except I couldn't see her. I never saw her. Does that mean what I see isn't real or does it mean she did leave? Or is there something beyond that even I don't see?

SPIRIT TALKER

The winding circle of my chaotic thoughts are interrupted when Dad speaks again. "I don't want her going around thinking she really talks to ghosts, Rich. If you feed into the delusion, it's only going to get worse. She had an appointment with Dr Hymore today. He called to tell me that he thinks I should check her into a private facility. He wants to be more rigorous in sorting this out. He thinks they are starting to get her medication right but thinks they'll have better success if she's under full medical supervision."

And with that I'd had enough. I didn't want them making decisions without me. I hate that Dr Hymore went behind my back to my dad. When we'd first begun, he said he wouldn't do that. Not unless he thought I wasn't safe. It was supposed to be my decision. He didn't even give me a chance to talk to my Dad about it myself.

I slide the door aside. I wished I could slam it open and stomp my way into the room, but a glass door wasn't the best for making dramatic entrances.

"Stop talking about me!" I shout, fixing my Dad with a glare. "You don't even know!"

He swallows and I see the colour flood out of his face as if it's dropping right to his feet.

"Sara, I didn't know you were home." I can see the instant he decides to try and cover what he and Rich had been talking about because his cheeks begin to flush. "How was your session?"

I shake my head. "The medication doesn't even work Dad?"

His mouth drops open, then closes, then opens. He looks like a fish, gasping for air, except his chest isn't drawing breath when he does it.

Eventually he finds words. "It's only been a few weeks, Sara. You have to give things a try. Dr Hymore said—"

"It makes me feel awful. I'm barely even alive on those tablets. I try. I try to pretend for you, and for my friends, for Will," I glance at Rich but quickly divert my gaze because his eyes are too full of kindness and compassion, even a hint of quiet pride which I don't understand at all. He doesn't even know me. Not really. Why the hell would he be proud?

"Sara," Dad begins but I cut him off.

"No, listen." I reach a hand up to touch his arm. "What if what I'm seeing isn't fake, Dad? What if it's real? Maybe it could be, couldn't it?"

I hate that there's desperation and pleading in my voice. I hate that I sound like a little girl wishing her Dad would tell her Santa Claus really is real. I hate that I can feel the warm trail of tears on my cheeks and that I'm crying in front of him and Rich.

And I hate it all more when Dad's chin turns side to side. He shakes his head. He sighs. "You know how crazy that sounds, Sara." I see the second he realises he's said that other taboo c word. He winces and grips my hand so that I don't pull away. "I didn't mean that."

I yank my hand out of his and glare at him.

"I'm not crazy." Except maybe I am.

I want to close my eyes and pretend this whole world doesn't exist anymore. But I can't fall apart, not really, not in front of my dad. So instead, I just glare at him for half a breath longer, then turn and stalk away. I keep my back ramrod straight. I keep my gaze fixed to the exit and refuse to let myself look at Rich as I march past.

"Sara," Dad calls to me, but I ignore him. By the time he reaches the kitchen door I'm running upstairs. I slam my bedroom door and throw myself down on my bed.

Downstairs I can hear Dad's murmured apologies. I hear Rich make his excuses and leave. I brace myself, expecting Dad to knock on my door. I hold back the tears and the long sobs, instead forcing myself to breathe deep breaths while I hold myself together.

But he doesn't come. The house falls silent. And when a few long minutes have passed I can't hold myself together any longer, so I tug my pillow close and let myself fall apart into it.

29

The rest of the week is a bit of a nightmare. Double Art feels strangely lonely as I paint Grae's face. His memory haunts me and I wish he were here. I don't really know his situation and I wonder about his reason for wanting to stay. For wanting to be a ghost instead of moving on to whatever comes after. He'd talked about wanting a voice. He'd been a poet, so maybe he'd actually had one. I didn't really know what legacy he'd left behind. I don't think he really knew either.

I gaze at him in the picture I'm painting. I can picture him vividly in my mind, so I keep tweaking the colour of his eyes. In my painting they're the stormy grey-blue of his anger. But I don't want that. I want the water-deep blue of his laughing eyes. I want the happy memories. I want his smiles, and his poems, and his raptures over Ella-May. Those were my Grae.

Thankfully, Dad doesn't instantly agree with Dr Hymore. During our long session on Tuesday afternoon, Dad and Dr Hymore do most of the talking. They weigh up the options. For the most part they talk about me not to me and I hate it. But I listen, and I think, because I know Dad at least cares about me and maybe this is important. Still, I make it very clear to both of them that I don't want to go into an institution. And I explain all the reasons why.

Dr Hymore tries to defend his position. Explaining how progressive his private clinic is and that any social damage can be repaired once I'm well. Some of it I believe. Some of it Dad believes for me. But I keep shaking my head.

Dad, clearly concerned about the rocks between him and me, says, "Thank you, Doctor. We'll talk about it and think about it," he glances at me and fixes me with a look that says we 'will' think about it, "and we'll decide together." I'm thankful, truly. I know he wants to agree with the doctor but now that it's just him and me against the world he doesn't want to risk making things between us impossible.

SPIRIT TALKER

Before Mum died, we didn't need glue to keep us together. When I was a little girl, he'd been my everything. He and Mum and me against the world. We were one rock, together. Now, everything is fragile. Because of me. Because of all this.

Wednesday isn't much better. As I walk toward them in the terraced garden for recess, Georgia can't even meet my eye. Synthe leans over to whisper in her ear and I feel the cold shoulder crawl down my back. Jenn keeps her gaze fixed on the floor but she's clearly listening to Synthe too. I glance around, hoping that either someone else will save me from my social pariah status or some hole somewhere could swallow me up.

Normally I'd be able to find Will here somewhere too, but I hadn't seen him in days. He'd gone so far to avoid me that he hadn't even been at school which I bet made Rich really supportive of the way I'd blown up their life. Will definitely isn't doing better because of me.

By lunch I don't even bother heading for the garden. Instead, I make straight for the library and the quiet stacks where my only company is ancient ghosts, who don't even notice me there, and the books. The rest of the week goes on that way too. The ghosts are there, around the hazes of my medication, and the hurt is there too. But over time the rumours do start to die down. The other students take less and less interest in me.

Georgia and the others still avoid me. Synthe still whispers behind my back. Will is still a complete and utter no show. But other than that, things start to go back to normal. Or a new normal. It's lonely, but it's not as unbearable as I thought it would be.

30

"Sara!" Bobby's urgent voice startles me out of sleep. The week had been quiet with no Grayson, no Bobby, not even a visit from Thea although I knew that woman was hovering around the edges. She'd told me her story but somehow I still felt like she wasn't ready to let go. "Sara!" Bobby shouts again.

I drag my eyelids open with a groan. "It's nighttime, Bobby. I'm sleeping."

"You have to save him!"

That had me more alert. Save him? Who?

I sit up on my bed and push back the covers. "What's going on?"

"It's Will. He did something. You have to help him!"

I kick the blankets aside and put my feet on the floor. "What did he do?"

"He took all the tablets!" Bobby dances foot to foot as if his whole body is urging me to get up. His words tumble out of his mouth, so fast that I'm surprised because he'd never talked like this before. I didn't even know he could speak so many words. He was nothing like the reserved, quiet and slow to speak boy I'd come to know. "He's supposed to take one. He takes one every day. It's supposed to help make him feel better. But he took all of them. Every single one. And then he got all dopey and tired. He groans and grabs his belly like he's really, really hurting but he won't go tell Dad. I can't wake Dad up. He doesn't hear me. I can't do anything."

I feel my gut sink. I hope I hadn't understood him. All of them? All of his tablets. That could mean...

I don't even grab the dressing gown out of my closet and instead dash downstairs and out of the door. I race across our driveway and jump over the little garden strip between our houses. I feel the scratch of the hard driveway on the bare soles of my feet and wince but even that doesn't slow me down.

I hammer on the front door when I get there. Even though I know it's probably locked I try the handle. When it won't open, I hammer again, louder. Inside Nikki starts barking.

"Yes, wake them up," I whisper, urging the dog to do her thing.

Bobby disappears straight through the door, he's back moments later. "Hurry, Sara. Hurry!"

It feels like ages but eventually the door creaks open. Rich stands there, bleary eyed and frowning. "Sara?" he asks, clearly confused.

I push past him, following Bobby who is already trying to urge me up the stairs. "It's Will," I say as Rich reaches out to grab my arm. I shake him off and instead follow Bobby who disappears through a door in the upstairs hall. I push through, not even knocking.

Will is sprawled across the bed. His fingers are clenched around a medicine bottle and he gazes at nothing. His whole body seems to twitch like he's strung too tight. He shivers and gasps, clutching a hand across his stomach as sweat streams down his face.

"Will!" I cry, rushing forward. Rich beats me to Will's side. He reaches for the bottle, but Will's fingers are so tightly clutched around it that he won't let go. Or can't let go. "He took all of them," I say, my voice so tight it's barely a whisper. "Will?" I ask, urging him to answer me but he doesn't respond. He doesn't even look at me. His eyes are glassy and fixed as if they're looking at something far, far away. I turn to look at Rich. His skin is pale, and he looks so much older. "Is he going to die?" I ask.

Rich just stands there, looking lost and helpless. Bobby gazes up at him as if he's waiting for his hero to know exactly what to do. "We have to save him. Daddy, save him!" Bobby urges.

"Rich?" I ask. He blinks at me, seeming to come back to himself, and nods his head.

"Stay with him. I'm calling an ambulance. Keep him awake."

I nod as Rich rushes out the door and disappears up the hall. I don't know if there's anything I can do. I grip Will's hand, holding it around the bottle. His fingers are stiff and tight, but his skin is soft. I stroke my thumb up and down the curve of his wrist. "Stay with us Will. Don't give up. Help is coming."

Moments later Rich returns with his mobile phone. He's already speaking in a hushed voice to the operator on the other end. He gives them the details in short, sharp responses. His deep voice is flecked with worry. From time to time he nods as if responding to questions I can't here.

It feels like an eternity as we wait together. Rich continues to murmur from time to time to the operator on the phone. I keep my gaze fixed on Will, willing him to respond, to look at me. "Come on Will. Come back to us."

Beside me, Bobby sobs quietly. He stands in vigil beside Will's bed and keeps swiping at the tears that trickle down his cheek. I want to comfort him too but I'm conscious of Rich with us. Instead, I keep my comments broad, as if I'm talking to both of them.

"He's going to be okay. Will is a fighter and we got here in time. The ambulance is coming. They'll be able to make him better."

Bobby seems to react to my words, so I just keep muttering them on loop until eventually we hear the quiet wail of the ambulance in the distance. Rich disappears downstairs and moments later returns with two paramedics.

Everything becomes kind of surreal then. I want to stay with Will, clinging to his hand, but they edge me back, clearing space around him as they quickly check him over. I step to one side of the room and Bobby comes to stand beside me. I reach down, clinging to his cold hand and willing myself to feel him. He needs me too. His fingers clutch back and grip tight. His breath is fast and his eyes wide as he watches the paramedics.

"He's going to be okay," I whisper. I'm talking to Bobby, but I'm also trying to reassure myself. I hope we got to him in time.

"You're Sara, right?" The female paramedic asks. She'd introduced herself as Mia when they'd first arrived. The other paramedic, Tim, glances at me too. I nod my head. She smiles. "Will's lucky to have a friend like you."

She turns to Rich. "You said you'd only recently refilled his prescription?" She asks. He nods. She sighs. "We're going to take him in. Get him on fluids, charcoal. They can handle it better at the hospital. Besides, they'll want to refer him."

Rich nods as if he already knows the process. In the time they'd been there he'd become even more withdrawn.

The paramedics load Will onto a gurney and take him downstairs. Bobby and I stay as close as they'll let me but as they load him into the back of the ambulance one of the paramedics waves me backward. "Only family can come with us," he says, looking to Rich.

Rich puts a hand on my shoulder and I look up at him. "I want to come," I whisper to him. "I need to know he's okay." I hate feeling like I'm begging. I hate the way my voice breaks. I hate that I'm crying.

SPIRIT TALKER

"Thank you, Sara. I don't even..." He shakes his head, his hand falling away as he lifts it to his mouth. I wonder what he was going to say. He swallows as if he can't get the words out of his throat. He glances to someone behind me and I feel a pair of warm hands take my shoulders. My Dad. I lean into him as he stands behind me.

"I'll bring her, if that's okay, Rich," Dad says. I feel a rush of gratitude and turn to give him a quick hug before returning my pleading gaze to Rich.

"Please, I need to come. I need to know."

Tim, the paramedic, closes one of the rear doors. "We need to go," he says softly to Rich.

Rich nods. I'm not sure if it's for the paramedic or for me. But then he nods again, looking at my Dad. He fixes his gaze on me and whispers, "thank you," again, before turning to climb into the back of the ambulance.

Bobby stays close to his Dad but, as the paramedic goes to close the door, he calls out to me. "Thanks Sara. I mean it. Really."

Dad has a quiet word with the paramedic as he secures the rear doors. Then Tim climbs into the driver's seat. Dad and I both step away as the ambulance pulls out onto the road. We watch it, sirens wailing and lights flaring, disappear down the street. I want to run after it, but I know that's ridiculous. As it turns the corner Dad squeezes my shoulder.

Finally, I begin to notice everything around us again. It's dark, the streetlight penetrating the scatter of trees that shade Will's front yard. Nikki hovers in the driveway. She whines, gazing down the street as if she's been abandoned. Their front door hangs wide open with lights on all over the house. Our own front lights are on too with the door slightly ajar.

"Come on," Dad says. "Let's get their dog inside and lock up. We'll grab some things and then get going. It'll take time for them to get Will sorted before anyone can come talk to us about him and it's better we make sure everything is good here first."

It makes sense, but feels interminable as Dad systematically checks through, making sure their house is secure and the lights are off. Rich must have had his phone with him, but his keys are still hanging on the hook in the kitchen. Dad even packs a bag of clothes and a toothbrush for Rich and I realise he'd gone to the hospital in his pyjamas. I glance down realising I'm still in mine.

"I'll go get dressed," I tell him, and he nods at me.

"Shoes too, sweety."

SPIRIT TALKER

I nod back and cross to our own house which seems normal, and quiet, and calm after the strange chaos. My bed is still a mess, the indent of my head still on my pillow. It's dark, and quiet. I hadn't even turned the light on.

I hear Dad come into the house as I'm changing. He heads to his own room and I meet him in the hall, both of us dressed. He watches me and I know there's a question on his mind that he's refusing to ask me. I ignore it, because I don't want to have to explain when he probably won't believe me.

Instead of asking he smiles at me. "Ready?" I nod.

The trip to the hospital is strangely eerie. The freeway, while not completely empty, is oddly quiet. The bright lights create intermittent shadows. I gaze out of the window, wishing Bobby would come back and tell me what was happening. But it made sense that he'd stay with his brother.

By the time we get to the hospital the sun is starting to rise. It must be about five a.m. The bright lights of the hospital make it feel like it's full day. I stay close to Dad who leads the way. He moves confidently, finding the way via signposts and asking directions at reception. Eventually he leads us into a quiet waiting room somewhere in the hospital. I have no idea where I am, but Rich isn't here. Neither is Bobby.

Dad leads me to a chair and sits down. I glance at him in confusion. "Can we see Will?"

He taps his hand on the chair next to him. "We have to wait. Hospitals are a lot of waiting. But I'm going to message Rich to let him know we're here."

I nod, glancing around the empty waiting room. I spend a few minutes pacing but eventually take a seat next to Dad.

I sit there, realising I hadn't brought anything to do. I pick up a magazine from the table, then toss it back down again. I glance down the corridor, wondering which way they'd come from when they came for us.

"Do you think Will is going to be okay?" I ask.

Dad tucks his phone into his pocket and grips my hand. "I think you did everything possible to help him. Now it's up to the doctors."

"And up to Will," I whisper, realising that the helplessness in that was the worst thing. Because Will didn't want to live. And I hate myself for not even realising that. How come I hadn't seen it? We'd chatted. We'd had that really great day together. I knew he felt bad about his brother's death, but I didn't know.

Didn't someone's will to live make all the difference in the world when it came to getting better?

"They'll get him help, Sara."

I nod. Inside I feel the war because he'd already been getting help. He'd had tablets too. Tablets that were supposed to help him. But then I'd opened my big mouth. I'd pushed his buttons and made him feel it all again. If I'd just shut up, not mentioned Bobby, not gone on and on about how Bobby wanted to talk to him. If I'd never even seen Bobby, never even talked to him. Maybe none of this would have happened. Maybe Will would be okay. Maybe he'd even be happy.

Or maybe he'd be dead.

The dark voice in my head makes me shiver, because maybe he would be. His Dad had already gone to bed. No one would have come for Will. He wasn't trying to save himself. What would have happened? Would Rich have found him in the morning? Would it have been too late?

I swipe away the tears on my cheek and lean into my Dad. He puts an arm around me. "You did a good thing, Sara."

And I hear it, there in his voice, the question he won't ask.

We glance up as someone comes into the room. Rich looks exhausted. His face is drawn, and his eyes are rimmed with red. He comes and sits opposite us, leaning back in the chair.

"How is he?" Dad asks.

"They're doing everything they can," Rich says.

I wonder where Bobby is. He's probably still with Will. I wish he didn't have to be alone, but I can't exactly say that I need to go keep Rich's dead son company while we wait to see if his other son is going to live or die. I can't even imagine it and another flood of tears overwhelms me. I turn my head into my Dad's chest. He lifts a hand to wrap the back of my head and strokes my hair.

Eventually the sobs start to subside again, and I take a deep breath.

"I'm sorry I didn't come sooner. I should have tried to talk to him during the week. I shouldn't have let him stay angry."

Rich shakes his head. "This wasn't your fault, Sara. If you hadn't come..." his voice fades off because like all of us, we can't voice the maybe. We just have to keep hoping that he'll be okay. That we got there in time.

Silence falls between us as we sit, quietly waiting together, hoping together.

Eventually, Rich breaks it again. "Sara, I," he pauses, searching for the words. "I just can't figure out. How did you know? Did he message you? I didn't think to grab his phone."

I shake my head. Part of me wants to use that excuse. A nice, neat little way to explain it. But I couldn't lie. I glance at my Dad, feeling awkward. He won't understand and I hate making him uncomfortable. But Rich is watching me, waiting for an answer.

I swallow, pushing back the churn in my gut, and swipe the sleeve of my shirt over my cheek. Dad puts a hand on my knee, giving me strength. "Sara?" he asks, finally asking too. I wonder if he suspects but doesn't want to believe.

I take a deep breath, then answer, "It was Bobby." I whisper the words and hate the shadow that passes over Rich when he hears his youngest son's name. "Bobby told me."

Both men still and the confession sits there in the quiet between us all.

I wonder what Rich thinks of it. He sits there, gazing at me, but I'm not even sure if he really sees me. Behind his eyes his mind must be churning away. I wish the floor would open up and swallow me. I hate being this freak.

But Dad pulls me tight against him again and I lean into him. There was something in that hug, an acceptance, and I find my eyes fill with tears again. I turn and sob into his chest once more. "I'm sorry, Daddy," I whisper.

He pulls back, lifting my chin with his fingers so that our eyes meet. "Hey," he says, his voice firm. "You did a really brave thing. I'm proud of you."

"But I try not to see them. Or I did. Really."

He shakes his head. "I don't know what you experience, Sara. But today..." He sighs, then continues, "Maybe it was intuition, or hell, I don't know, but today you helped Will. You might have saved his life. That's really special. Whatever it is. It's special."

Across from us, Rich nods. "Bobby?" he asks, his voice quivering and his eyes large. "My Bobby?"

I nod. His gaze is hungry, so I tell him some more. "We talk sometimes. He's been real worried. About Will."

Rich draws a breath and runs a hand through his hair. "Will has had a hard time of things. A few–" his voice quivers and he sucks another breath, steadying himself so that he can continue. He swallows, then says again, "A few months ago Will tried to drown himself. We weren't sure, not entirely, that he did it on purpose, but his friends said he'd been deliberately reckless. And I'd known, you know." He glances at Dad who nods. Somehow their 'just knowing' must have been a parent thing. "But then we've been seeing Dr Hymore and I thought he was doing so much better. Especially since you, Sara."

I nod and feel a quiver as I remember. "But then we had a fight. I told Will, you know, about me seeing ghosts. He was okay with it. But then Bobby," my voice hitches because it still feels weird to talk about it, "Bobby wanted me to talk to Will for him. To tell him stuff. But when I tried Will blew up at me. He said I was crazy." I dip my chin, feeling it all over again, and hating myself just that little bit more. "I really thought he believed me, but he wouldn't even listen."

Rich sighs and shakes his head. "I think he does believe you, Sara. I don't think he really thinks you're crazy. That's just something people say when they're lashing out. And Will has been feeling a lot of anger, mostly at himself. I should have talked to him."

We sit there, and the quiet between us grows. But it feels comfortable to sit in silence. Each of us drawn up into our own thoughts. I still can't help thinking of all the things I could have done, everything I should have done differently. I wonder if Rich is thinking the same.

Eventually Bobby appears across the room. He walks toward us quietly and pulls himself up into the seat beside his Dad. He leans close, not quite touching. I watch him. His eyes are sad.

"Is he okay?" I ask.

Rich shakes his head. "I don't–" he begins, then blinks at me when he realises I'm not looking at him. "Oh," he says, suddenly stilling.

I nod. Bobby glances between us and I nod at him too. "He knows," I say. A wave of joy flashes over the boy's face but then the sadness returns.

"The doctors did lots of stuff. I don't know. But he seemed to be a bit better. And they're letting him sleep. Is that good?"

I shrug. "I don't know. But if he seems better maybe he is."

"They gonna come talk to my Dad."

I nod. Rich leans forward. "Sara?"

"A doctor should be coming out to talk to you. Will's okay, we think," I tell him and even as I say the words the doors behind us swing open and a man in a white coat comes into the room and crosses to sit with us.

"Mr Saint-James?" he asks. Rich nods.

As the doctor talks about Will I find myself relaxing. We didn't know for sure. Things can still go bad. But Will seemed to be responding well to treatment and they were very hopeful.

"We're going to keep him in at least a few days. We've already talked to Dr Hymore. He and a team will check in on Will either later today or early tomorrow to discuss next steps. Right now, it's important that Will get some rest, his body has been through a lot these last few hours. I'm sure you could all use some more sleep."

Dad nods and Rich does too.

"Can I sit with him?" Rich says, "I want to be there when he wakes up."

The doctor nods. "We are going to transfer him to a room, but that might be a while. You could go home and get some sleep first. You'd be more comfortable, and Will is probably going to sleep for at least a few hours."

Rich shakes his head and the doctor seems resigned to the fact that his patient's worried Dad would linger in the halls if he had to but wouldn't leave his son alone.

"Can I see him?" I ask.

The doctor looks at me with compassion. "He's sleeping–"

"I just want to see that he's okay," I say, interrupting the doctor before he can say anything else.

The doctor turns to Rich. They seem to communicate silently between each other. Eventually, Rich turns to me. "How about I call you once he's settled in. They don't let non-family into the room he's in, but I think, when he wakes up, he'll be glad to see a friend."

Bobby reaches out, touching my hand. "And I can come and let you know. Really quick and stuff."

I gaze at the little boy. He'd become such an important part of my life. They all had. I force a breath past the tightness in my chest. I hope, deep into the very core of myself. Hell, I hope out to the edges of the universe, out through the strange 'other' that Grae talked about. I hoped with everything in me, that Will would be okay.

31

By the time we get home I realise I really am exhausted. School had already started for the day, but Dad called them to let them know I'm not coming. I head straight up to my room, kick off my shoes, and lay in bed a while before I finally fall asleep. I must have slept a few hours because by the time I wake up the sun is setting.

Everything seems so ordinary and normal in our house. It's like everything that had happened last night was just a dream. I splash water on my face in the bathroom before heading downstairs to join Dad in the kitchen. Dad watches me carefully as I set the dining table and I eye him warily as we sit down to dinner. He'd done a really nice white sauce fettucine with a side salad just like Mum would have made with extra cherry tomato halves and cos lettuce. There was even a drizzle of the vinegar dressing she loved. The smell of it reminded me of her. I close my eyes, inhaling, before taking a bite.

"Sara," Dad begins. "About what Dr Hymore wants for you. The in-patient clinic..." I'm not sure I want to open my eyes because he'll be giving me that look again. The one he'd given me every night this week. The concerned one, that wanted to be fair but was equal measures frustrated at my stubbornness. The bullheadedness I got from my Mum and it had driven him nuts with her too.

I carefully chew the bite of lettuce. I wish my mouth wasn't full so I could tell him to just back the hell off and that I hadn't changed my mind. If anything, after everything that happened with Will, I wasn't even sure I liked Dr Hymore anymore. He out of anyone should have known Will needed help. I'm actually kind of glad I can't talk because I'm pretty sure I'd be a real bitch about it. Especially now.

When he doesn't continue right away, I risk opening my eyes. He is giving me that look but there's also a really deep sense of dark worry in his eyes. A wave of guilt sucker punches my gut and I force myself to swallow the now cardboard salad in my mouth.

"Please, Sara," Dad says, "I'm trying to do what's best for you."

I nod, because I know that. He loves me and I must be making him crazy with all the fruit loop stuff. I wonder if he's worried I'm like Will. If he thinks I might do something like that. I wonder how many times he'd heard me talking to things he couldn't see. I try to imagine what it must be like for him. Probably really scary.

"I know you are, Dad," I say, searching for a way to hold my ground. "I just honestly don't think this option is a right fit for me. At least not right now. I'm doing okay. Really."

The conversation isn't over. I know that. But Dad backs off again. We'd played this kind of table tennis with the topic all week long. He would push a little, or a lot, and we'd argue a little or a lot accordingly. Tonight, it seemed, he was vying for just a little. And if anything, that made me even more uncertain about my choice.

We finish dinner in silence. My mind whirls, weighing the options, but it keeps circling back to the idea that what I see must be real. It might be important. I'm making myself crazy with indecision and rather than get up and pace the house for hours I glance to the window that looks out on the street.

"Can I go for a walk down to the foreshore tonight?" I ask. "I want to clear my head, you know, think about things."

I was worried about Will. Rich had called earlier to explain that they didn't want him to have any visitors today. I wondered if that was just an excuse. Maybe Will just didn't want to see me and Rich was softening the blow by blaming it on the doctors. But Will is only some of it.

Dad watches me, carefully considering my question. That's another thing that had changed. I don't know if it was Mum's death, my breakdown, or the Will thing, but he was more careful now. I couldn't help wondering if he was afraid I'd fall apart out there by myself. Eventually, he nods. "Just promise me that you'll think about the clinic."

I nod back, picking up my plate and cutlery. I put them in the dishwasher then grab a jacket before heading out the front. It's still a warm night but the breeze off the water could be cool. I walk slowly, watching my long shadows on the pavement move as I pass under the streetlights. Only some of them are lit as if mimicking the varying degrees of light cast by the setting sun. The walk down the street is quiet, and calm, and peaceful.

SPIRIT TALKER

I hear the water even before I see it. The sunlight is a haze of orange glow on the distant horizon to the west and the water laps gently at the sand. I walk a short distance along the water's edge before finding a dry spot to sit and just gaze at the city lights across the river.

This side of the Swan is quiet and dark compared to the still thrumming churn of lights and motion in the city. The gentle shush of water adds to the calm and for the first time all week I feel like I can really breathe. The salty air is crisp and cool. Tension begins to fall out of my shoulders as if drawn to the sand. I didn't realise how uptight I'd been feeling until the weight of it lifted just a little.

It's an impossible situation, really. Right now, what did it really matter if I opted for the loony bin. I'd already been tarred with the crazy brush at school and I'd have to start over anyway. At least if I went, I'd get my life back. The life before I could see stuff. Would that be better?

But then I think about Will. I see him again in my mind, laying on the bed with the bottle clutched in his fingers. Will could have died. If I wasn't this thing, I couldn't have helped him.

My mind wanders to the others. To Thea, and Bobby, and Grae.

I feel the warmth of him before I see him because the sand doesn't shift when he sits down beside me. I'd been so preoccupied with my thoughts, as I gazed out toward the city, that I'd been completely oblivious to my immediate surroundings. Probably not the safest way to sit alone in the growing dark. But the instant I felt him I also felt safe, which was really weird because it's not like a ghost would be able to save me if anything happened.

"My dear Sara Brooks, I have been looking for you," he says. I swallow, pushing back the tears that want to fill my eyes. I can't believe how much I had missed his voice this week.

For the first time, really, I just feel a wave of welcome relief in seeing him. For the first time there isn't even a hint of fear or desperation. I don't want to undo this. I don't want to unmake it.

"I thought you'd gone," I say, my voice a little tight and my words barely a whisper. For the first time, Grae doesn't feel like a broken part of my brain. He feels real. Not in an alive way, but in a way that exists and is true.

"I need to express the very deepest of my apologies for my atrocious behaviour. Not just when we argued, but for the past week of your life." I turn my chin to watch the soft folds of his lips move. Every time he speaks it sounds poetic, like every word has been carefully crafted. He gazes out over the water, speaking to that rather than to me, but that's okay because at least he's here. "You have felt very alone Sara Brooks, and I have aided the cause of that by turning away from you." He turns to me then and our eyes meet. "I am truly, truly sorry."

I swallow and nod. "I'm sorry too. I shouldn't have pushed you like that. You've been around the world way longer than I have. I should trust you to know your own mind and the best decisions for you."

He seems to become very thoughtful at that and I can't help feeling a churning in my stomach as if the acid there is bubbling away over something. But he turns his chin back to the water and we sit in silence for a long minute before he finally speaks again.

"If only the number of one's orbits were the measure of one's wisdom," he says with a sigh. "You were not wrong to speak the way you did to me. You spoke from a true desire to be helpful and I appreciate that you care for me. Perhaps that is why the longing to stay is stronger than it has been in centuries."

"But you shouldn't stay for me if it's time for you to go."

"Always self-sacrificing." He smiles and the barest hint of a dimple creases his cheek. "I adore you, Sara Brooks, and I assure you, when I am decided my time has come, I will be ready to say goodbye. I promise you, I will do that, because disappearing from your life was unforgivable."

The comment brings Will to mind. He'd practically disappeared from my life too. He hadn't been at school all week and a big part of me had worried about him even then. I knew I'd made things worse for him. I knew he was hurting. The thought had gnawed away at me that maybe he was hurting way more than we all thought. He'd been seeing Dr Hymore after all, and you don't regularly visit a psychiatrist if there isn't something serious going on. If I'd trusted my instincts. If I'd just gone and seen him...

All of the what ifs swirl through my mind.

"Sara Brooks," Grae says now, gently bringing me back from the spiral of my thoughts. He pushes himself to his feet and turns to look down on me. "I will leave you to your solitude. You are amidst your own decision-making tonight and I am doing my best not to sway you for self-serving reasons. But I will say one last thing." He waits until I'm looking him directly in the eye. It's not the easiest thing to do because he's so tall but I crane my neck backwards and nod at him. He smiles, his gaze arresting mine. "You are utterly remarkable and sometimes hardship and challenge are an inevitable part of that. You are also courageous and strong. You can overcome any adversity you might ever face in your life." He pauses and I start to think he's finished but then he adds, "And Sara, those of us who aren't as strong as you," he fixes me with a look and I can't help thinking he's including Will in the 'us' when he speaks, "we appreciate the courage of people like you. You give us your strength. Your friendship, it matters to us. If I'd had a friend like you in my lifetime..." His words fade away and he doesn't finish what he was going to say. Instead, he shakes his head and says, "I'm glad to have the honour of knowing you."

My jaw drops open as he speaks but he doesn't give me a chance to recover enough to respond to his words. With a last, fleeting and slightly haunted smile he disappears, back into the nothingness or ether or wherever it is he exists when I can't see him. I swallow and feel a cool streak as the breeze touches my cheeks and dries the tears I hadn't even noticed were falling.

I swipe the back of my hand against the cool stains and draw a shaky breath. He'd said he was trying not to sway my decision and honestly, he had made me even more confused about it. On the one hand, if I accept Dr Hymore's offer then I'd never see Grae again. I knew Grae couldn't want that. But he'd said I had the strength and courage to face anything. Was he saying that I'd be okay, either way? I guess he was.

There are so many people in the world who would want this. The people who desperately cling to the hope of seeing their loved ones again. Even someone like Will. What difference would it have made if he'd been able to see and hear his brother himself instead of trying to believe that I could see for him?

It felt like the only one I wish I could see for me was the only one I never could. Was that because she was happy, and had moved on? Or did she worry I'd hurt to see her? Right now, all I wanted in the world was to be able to talk to her, like we did before. She always had exactly the right words to make me feel better.

"Mum," I whisper to the river, "I wish you were here. You'd know what I should do." I close my eyes, letting another tear drop. I knew I wasn't really alone and yet right in this moment I feel like I'm the only person in the world. I feel like all of it is on me. I drag a shaky breath into my lungs and let it shudder out of me, then draw another. Finally, I open my eyes again and whisper the real crux of the matter. "I don't want to be crazy."

A breath of air swirls the sand a little and a flutter of white fabric catches my eye out over the water. Impossibly, a woman stands there, shimmering as if touched by the setting sun, the water, the breeze, and the world around her. She walks across the water to me and I burst into tears because I can't really be seeing her. Just wanting to so much must have conjured her up in my broken mind. "Mummy?" I whisper, speaking like the little girl I'd been so long ago. I want to reach out and touch her, but I'm terrified she's not really there.

She kneels down in front of me. I can't bring myself to look at the sand because I know it doesn't move with her. She's not really here. I hold my breath as she reaches forward and then close my eyes. A fresh trickle of tears escapes my lashes as I feel her hands on my cheeks. She wipes away my tears with her thumbs.

I inhale a snotty breath through my nose and realise I can even smell her. Oh god how I'd missed her smell. Like a mixture of rose hip and juniper berries. It was a tea she'd loved to drink since I was a baby. The smell lingered on her hands.

"My beautiful little girl," she says, her voice the soft, calm melody it had been before she got really sick. There was no tightness from pain or sorrow in her words, just the golden glow of unconditional love. I draw another shaky breath and look at her. The light moves through her, just a little, but she smiles at me and everything feels like it's exactly as it's supposed to be. She shakes her head, her dark hair, so much like mine, scatters around her face as she adds, "You're not crazy, my love. Trust yourself."

I want to lean forward and just pull her into my arms and cry and cry and cry. I thought I'd done all my crying for her, but I guess that's not really what I'm crying about. I'd grieved my mother. I'd let her go. But I hadn't had the chance to let go of needing her. I don't think I ever can.

But I do need this. For the first time I realise exactly the gift I've been given. It will be hard. I'll see things and hear things, feel them and smell them too. And people won't understand. They'll think I'm crazy.

But some people won't. Some people, like me, like Rich and Will, like Bobby and Thea and Grae, they'll need me to be this new me. They'll need me to hold onto this precious thing I've been given.

It doesn't make any sense. And it is the definition of crazy according to medicine. But that doesn't make it not real. It doesn't make it dangerous. It doesn't make it something that ruins my life.

I'll need to learn how to use my gift. I'll need to learn how to live my life with it. But I'm already starting to do that. Maybe that's exactly what Grae had meant. Not to be strong and courageous enough to give it up, but to be strong and courageous enough not to.

I lift a watery smile up to my mother. She gazes down on me with all the love she'd ever had. "Are you okay?" I ask. I already know the answer. There's just some sort of instant knowing about her and I can feel it as if it radiates off her skin. She knows true peace. She knows true belonging. And right now, she's here just for me and can be here for me whenever I need her no matter what happens going forward. Even when I don't see her, she's with me.

"I'm okay," she says simply, because we both know it encompasses everything. "And you'll be okay too, Sare-bear."

I can already feel her letting go again. Fading away. The little girl inside of me wants to cry out and beg her to stay but I don't. She smiles again and I wonder if she knows that too.

"Be brave, my love, and remember," her words already feel like they're coming from far, far away. They echo more in my mind than in my ears. "You are never alone."

32

By Saturday morning, Rich still hadn't given us the all clear to visit Will so I head off for skating instead, hoping I could forget about him, at least for a little while. For the first time in a long time I'd had a really good sleep. Life was still complicated. Maybe it always would be. But right now, as I tug down the covers over my figure skates, I realise that I finally feel sure about what I am doing. Decisions are like that. They're impossible to come to but are like throwing down a heavy weight once finally made.

As I push out over the rink, I realise Synthe and Jenn aren't there. Georgia is warming up against the far rail with our instructor, Michelle. The rest of the students are scattered around. I take a long, slow lap around the rink to warm up a little then cross to the rail where Georgia is flexing. I line up beside her, stretching out my calves.

"Good morning," I say, not sure if she'll respond. She looks at me, so I smile. There's a slightly haunted look in her eyes. Her shoulders are tense, and she moves stiffly. She shifts on her skates, turning slightly away. I try not to let the snub hurt. Instead, I turn my attention to Michelle who finishes up our warmup exercises before moving on to reinforce some of the moves we'd learned over the past few weeks.

Over the course of the one-hour session, when Georgia and I are often left to continue practicing alone while Michelle circles among the other students, I notice Georgia slowly relax. "If you push your chest just a little more forward, you'll bring your hip into better alignment for your arabesque," I tell her. I'm almost surprised when she does just that. The arabesque levels out and her legs form a perfect ninety-degree angle. "That's it!"

The smile on her face is so lit that I feel the warmth of it through my own skin. I watch as she initiates a turn with the slightest twist of her body. Her standing foot wobbles a little and her extended leg dips just a little but she steadies herself into the turn and levels out again. The rink lights flash the end of our session. She carries her backward glide for another few feet then drops her extended leg and does a twin toe-stop.

"That felt amazing," she says, her grin even wider as she pushes off and skates back toward me. "My turn is still a little sloppy, but I think that's the first time I've had a full extension on the arabesque." She looks up at me, meeting my gaze. "Thank you."

I nod. "It's one of my favourite positions. Inside spirals. Outside spirals. If only I could make a convincing camel spin of it." I say. We cross the rink together, heading for the exit.

"You'll get there."

"Goofy foot and all," I say, giving her a grin of my own. She chuckles, then dips her chin.

"I've missed you," she says. She stops at the entrance and steps onto the carpet.

My smile fades. I feel suddenly very awkward. "Georgia, I wasn't–"

She lifts a hand to stop me. "No, I know. It's our fault. And it wasn't fair. You're going through stuff. You dad told us."

I shake my head and draw a breath before trying to explain. "My Dad doesn't really know what he's talking about." I wave a hand up to the kiosk area and our usual table. She nods and leads the way, so I continue. "I want to tell you about it."

SPIRIT TALKER

She takes a seat at our usual table and as I sit opposite her, she gives me a very sorry smile. "I'm sorry I didn't give you a chance to talk to me about this."

"I don't think it was you who made that impossible," I say. I let my gaze wander out to the rink. It was instinct to look for Will. I try not to let the disappointment of again, not seeing him, sit too heavy in my gut. I knew he wouldn't be here because he's still in the hospital. I hope he's okay. I mean, I know he's doing better, that he didn't die, but I'm pretty sure it's a longer journey back from what he's going through than just surviving.

Georgia sighs, drawing me back to our conversation. "Synthe means well," she says, "but she doesn't let her guard down very much. Her mother hasn't been a very stable influence in her life."

"Her mother?" I ask. I remember how awkward Synthe had been about her mother's visits.

Georgia nods. "Her mother is a bit sick, you know, in the head." She taps her own head. "She takes medication now but there was a time when it was really dangerous for Synthe to go home because her mum was prone to violent outbursts. She's always been really insecure. It's just a crazy situation."

I drop my gaze to the table, suddenly understanding some of Synthe's mistrust. She saw me take my pills that night. I bet it hit all kinds of raw memories of her mother. And then I have my freak out. It must have genuinely scared her.

"I'm really sorry. I should have explained to all three of you."

"Will you talk to me about it, Sara?"

"It depends. How open minded are you?"

"What do you mean?"

"Well, we were telling ghost stories the other day. Are you a believer?"

Georgia lifts a shoulder. "I don't know. I mean, I guess. It wouldn't be so scary if I didn't think it could be real."

I nod again. "Things have been a little strange for me the past year. When my mother died, I started to have–" I pause, looking for the right word, then settle on, "experiences."

Georgia leans forward. "What do you mean?"

"At first it was just strange things. Like seeing a cat out the corner of your eye but when you turn to look it's not really there. Sometimes it was just shadows, or even just feelings." I begin to explain, remembering some of the earliest experiences when I'd just put it down to feeling a bit out of my own skin. "But then it started to get more vivid."

"Vivid?"

I nod. "Yeah. The things I saw were more violent and gruesome. Like a soldier with half his face melted off. Or like last week, an old woman who could tell me the whole story about her murder."

A crease of confusion crosses Georgia's face. "You mean you see things and they talk to you?"

I nod again. I wait for her to process the idea. She's not laughing at me and she's not shaking her head. Eventually, I realise maybe she really is listening. Maybe she wants to understand. So, I continue, "When it first started happening, I thought I was going crazy. I've been seeing a psychiatrist because Dad was really worried about how the hallucinations were getting in the way of everything in my life. I'd wake up screaming because someone was whispering in my ear. Or I'd accidentally drop plates because I felt like I was about to walk into someone who suddenly appears in front of me that no one else can see. But now I'm not so sure you can call them hallucinations. Not really."

"You think what you're seeing is actually there?"

"What if it is? What if what I'm seeing really is ghosts?"

Georgia seems to think about this for a few minutes. The silence between us grows but isn't uncomfortable. I wonder what she's thinking, but can tell that when she's ready, she'll tell me.

Eventually, she nods, then says, "I guess it could be pretty cool."

I lift a shoulder. "I'm not sure cool is the word I'd use. It still makes me a freak."

She chuckles, shaking her head. "No, really. Just imagine what you could do."

"Like what?"

"Well, you'd be a real psychic, wouldn't you? And you'd be able to give people messages from their loved ones. You'd be able to find things people have lost. You'd be able to help people feel connected and not so alone in the world."

I hadn't really thought about it like that. I mean I'd wanted to try to help Grae and Will. I'd tried to do the message thing with Bobby. And it was though seeing Bobby that I was able to get there in time for Will. But I hadn't thought about the way other people might need this kind of gift.

"You said you saw cats? Have you ever seen mine? He's was a ginger tabby. I called him Claws."

I shake my head. "I don't know if it works like that."

Her chin drops for a moment, but then it lifts again, and she gives me a smile. "You've never been to my house. Maybe he'll be there."

I chuckle, feeling strangely warm and happy in the buzz of her energy. And somehow hopeful because at least there was one door that wasn't still shut in my face. Reconnecting with Georgia was a start. Synthe would be the harder sell, but with Georgia on my side, who knew? Maybe I'd have a chance to have friends again. Friends who supported my level of crazy in their own, odd way. And that would be okay.

And maybe, if Will doesn't forgive me, having other friends would make that okay too.

33

Will was definitely proving to be the tougher nut to crack. He'd missed another whole week of school and skating too after 'the incident'. So, as the stars start to outshine the city lights, I gaze out of my bedroom window and look down into his yard. He isn't there and I hadn't seen him, even in passing on the street, but I knew from Rich and Bobby that he was home.

He hadn't allowed me to visit him at the hospital. I was pretty sure it was him that didn't want me to come too because when Dad and I rocked up during visiting hours one day the staff gave each other a sideways look which spoke levels of pity.

But he'd gotten home yesterday, and I was tired of waiting. I just needed to see for myself that he really was okay.

I glance at the alarm clock on my bedside table. It isn't even nine yet so technically it's not too late to visit. At least I don't think Will's Dad would mind. Especially since Will had missed so much school. I could offer to drop him my notes from the classes we share. I gather them out of my file and slip them into a plastic sleeve before heading downstairs.

Dad is sitting in the living room reading another Saint-James book. I'm pretty sure he's read this one at least twice already. "Can I go next door for a little while? I want to take some notes to Will. He's missed a bit of school."

Dad lifts his gaze from the book and fixes it on me. "Sara," he says, his voice holds a hint of warning.

"I just want to check he's okay."

"You can't push him, Sare-bear."

"I know. I just want to take him my notes."

Dad knows that's not all I want. He keeps his gaze fixed on me until eventually I drop my chin and look at the ground.

"Fine, I just need to see him. Okay? I need to know for myself that he's really okay."

Dad's brow furrows. "Maybe you're better off keeping out of his business. You have your own wellbeing to consider."

I sigh and plop myself down on the couch beside him. "He's my friend, Dad. I'm worried. Being worried is not good for my wellbeing." I slip him a cheeky smile and he shakes his head with resignation.

"No later than ten, remember. Or I'll come beating their door down for you."

"I remember." I lean forward and kiss him on the head. "Thanks for being patient with me Dad. I know you've been worried too. Worried about me. But I really think everything is going to be okay."

He watches me, a small crinkle between his eyes as he tries to figure me out. He squeezes my arm as I stand up. "I just want you to be happy, Sare-bear."

I smile at him. "You know, for the first time in a long time, I think I really am happy. Or I will be, when I know Will's okay." I fix him with a meaningful look.

He rolls his eyes and drops my wrist, waving me away. "Fine, fine. You go check on your young man." As I reach the door, he calls out to me. "Ten o'clock, not a second later!"

SPIRIT TALKER

I chuckle as I slip outside. Odds are we'd probably still talk about the in-patient thing. But more and more I feel confident he'll side with me on it. Especially since, now I finally feel sure about myself, I really am feeling happy for the first time in a long time.

I just hope I can help Will find this feeling inside himself, too.

His front step is dark and the house itself seems quiet although light seeps out around the curtain across the upstairs window which I'm pretty sure is Will's. I knock, trying not to make too much noise. I hear Nikki snuffle the door and moments later it opens. Rich stands there, he greets me with a smile that doesn't quite reach his eyes.

"Hi, Sara."

"Hi Mr Saint-James." I suddenly feel more than a bit awkward standing on Will's doorstep. He probably doesn't even want to see me. My fingers clench and I feel the plastic slip as I fidget with the pages. "Um," I say, trying to find a valid way to ask to see Will but no longer sure I even wanted to. "Will wasn't at school this week so I thought maybe he could use some notes from our classes." I reach forward with the notes half hoping Rich will take them and say goodbye.

Rich glances back into the house. His gaze lingers on the stairs for a long while before he sighs and pulls the door open a little wider. "Come in, Sara. Maybe you'll have more luck with him than I have."

"What do you mean?" I ask, crossing into the entry. Rich hadn't taken my class notes, so I keep them awkwardly clutched between my own fingers.

He runs a hand through his already messy hair then closes the door behind me. "He hasn't done much talking this week," he says, crossing to stand by the stairs, "at least not to me. Dr Hymore cleared him to come home. But today he barely ate a thing and he hasn't come out of his room, not even to walk Nikki." The dog whines, perhaps sensing her owner's misery or just sharing her own doldrums at not getting her normal walks with Will. "Maybe they should have kept him longer."

Rich sinks down on the stairs and leans forward with his elbows on his knees. "He tells me everything is okay and that he's just tired, but the niggle in my gut says it's more than that. I just wish he'd talk to me."

I put a hand on Rich's arm. "Maybe he needs more time."

Rich shakes his head. "It's just," he pauses, his features marred in a gut-wrenching grimace of anguish, "we almost lost him. I know he's taking his medication. I watched him take it at dinner and the doctor made sure we can keep everything locked away so he can't hurt himself again."

Rich shakes his head letting his chin dip down to his chest as he stares at the floor. His jaw flexes and I wonder if he's trying to tell me something else but can't find the words. A sob hitches his voice and I suddenly feel helpless and frightened.

"Should I get my Dad?" I ask, wondering how on earth I could possibly help these people.

Just then Bobby shimmers into view. His wide, child's eyes are like saucers as he gazes at his distraught father.

I fix my sights on him. "What can I do?" I ask, hoping he'll have an answer. Surely being connected to the other side gave him some kind of powerful insight we could tap into for dealing with a grown up falling apart on us. He shakes his head but steps forward and lays a hand on his father's head. Rich sniffles. I wonder if he senses the touch of his youngest son. He drags a deep breath into his lungs, gaining strength and composure.

"No," Rich finally says, "Will's going to be just fine." He lifts his chin and fixes me with his stormy ocean eyes. They're still full of a father's worry. "Go and speak with him. Be there for him.

You're a good friend for him and I'm not going to keep helping him push you away. Can you be brave enough not to let him push you away either?"

I wasn't so sure about that. I'd caused these past few weeks of crazy emotions for them both. The Bobby thing besides, it's just a shock to hear your neighbour is certifiably insane and I didn't mean Will. Whatever he saw Dr Hymore for he had legitimate reasons to feel the way he did. And if I make him feel worse, if I make it harder, then he really should push me away and I shouldn't try to stop him.

Still, I pushed myself back to my feet and turned to head upstairs, because if it were me, I'd want a friend to be there. Even when I was raging at my Dad, knowing he would never give up on me, no matter what he believed, made all the difference in the world. Bobby reaches for me before I've gone two steps.

"Sara," Bobby whispers as if his father will overhear him. I turn slightly, just to show him I'm listening. "Will's really not okay, is he?"

I close my eyes. How was I supposed to know? I sigh, shrugging my shoulders. "I'll go talk with him."

34

As I reach the top of the stairs Bobby is already there. He gestures to one of the closed doors. I approach it carefully and knock gently.

"Go away, Dad. I said I'm not hungry."

I swallow and jiggle the handle but it's locked. "It's not your Dad. It's me, Sara. I was hoping we could talk."

The silence from the other side of the door is deafening. A long minute passes and I start to wonder if he will even open the door. I try again.

"Will? I, um, brought you some school stuff. Your Dad said I should give it to you."

The silence drags on. I shift from foot to foot wondering if I should just give up but just as I bend down to slip the pages under the door it opens.

Will gazes down on me. He looks strangely hollow and I feel that deep in my gut.

Still, I try not to let it show and instead offer him a small smile. "Hi," I say.

I feel his eyes on me and there's an itch on my skin like the insides of me think he's trying to devour me. It's a really odd feeling. I feel wanted, but I can't help also feeling like the sight of me is torturing him. He swallows and his Adam's apple bobs in his throat.

"Sara," he says. My name is a rasp on his voice.

My smile wobbles and I bite my lip to push back my tears then say, "I'm really glad you're okay."

He nods, and swallows again but still says nothing. I stand there, awkwardly holding the papers in my fidgeting fingers. I hear my own breath between us. It feels loud in the silence.

"Can we talk? Just for a bit?" I say. "I've missed you."

He glances away, looking down the hall and I can tell there must be a thousand thoughts stampeding through his head, but eventually he pushes the door open and nods.

I let go of the breath I hadn't realised I'd been holding. We sit down, side by side on his bed.

"I'm glad you're okay," I say again.

He leans back against the headboard of his bed and I turn to face him. He looks down at his hands as he clutches them in his lap.

"Is it okay that I'm here?" I ask, trying to get him to say anything at all. "Is my being here making it worse? Should I go?"

He glances up at me and his eyes are hungry again. "Yeah," he says. I feel the sting of pain and go to stand but his hand snatches out and he grabs my arm. "No, I mean, yeah, it's okay that you're here. Don't go."

I draw a shaky breath and nod my head, settling back on his bed again. The mattress shifts under my weight and I realise how soft the blanket feels under my legs.

"Are you doing better?" I ask, not really sure how to talk to him.

He smiles at me, but it doesn't quite reach his eyes. "I'm trying to be," he says, and the word trying says a lot. I feel a weight lift from my shoulders because all week long I'd been so worried that he'd hate me for saving him. That he didn't even want to try any more. That he'd had enough and just wanted to be with Bobby.

I smile at him, feeling the first true smile about all of this stuff with Will. "Me too," I say. "Trying."

We talk for a while, just about school, and skating, and the simple stuff. The hard stuff is still there, under the surface, waiting.

It's gone ten by the time Dad really does come over to get me, but he comes in quietly. I think he understands how important it is for me and Will to have this time. It's like the door between us is opening again, at least just a little.

Right now, just being able to talk with Will, just trying to be okay together, was enough.

For both of us.

35

I spent most of Sunday at Will's house too and by Monday he'd decided on heading to school. Dr Hymore had been pushing him to get back into routine. The doctor had said that finding a new normal in his life was the best way to go forward and for a change I agreed with him. At least, on Will's behalf.

Over the next week we'd fallen into a pattern of going to and from school together. By the following Tuesday afternoon, I feel kind of awkward when I remember that I'm supposed to go see Dr Hymore after school. Will and I hang out at lunch, so I bring it up with him.

"I really don't want to go anymore," I tell Will after explaining.

"Why not?" he asks. He unwraps his sandwich, a chicken mayo, and takes a bite.

I sigh, fiddling with the plastic wrap from my own lunch. "He keeps pushing me to do an inpatient clinic. He wants to do some radical medication adjustments because he doesn't like that I'm still seeing things after so long."

Will nods. "But you don't want to?"

I shake my head but am suddenly wary. Despite spending so much time talking to Will the past week, we hadn't talked about what I could see. We hadn't talked about my bringing up Bobby. We hadn't talked about ghosts. I wasn't sure I wanted to bring it up again because of what happened last time.

I take a bite of my sandwich, buying myself time before responding. Will puts a hand on my knee and squeezes it. "It's okay you know," he says. I look up at him, wondering exactly what was okay. Seeing the confusion in my eyes he sits back, wrapping both hands around his food, and sighs. Then he looks at me again. "I'm really sorry, Sara. About the way I acted that night." I swallow the food in my mouth as I nod, but before I can speak, he continues, "I thought about it. A lot. You know? That week, I thought about it. But then, in the hospital too, after."

"Did you talk about it to them?" I ask, feeling suddenly worried that my crazy might even contribute to his. What would people think of either of us if he talked to them about it.

"I had to talk to Dr Hymore about it," he said. He tugged a section of bread off his sandwich. "He doesn't believe, of course. And he couldn't talk specifically about you or your case because you're his patient, but he talked about how it didn't really matter if I believed, or even if you believed in what you were saying or seeing. What mattered was that I believe and come to trust that what happened to Bobby wasn't my fault."

"That's what Bobby was trying to tell you."

"I know. I get that now. I guess at the time I wasn't ready to hear it. I didn't want to believe it because I didn't believe he could believe it." He pauses then shakes his head. "Does that even make sense?"

I smile despite myself. "It actually does."

"I've had to do a lot talking the past couple of weeks," he says. He shakes his head and chuckles. It feels good to hear him happy. I knew he wasn't fully back and maybe it would take a long time before he could be, if he ever would be. Losing someone is like that. It changes us. We have to be different people to live without them. The hole where that person belongs never really heals over. Not completely. But I could really believe that Will was starting to live again. Or at least believe he deserves to.

I think about home truths, and Dr Hymore, and sigh. "I guess I'm kind of over the home truths when it comes to Dr Hymore. I don't think he could ever believe me, and I don't like how talking to him makes me feel like I must be broken."

"He just wants you to be safe."

I nod, understanding that. "I know. And you know at first, I guess it did matter. When this first started happening it changed everything in my life. I couldn't focus at school. I was anxious. I'd drop things. I'd freak out. But now I feel like I'm getting a handle on things. Life is good again, even with this thing that makes me crazy."

Will flinches and shakes his head. "I never should have said that, Sara. You're not crazy."

I smile at him and squeeze his arm. "I'm okay with it now. I think maybe there are two definitions of crazy. The Dr Hymore kind, and then life."

He chuckles. "Well in the life part I think we're all a little crazy."

"Exactly."

"So, what are you going to do about Dr Hymore?"

"Well I have to go."

"Do you?"

"I'm still not off the hook with Dad. He'll be there today. One last ditch effort for both of them to talk me into volunteering for the loony bin."

"But your Dad will understand. He won't force you."

I grin. "He might even be coming around on the whole not believing thing. Or at least not thinking that my seeing stuff means I'm going to go completely insane."

"So, there's some hope for you."

"For us both, I think."

36

Dr Hymore's office was strangely quiet. I felt kind of weird because although there had been a few weeks when I didn't cross paths with Will between his session and mine it felt odd to know this week that he wasn't there. Still, I take a seat in the waiting room and glance at my phone, wondering where Dad is. He arrives just as Dr Hymore opens his office door and I breathe a sigh of relief. I'd been worried I'd have to face the doctor alone.

"Sorry I'm late," Dad says. He rushes over to join me.

"Perfectly on time," Dr Hymore says to him. "Come through, both of you."

We sit down, side-by-side, on the long couch in the psychiatrist's office. Dad settles back in the chair. I tuck myself back too and cross my legs in front of me. Dad squeezes my knee and gives me an encouraging smile.

"So, I hear you've had a busy couple of weeks, Sara."

I swallow feeling strangely guilty then feel angry at myself for feeling guilty. What the hell did I have to feel guilty about? I'd saved Will. But Dr Hymore knew about my ghost talk with Will. He knew about Bobby and maybe he blamed me and my crazy for what happened to Will. I shrink back in the chair. Maybe he was right to blame me.

When the silence between us stretches Dad fills it. "She saved our neighbour's life," he says, his voice full of pride. "I understand Will is a patient of yours too."

Dr Hymore fixes him with a look. "I can't talk about that. But I'd like to hear from Sara. Do you feel like you saved him?"

I lift my chin to glare at him. He can see the defiance in the set of my jaw and shoulders. "I think Bobby saved him."

He flinches and I feel a little spark of righteous victory. "Sara-" Dr Hymore begins but I cut him off.

"I know you don't believe me, Doctor, but if it weren't for Bobby, I would never have known Will needed help. How could I have possibly known that?"

Dr Hymore gazes at me for a long minute. His ankle rests across his knee and he holds the notepad with one hand, the other rests along the arm of the chair. I can tell he's thinking. Eventually, he puts the notepad aside, puts both feet on the floor, and leans forward in his chair. "The human body has amazing senses for instinct. You and Will have been friends quite a while now from what I understand. You're close."

I shake my head. "Close enough that in the middle of the night, while I'm fast asleep, and dozens of metres away, I feel enough urgency to go bang on my neighbours door just to check my friend, who I hadn't talked to for almost a week, isn't trying to kill themselves?" I deliberately use the jarring language. I hated it but I wanted Dr Hymore to really hear it. To hear how equally insane it is to think my knowing was just instinct.

"Sara," Dad says, his voice a reprimand, probably for my attitude more than what I'd said.

Dr Hymore raises a hand to silence him and instead fixes me with a look. "Is it more likely that a dead boy told you?"

"Isn't it? Or at least just as likely."

He shakes his head. "Hallucinations can be very visceral. They come from a deep core within your psyche. You believe them because your mind needs to believe they are true, but Sara, your inner knowing gave you that voice. Ghosts aren't real."

I swallow, feeling a pit of doubt because it sounds so logical when he says it like that. My mind made up Bobby to voice what I knew inside. That Will was in danger. I push the doubt away, because while it could be true for Will, it didn't explain Grae or Thea or the other things I see. And I'd seen Bobby even before I knew Will. I'd known Bobby even before I knew Will had a brother. My brain couldn't have made any of them up because they were all too real.

Instead, I shake my head, pushing back at what he said in my mind, but to him I simply ask, "Does it really matter if it's real or not?"

He blinks at me and I wonder if he's hearing his own conversation with Will. I lean into it because that's exactly what I want him thinking about.

"It's not hurting me, Dr Hymore. Seeing these things doesn't harm me, or anyone else."

"What about Will?"

"What about him?"

Dr Hymore fixes me with another one of those looks. I can tell he doesn't want to voice the question because it invades the privacy of Will's session with him. I want to push him to do it too because I want to feel angry at him. I want a reason to trust him less. We stare at each other so long that my dad clears his throat.

"What about him?" I ask Dr Hymore again.

He takes a breath and I can see the way he's forming the sidestep in his mind. "Sara, you might never know the emotional mindset of another person. When you talk about these things, when you talk about things that touch on someone's grief and longing and pain, it can be dangerous. It can do harm." I go to argue with him, but he raises a hand. "I know you wouldn't mean to. You have good intentions. But when you choose to believe in your hallucinations, when you act on what you believe you're seeing, it can be dangerous."

I can feel my dad shift uncomfortably in his seat. He doesn't know about the conversation I'd had with Will. I glance at him and he's watching me. I drop my gaze to my lap where I'd been unconsciously twisting my bag of dice in my fingers.

The silence grows between us another moment until Dr Hymore leans back in his chair and pulls his pad of paper back onto his lap. "Sara, I still want to talk to you about the inpatient–"

"No," I say, probably louder than I needed to. It cuts him off and he seems surprised by how adamant I am.

Even Dad shakes his head. "Dr Hymore," he begins. The doctor looks like he's going to cut him off again. He fixes him with another look, but this time Dad stares him down as he continues, "I've discussed this at length with Sara for the past few weeks. I've come to agree with my daughter that it is not the right option for her."

I can see Dr Hymore's jaw clench. He drags a breath through his nose then opens his mouth to release it before speaking. "I understand. But please tell me you're not feeding into your daughter's delusions. It is important that the people around her keep her grounded in reality."

Dad shakes his head. "I don't know what I believe at this point." I feel a kind of win in that statement because it's not the absolute disbelief it used to be. "What I know is that Sara is doing better in school. She's making friends. She's enjoying hobbies. She's eating and drinking and sleeping well. She's happy again, like she hasn't been in a long time. Believing in what she sees is helping her live with it."

"It's not healthy," the doctor says but Dad shakes his head.

"She seems pretty healthy to me."

"I just want you to understand that hallucinations are caused by chemical imbalances in the brain. Fully functional people do not experience them. And there are other treatments we can try since the medication she's currently taking does not seem to be having any effect on reducing her episodes."

I hate the way he says episodes because although I didn't always see ghosts, it wasn't like something that switched on and off. When I didn't see them, it wasn't because I couldn't see them. I wonder when I'd started realising how much control I actually have over the ability. The thinness of the veil was something I could influence.

It takes me a moment to realise the doctor had kept talking, "... ECT."

"What is that?" Dad asks.

"ECT or electroconvulsive therapy is a treatment where we stimulate the electrical impulses of the brain. It's proven to be relatively effective for a range of mental illnesses."

"You want to electrocute my brain?" I ask, rising to my feet. I feel my hands on my hips even before I think to do it. I can't help wondering if I'd really heard him correctly. I turn to my dad. "You want to let him do that?"

"We're just talking, Sara," Dad says. His voice is calm and rational in that way I hate.

I shake my head. "Seriously?" I raise an eyebrow at him then slam him with the thing I know will hit the most. "Mum would be ashamed." Dad flushes with guilt and I feel a wince of guilt too for putting that on him. Instead I turn to Dr Hymore and glare at him. "I think we're done."

I lift my chin and turn from both of them to storm out the door. I slam it behind me and march out of the waiting room too. By the time the anger starts to cool a little I'm standing on the footpath outside in the sunlight shaking my head.

A car passes on the street and life in the city buzzes its same kind of normal. It feels good, like real life, instead of this strange haze of wrongness I'd been feeling even just talking to Dr Hymore. I still feel guilty for saying that to Dad. He was trying to be on my side, and it can't be easy when an expert tells you one thing and your daughter tells you another. Still, I was right. "Well you would be," I mutter to Mum, even though she's not really there.

I lean against a tree for a few minutes until Dad comes outside. He's alone and I'm glad. I wonder what he said to Dr Hymore after I left. I know he can force me to keep going but he can't force me to talk during the sessions with the doctor.

"Ready to go home?" he asks. I nod.

As we walk to his car I can't resist asking, "Do I have to go back?"

He pulls me in for a sideways squeeze. "I'll leave that up to you. You really are doing good now, aren't you?"

I stop in the street and look up at him.

"Yeah Dad," I say, "I really am."

37

Even school becomes good again. Will and I hang out a lot and after my talk with Georgia she and Jenn had started to spend more time with me. Synthe too wasn't the hard, cold shoulder she'd been for a while. She'd returned to the reserved, grudging, sarcasm-laced acceptance of my presence. I think hanging out with Will was at least scoring me points with her. Especially when one of his friends joined us at recess on Thursday.

Jackson was a warm, friendly, easy-going guy. The way he kept having to flick the brown threads of his fringe out of his eyes reminds me of Grae. Synthe kept leaning in to join the conversation he and Will were having.

"I've learned so much this year, Will. I swear, if we incorporate my new art style with an edgier storyline, we can turn this thing into something phenomenal."

"We're not trying to break ground, Jack. It's just a little indie game. Breaking teeth, you know?" Will argues back, clearly not too comfortable with the wave of energy and fresh ideas Jackson keeps throwing his way. Will and I had talked late into the night after my appointment with Dr Hymore on Tuesday. Jackson had been his best friend since they were little, but they'd drifted apart after Bobby's accident. I was really glad Will had taken my advice to reach out and it was clear Jackson was thrilled about it too. There was an urgency, a longing, in his voice. He'd missed his friend. A lot.

Will was more reserved. He was doing better but I could tell that he felt a bit overwhelmed by all the changes Jackson was talking about.

"I'd love to see your art," I say to Jack. I let my arm brush Will's just a little and hope he doesn't notice.

Jackson looks at me and grins. "Sure!" He goes on to talk about his art classes, letting the video game topic drop and I feel Will relax beside me. Synthe keeps feeding him into the topic and he glows under her attention. Even Georgia seems fascinated. I feel a little pang of jealousy because they hadn't shown that kind of interest in my own art. Maybe digital art is different. Or maybe I hadn't really talked much about my art. Except to Grae.

Jackson flicks his fringe again and I think of the strange centuries-dead poet. We'd mended fences, mostly, but I still couldn't put aside my curiosity. He was clinging so tightly to what was left of his existence instead of letting himself discover whatever waited for him beyond it. What had he said he wanted? Legacy? Could that be unfinished business? And if it was, how on earth could a dead man ever leave behind something lasting.

"That's why I've always loved the greats. I mean, I use cutting edge technology to design my work but at the very core is the basics. That comes from the foundation of work from the likes of Pollack and da Vinci, van Gogh, Monet, Picasso."

The greats, I think. Personally, I was more partial to female artists like Frida Kahlo and Élisabeth Louise Vigée Le Brun but that's because I resent how little recognition and even opportunity women had to paint their truth over the centuries.

But thinking about that got me wondering about legacy. Because, although underappreciated, particularly in their time, there were women artists deserving acclaim even during the Renaissance era. Their legacy lasted the ages, at least in part but they may never have known the impact of their work on artists, particularly female artists, centuries after their death.

I jump to my feet. Scattering the crusts of my sandwich on the floor then flush as the others all stare at me. I hadn't heard a word any of them had said in ages. "Sara?" Georgia asks. "You okay?" There's a look of concern on their faces as if they think I'm having another freak out.

I bend down to pick up my crusts. "Yeah, I just had an idea." I glance at my watch. "We've got what? Ten more minutes before the next bell?"

Synthe pulls her phone out. "More like eight."

I frown. "What is it?" Will asks.

"I wanted to go to the library. There's something I need to look up."

He tilts his head a little as he watches me. "Lunch?"

I sigh but nod. Really, I wished I could just blow off English and Health, but I try to remind myself that Grae had already waited decades. A few more hours wouldn't make a difference.

38

Will and Jackson are already waiting for me when Jenn, Synthe, and I finally reach the library after the end of fourth period.

"So," he asks, "what are we looking for?"

I grin at him. I hadn't thought to rope him in as an accomplice in my search, but it felt good to have him with me. Jenn and Synthe seem really curious too and the way Georgia bursts through the door as if she's hoping we haven't left her behind makes me realise the whole crew actually care. It felt really good to connect with them. Although, I was suddenly really anxious about telling them. Could they handle my crazy?

I dip my chin, swallowing.

"Hey," Will says. His warm hand touches my arm, just below the elbow. "You don't have to tell us if you don't want to. We can leave you alone if it's private."

His gaze is so warm and understanding that I feel really touched. We'd come so far, understanding each other. Even Erica and I hadn't been as in tune as Will and I had become over the past days, maybe weeks.

"It's just, my crazy, you know. I don't want to freak anyone out."

He smiles. "I love the way you talk about it like that. You're not scaring me off, Sara. I'm all in on the crazy."

"Hey, I love crazy," Georgia says too. She puts her arm around me.

Synthe shakes her head. She shifts her feet and I can tell she's still a little uncomfortable about it. "I'm gonna find some sushi. Anyone want anything?"

It was a concession of sorts. She couldn't hang out for the crazy, but she wasn't actively snubbing us either. Progress.

Jenn smiles at me. She'd been kind of shy since the mending of fences. She'd always been the quietest of us, but her reserve was more pronounced. "I'll go with you Synthe. But we'll be back. I still want to know."

Beside Will, Jackson seems kind of confused by the dynamics. He doesn't know us like the others do, but he hovers close to Will as if worried turning his back on his friend now would sever their friendship again. "I'm up for crazy," he says, "whatever that means."

I take a breath, looking at my friends and then glancing behind them to the rows of stacks. "This could be a fruitless quest. I have no idea if we'll find what we're looking for. It might not even exist and even if it does it might not exist in this library."

Will turns to look at the stacks too. He waves his arms out to encompass the array of books and journals stocked in our school library. "Well," he says, "we have a wealth before us. Besides, if we can't find it here, we have the State Library, and the National Library. We even have the whole world at our fingers," he adds, gesturing at the computers.

I nod. Resolute.

"So?" Georgia asks, "What are we looking for?" They all turn back toward me, watching me carefully while they wait for my response.

"Grayson, um," I pause, trying to remember the way Grae had introduced himself when we first met. "I think his last name is White. He's a poet."

Will raises an eyebrow. "Please tell me you have more than that to go on. Do you know how many people there are in the world with the last name White?"

Georgia's eyes sparkle and she shakes her head. "Right, but when you narrow the field to those who've ever written or published poetry that has to be a significantly shorter list."

Jackson shakes his head. "I still don't get the crazy."

I glance at him and then at Georgia and Will in turn.

"Oh," Will says, suddenly clicking. "Narrow it a little more to dead?" he asks.

I nod and add, "And a little bit more to about two or three hundred years ago."

"Wow," Georgia says, her voice breathy with excitement. "It's like a real mystery. We're uncovering a historical legend."

"Where would you even start?" Jackson asks. He looks around the shelves.

"We divide and conquer," Georgia tells him. "I'll start in the English works section. You do a catalogue search to see if he has any published work under his own name." Jackson nods, following Georgia's lead as if he appreciates the direction. He heads to the catalogue computer and starts searching.

"And us?" Will asks.

"Internet," she says, pointing to Will.

SPIRIT TALKER

That doesn't leave much else for me to do. It's not like I could start scrolling through microfiche. I don't even know if our school still has those ancient archive technologies. But Georgia doesn't leave me hanging. "And you," she says, pointing at me, "you need to get some more facts." She grins as if she's in on some big secret.

"What do you mean?"

"Go to the source. We need more detail. When was he born? When did he die? Did he write under a pen name? What did he write about?"

My gut sinks. She wanted me to actively call up Grae, to ask him. First, I don't know if I can even do that. They'd always come to me, not the other way around. Well, except for Mum. Besides, when I'd had the idea earlier in the day, I'd been excited that I might find something that would unlock him from the battle within him that said his life had amounted to nothing. It was a long shot. It's entirely possible there's nothing in history that was a direct ripple effect of Grae's life. I don't want to get his hopes up because this crazy idea might not pan out.

"You can talk to him, Sara." I'd told Georgia about Grae. The boy who hung out in my room scrawling poetry while I slept. She'd thought it was romantic. I'd told her it was weird.

"But what if this all leads to nothing? I don't want to hurt him."

"So, don't tell him what we're doing." She rolls her eyes as if I were the dimmest person in the world. "Obviously."

"Just talk to him?"

"Yes. Talk to him."

I glance around the library. "Here?"

"Why not?"

"It's kind of weird. People freak out when I talk to myself."

Will chuckles. "Hang out with me while you do it. I can even take notes so you don't have to try and remember what he tells you. Just repeat it back each time he gives you a detail that matters. I'll pretend I'm doing some work on the computer."

This had to be one of the weirdest conversations of my life. My friends were actively encouraging me to conjure up a hallucination. To have a conversation with it. I try to remind myself that because he's a ghost he's not technically a hallucination. It doesn't help much. I swallow.

"Come on, what have you got to lose?" Will asks.

I shake my head, but I can't help smiling. "My sanity?"

He chuckles. "Sanity is overrated."

SPIRIT TALKER

He was right. They both were. And we didn't have very long to do this thing, so I really needed to stop putting it off. I nod, giving in, and for the next twenty minutes we do. Georgia disappears into the sacks, headed for the English Literature section. Will and I settle in at one of the internet-enabled computers and I think about Grae. I wasn't really sure how to go about calling for him. I start with his name, tentatively at first, and then with more urgency. I'm more surprised than him when he suddenly appears.

"That worked?"

He beams at me. "Sara Brooks!" he says, clearly delighted to see me. "You called?"

"How does that even work?"

He blinks. "I don't entirely know. I felt a pull here," he puts his hand on his stomach, over his solar plexus, "and when I followed it there was you."

"Has that ever happened before?"

"Not in a very long time. It used to happen, occasionally, for a while after my demise. I thought perhaps it was related to those I left behind. Like a longing. But, of course, I could never ask them if they initiated it or if I did."

"And this time?"

"Well, it seemed you were waiting for me. So, I can only assume that you called upon me."

I imagined it like calling a dog and felt guilty. "Did I pull you away from something?"

"Not at all. Indeed, did I not believe you'd be otherwise engaged with your friends," he glances over my shoulder at Will. Will was slightly angled toward us with the screen facing away from Grae. I could sense him behind me, like there was a buzz between us. A tuning in or sensing of each other. It was nice. Warm. Comforting. "I would have come for some company. I've missed our painting together."

I smile. I'd missed that too. "I'm almost finished. You should come by next time to have a look."

"I will do that Sara Brooks. But do tell me what it was you wished to see me about. I cannot imagine there is no purpose to your call."

"Well, I was curious. I wasn't sure I could, you know?"

He nods so I continue. "And I got to wondering about you."

Both of his eyebrows raise at that. "Wondering about me? Whatever for?"

"Well, I know all about Bobby. And Thea told me all about herself too. But I realised I still don't know anything about you."

He smiles, clearly amused. "You wish to know about me?" There's almost a sense of preening in his voice as if I'd touched on his pride. For someone who wanted to leave a mark on the world I could tell he was delighted by the idea of someone caring about his life centuries after his death. It wasn't the same as having had an impact, not when all he could do was talk about it with me, but maybe even that much fed the yearning in his soul.

"Will you tell me?"

"For you, my dear Sara Brooks, I am an open book. What would you like to know?"

For the next several minutes we talk. I try not to sound like I am grilling him, and I really am fascinated to hear all about his life. He is animated and entertaining. His eyes sparkle as he looks back, remembering. From time to time, when I get too enthralled by what Grae is saying that I stop responding, I feel Will nudge me from behind, reminding me to restate the parts that might help our search.

It's too soon when the bell rings, calling us out to fifth period. I'd never wanted to attend Music less, but Georgia and Jackson join us immediately. Georgia clutches a book in her hand and there's a sheen of tears in her eyes.

"You okay?" I ask. Beside me, Grae seems curious. We'd not really interacted around my friends before, so it was kind of weird to include him but not include him at the same time.

"We've got to borrow this," she says, keeping it vague. She glances around as if looking to see if Grae is still with us even though she can't possibly see him. "And we need to get to class."

I nod, turning to Grae. "Talk more later?" I ask.

The warmth of his smile is radiant. It steals my breath and I blush, then feel doubly embarrassed when Will, who had already shut down the computer, closed his notebook, and was waiting for us, raises his eyebrow at me. "Sara Brooks, I am at your service, any time. As always, it is an honour to speak with you." His cool fingers reach up and stroke my cheek. I wonder if he can feel the heat of my flush.

I smile and step back. "Bye," I say, feeling suddenly kind of shy. He nods and watches as I turn to my friends. The four of us, Will, Georgia, Jackson, and I walk out of the library together leaving Grae in our wake.

The others buzz with excitement.

"Did you find something?" I ask, glancing at the book still clutched in Georgia's hand.

"It's absolute gold," Will says, jumping in first. The second warning bell goes off and we realise we're already late for class. Will shakes his head. "I've got to go. Ferry after?" I nod. He reaches out to grip my hand, squeezing my fingers lightly as he gazes into my eyes. I feel pinned in his look as if he's trying to say more without saying anything at all. He sighs, squeezes my fingers again and shakes his head. "After," he says again, then turns to head toward the technology building with Jackson.

Already late, Georgia and I don't have time to talk about her book as we run to class. But, after profuse apologies to Miss Carnelian we settle into music. Somehow, we manage to make a plan to head to my house after school. Her excitement is infectious, and I can't wait to discover what she and Will had found.

Somehow, I just knew Grae had left a mark. There was no way a man like him had lived an unextraordinary life. He was too vibrant and charming and talented.

39

Will, Georgia, and I had headed back to my house after school. On the ferry, Georgia showed me the book. It was full of poems for a dear Ella-May. Grae's Ella-May. They were passionate and pained. Full of stolen moments, secrets, and heartache. They were Grayson, deep to the core, and so very much in love.

Will had found him too and instead of hanging out at my house we head over to his so that he can print out what he found. There were pages and pages of it. True legacy. Not just Grae's own work but his whole life, laid out in so many ways. He'd had friends and colleagues. People admired his work and decades after his death they recounted the story of his life through dramatic art.

SPIRIT TALKER

There was even a play, still performed today, that honoured the life and lamentable death of Grayson Thomas White.

It was a tragic story. A bright spark diminished too soon. I glance at Will when we learn about his death. Will shifts, uncomfortable, but seems to handle it okay. Still, the idea is raw, and I hate Grae just a little bit for it, then feel mad at myself because I have no right to judge him. There isn't weakness in suicide, not really. But there is so much pain and I see it in the memories of the people who had loved him. I can't help wondering if he'd even seen and felt their love while he lived, or after. How could he not know about this outpouring? How can he still be lingering in an afterlife of loneliness wishing his life had made a difference when there was all this.

I remember back to a conversation I'd had with Grae. He'd had sad eyes then, too, like those in the portrait we'd found of him online. What had he said? 'If I'd had a friend like you in my lifetime...' Would it have made a difference? Could I have saved him, like I'd saved Will?

After Georgia heads home I sit with Will on their back porch. I try not to remember the last time we did this. It feels like an age ago, and a breath ago. He's doing better, I remind myself.

"It's really sad, isn't it?" Will says. I glance at him. He's looking up at the fluttering leaves from the white gum that hangs over our fence from my yard. Through it we see the start of the night's stars. "For hundreds of years he's been alone, imagining that no one loved him in his lifetime. What do you think he thought about, toward the end I mean?"

I swallow, hating how close to the surface this subject feels. There's a knife edge here and I feel like I'm cutting my feet as I walk along it trying not to tip the conversation too far either way. "I don't really know," I begin, then realise I can't give myself that kind of out because Will needs to talk about it. He must need to, or he wouldn't have asked. So instead I let myself think about it. "I guess, he must have felt helpless. They talked about his debts mounting and that he hadn't been earning what he deserved for the work he was doing. Perhaps he felt as worthless as the scraps and pennies they paid him."

"And guilty, that he couldn't be for Ella-May what she needed him to be so that they could have their love?"

I hadn't really thought about that. She'd made her own choices, marrying for a comfortable future rather than risking it all for love. But there wasn't anything of Ella in what we'd found. The poems were all Grae's. Did she love him as earnestly as he loved her? I couldn't imagine marrying someone I didn't love when my heart was taken. I glance at Will. He turns to look at me and I glance away before our eyes meet.

"Sara?" he asks.

"Mmm?"

"He's lucky to have you." There's sadness in that which feels odd. I glance at Will and he's looking at me. I don't know what I see in the depths of his eyes, but it makes me want to lean into him, to reach out for him and just pull him close. I wonder if he feels that pull between us too. I don't of course, because it would be weird, and I didn't want to risk the friendship we had because of some stupid crush that seemed to swirl up in my belly any time he looked at me like that.

I swallow, remembering that we're supposed to be talking about Grae, not us. "I just want him to find peace. It must be out there. That's kind of the whole point, isn't it?"

Will shrugs. "I have no idea. I guess I hope so. For Bobby."

We both fall into a companionable silence. It doesn't feel strange. As the night darkens above us, we find ourselves talking of other things again. But before it gets too late Nikki scratches at the back door, reminding us of the time.

"I better go before my Dad, you know."

He smiles. "Think he'd really do it?"

I roll my eyes. "You have no idea."

Will walks me out. Just as I think he's going to close the door behind me he steps out and walks across with me to my own front door. Our hands touch as we walk. It's just the faintest brush of his against mine. I glance at him with a smile and feel strangely shy because of it.

"See you tomorrow?" he says when we reach my door. I nod.

"Tomorrow."

40

The morning light is warm on my face when I stir from my dreams. Fragments of them linger in my mind. Grae and Will seem to ebb and flow through my thoughts. When I try to grasp the memories, they disappear, and I'm left with this helpless curiosity as the dream escapes me.

I hear the scratch of the pen on parchment before I even open my eyes and I smile. It had been so long. I can't even guess how many weeks it had been since Grae had spent the night.

"Good morning, Grae," I say as I open my eyes.

He turns at the sound of my voice and the very serious look on his face disappears in a bubble of joy. "Sara Brooks!" he crows, clearly delighted. "You stir from slumber. I've been waiting for you."

I glance at the clock. It's a little after six. "It's barely morning."

He frowns at that and shakes his head. "One cares not for the hour, Sara Brooks. I've penned you a poem."

I arch an eyebrow at him. "You what?"

"Indeed, a poem, one for you and you alone. It rivals even those I once penned my dearest love although of course it speaks only of our dear friendship and the true treasure that is you for I cannot betray my Ella-May. Even if my heart is tempted." He grins at me but even I can tell the flirt is in full play. Grae was gorgeous in the way that would turn heads even in this century but there had never been that between us. Not really. Heart flutters aside it was like the bubbles you feel when the lead singer in a boy band flutters his eyes at the camera. Surface and charm. Not that there's anything wrong with that.

"Shall I recite it for you? Perhaps you would honour me to make a copy in your own hand so that it might be preserved?"

Ah, so that's his real angle.

"I might be persuaded. But after my shower. I need to feel more human first."

He sighs. "Hours of slumber and then your biological needs come before the perfection of my artistry. I see how I fall in the ranks of your priorities, Sara Brooks. You've no compassion for me at all." He puts a hand to his heart and another to his forehead as he feigns a faintness with all the melodrama of a soap opera swoon.

"Oh please, you've enough ego for the both of us."

A shadow haunts his eyes and I realise that's probably not actually true. As much as Grae postured there was always this edge of desperation that brushed the surfaces of our interactions. He had a deep insecurity and three hundred years of afterlife hadn't healed the ache in his heart to be seen, to be heard.

"Five minutes," I promise. "Then I'll copy every single word."

My shower takes more like three because I hate making him wait and I know we don't have too much time before I need to get off to school with Will.

As I write the words of his poem, I feel my heart breaking just a little. It really is beautiful and although I might be biased because he's writing about me, I can't help thinking it actually is even better than the poems he wrote for Ella-May. Then again, he'd had three hundred years to hone his craft, so his ghostly self had an unfair advantage over the boy he'd once been.

"It's beautiful," I tell him as I place the final full stop. I write his name at the bottom. Grayson Thomas White.

Grae scowls at the letters of his full name. "How do you come to know that name?" I flush, realising he'd never told me his middle name. I guess now was as good a time as ever.

"Actually," I say, turning in my chair to face him, "I wanted to talk to you about that."

He shifts on his feet. His eyes flick and I hear the race of his breath. He looks like I'd imagine a hunted animal might look and I'm suddenly afraid he'll blink away before I can talk to him. I reach out, putting my hand on his arm and gripping his shirt between my fingers as if I can hold him in place. "Sara Brooks." His voice holds a warning. "What did you do?"

"You need to know, Grae. Really. For so long you've wandered like this, like you are. Have you ever wondered what you're giving up by staying?"

"We have already spoken of this, Sara Brooks. Indeed, if you will remember, we argued about it."

"I didn't understand then. But I thought about what you said, and it got me wondering if maybe, I don't know, maybe there was more to your life than even you could ever have known."

Grae steps back. He feels the end of my bed behind him and bends to sit. His gaze is fixed on me, staring at me a long moment before he shakes his head and finally speaks, his voice soft. "My life was at best brief and meaningless, at worse wasted. It is a regret that cannot be undone, Sara." There's so much sorrow in the words and tone.

I lean forward in my chair. "What if it wasn't?"

There's a spark in his eyes and I'm not sure if it's anger or grief. He swallows and blinks his eyes.

"No, listen," I say. I cross the room to pick up the pages, the book, and the photographs we'd printed the day before. Grae turns to face me as I cross to the bed and lay it all out between us. "I have to show you."

I can feel his hesitation. There's a twitch in his jaw but he doesn't disappear, so I push, just a little more. I take him through it all, piece by piece. By the time I hear Will's voice downstairs Grae is staring at all of it. I glance at the clock, frustrated because I have to go to school.

"Say something," I beg. I want to reach out to him, but he's still tightly wound, and I worry that if I touch him, he'll run away.

Still, he says nothing. "Don't you get it, Grae? Don't you see what it means?"

He shakes his head. I'm not sure if he's saying he doesn't see or if he's just struggling to take it all in.

"You were remembered. Your life mattered. It still matters." I flick my fingers toward the play bill. It was dated just weeks ago from a small indie theatre in London. It wasn't Broadway, but it was something. Across the world dozens of people had been immersed in his life. Hundreds, maybe thousands or even tens of thousands over all the years between.

"Remembered," he echoes back at me, clearly still in shock.

"Sara!" Will shouts from downstairs. "We're going to miss the ferry!"

I glance at Grae. A tear trails down his cheek, and he looks at me, seeing me for the first time in the past hour since I'd started to show it all to him. I nod. "This is your life, Grae. You left your mark."

Grae seems to finally hear it. He reaches a hand out to touch mine and the barest hint of a smile tips the corners of his lips. "My dear Sara

Brooks," he says. He shakes his head, but his smile grows as he does it. "Thank you."

I feel a sudden pull in the gut and lift a hand to my mouth because I suddenly realise what I'd forgotten when I'd gotten lost in all of this. He reaches up and touches my cheek. The warmth of his thumb smooths the cool streak of my tears.

"Thank you," he whispers again.

"You can't go yet, you promised," I say, gripping his fingers in my hands. Suddenly, it's more urgent than ever that I cling to him. "We don't have enough time to say goodbye. I have to go to school."

He glances at the pages on the bed. "Then go to school."

"Will you wait?"

He smiles. "I'll wait. But really Sara, you have no idea of the gift you truly are. I think I will languish in this the whole day. And I will wait for you, to say goodbye."

41

School sucks. Nothing Will or Georgia do can pull me out of the wallowing despair that haunts me all day. There's an edgy feeling and I can't help wondering if Grae really will still be there when I get home. I rush out of school so fast that Will calls after me and has to race to catch up.

"Where's the fire?" he asks.

I dip my head. "I just need to get home."

"Hey," Will says, gripping my hand. He pulls me to a stop while we wait for the ferry to dock. "He won't leave without saying goodbye."

I gaze up at him. "What if he does?"

Will's brow furrows as if he's concentrating or trying to remember something. "You told me something once. About your Mum. That she's still here." He puts a hand over my heart, and I draw a ragged breath.

"But—"

He shakes his head. "No, no buts, Sara. Grae cares about you. There's a connection. Even when he finds his peace, the peace you've helped him find, he'll be there for you. Always."

I want to believe that and just hearing it helps me believe it a little. As we ride the ferry across the Swan, I feel myself leaning into Will's strength. It didn't feel strange at all to rest my head on his shoulder. It helped me hope.

Besides, Grae had promised. He wouldn't go without saying goodbye.

42

In the end it seemed he wasn't in any rush to do that either. There was a playful joy in him when I got home. It was as if he wanted me to experience the adventures he'd known in his three hundred years. We stayed up all night talking. He told me all of it and I watched the bliss in his face.

There was something free about this Grae. The haunting was gone and his skin almost glowed with his contentment. Eventually, I crash to sleep as the sun is rising and it's hours and hours before I wake again.

I feel a wave of panic when I stir and my gaze flicks around the room, searching, until they fall on Grae. He's watching me sleep again.

"You know that's a little disturbing," I say with a smile as I stretch my sore muscles.

"I've been memorising every detail of your face, Sara Brooks. I had been tempted to write a sonnet on that subject entirely but felt too at peace that I did not wish to disturb either of us with the scratching of my pen."

"What time is it?" I ask, glancing at the window behind him.

"Late in the day indeed. Your father briefly looked in upon you, but I suspect he heard your late night and begged mercy upon you because he let you sleep. Apparently you were supposed to be somewhere this morning."

I flush, remembering. "I was supposed to go skating."

He nods. "Another time. I'm sorry for stealing your slumber hours." He glances down at his hands and a shadow crosses his features. I sigh, because I already know what he's going to say. I don't feel the same panic as I'd felt yesterday. I keep Will's words close.

"You have to go, don't you?"

Grae looks up at me. "You once talked about a greater adventure in exploring whatever comes after." I nod. He smiles. "I think I'm ready for another adventure."

He stands up from my chair and motions a hand to call me over to him. I climb up from the bed and meet him in the centre of my room. "Time for goodbye?" I ask, my voice small. I'm ready, I tell myself, but I don't even half believe it.

He gazes at me a long moment, draws a deep breath, and then sighs. "My dear, sweet Sara Brooks. It truly has been an honour to know you and I must tell you that whatever comes after, I will never forget you or the gift you've given me. You have a remarkable life ahead of you and I feel blessed to have had even so small a part of it."

I feel the tightness in the back of my throat. He pulls me into his embrace and I breathe deep against his chest. Everything about him surrounds me. His smell, his touch, the softness of his breath against my ear. There's so much strength in his arms and it shores up the heartbreak of losing him.

Eventually, I step back and force a watery smile to my face. "I'm going to miss you," I say.

His smile is gentle and warm. "I'm with you, Sara." He pauses, then shakes his head. "I have to break a promise because I told you once, that when I was ready, I would say goodbye. But I stand here before you, ready to see what comes after, ready to let go, yet I cannot say those words. I don't think it is goodbye, not really. We may not have this any longer because you have so much more of your life ahead of you and I have whatever comes after mine, but somehow, deep in the very core of my being I feel like we'll never really be apart. There is no goodbye because I carry you with me. Always."

I gaze at him and nod my head. "Always," I whisper. His lips quirk as he gives me one last cheeky grin and the warmth of him seems to fill every place in the room before it fades from sight. I stand, alone, feeling the trail of a final tear on my cheek and smile. Because he's right. Even though he's gone, I don't feel alone. Not really.

43

When I wake up with the sun the next morning it feels almost surreal. So much had changed and yet so much was the same. I stand at the window, gazing out to the water in the distance. How long ago was it that Grae and I stood here together doing just this.

He'd smiled and teased me about my routine of walking down to the river. It had been different the past few weeks, since Will, but after getting dressed and brushing my teeth I pull my sandals over my toes and head downstairs. It was silly to try and keep that little part of Grae alive by keeping to the routine he'd teased me about, but it made me feel close to him.

As I walk down our street, I notice the there-not-there world around me. It's different now too because I'm not afraid anymore. Instead, I see a story in every face. Even in the sad little bird that chases a bug on loop, over and over again. Maybe I can't help him find his peace. Birds might be tricky. But I wasn't going to set myself up for failure thinking I could help them all. But each one? Each one I could save would be worth it.

I feel the sand between my toes as I near the water. I smile beside myself when I see a familiar trio sitting right near the water's edge. Nikki's ears perk as I approach and she turns her head, tongue lolling. She bounds over toward me, but she doesn't jump up. She nudges her head under my hand, and I scratch her ear as we keep walking over to Will. I sit down next to him.

"Hey," I say, greeting them both.

Bobby smiles at me but it's Will's grin that makes my heart stutter. There was a familiar glow about him that reminded me of Grae too. A sense of peace that had been eluding Will for all the months I'd known him.

"You seem happy today."

He chuckles. "Yeah, it's odd, isn't it? For so long I'd forgotten this feeling."

I lean over and nudge his arm with mine. "It looks good on you."

"Did you say goodbye?" he asks, his voice soft, in that compassionate, considerate way he has. I nodded. He puts his arm around me. "He was good for you," he adds. "And it was good to know him, even if I couldn't really know him the way you did."

We sit, quiet together for a while watching the water shush against the sand.

"I'm ready you know," Will says. I look up at him, not sure what he means. There's still a hint of apprehension on his face so whatever it is he's not entirely ready, but I can feel the way he sits just a little taller as if pulling some steal into his spine.

"Ready?" I ask.

He nods. "To talk to Bobby."

"Oh."

Bobby's eyes widen and his mouth pops open. He shakes his head. "But what if it makes him bad again."

I give Bobby a smile and wave a hand to him. He wiggles around to sit beside Will and me so that we form a strange kind of triangle. I try to imagine how it looks to others with one corner incomplete. Like two young people sitting together looking out over the water. And that's okay.

I reach a hand out to hold Bobby's hand in one of mine. It rests close to my knee and he clings to me. I grip Will's hand in my other and look at Bobby. "He's ready," I tell him, lending him my strength.

Bobby swallows and I can tell he doesn't know what to say but it doesn't matter because Will starts talking.

"I wasn't the best big brother in the world, little mate. But I loved you, I love you, more than anything. You know?"

I squeeze Will's fingers and he squeezes back. Bobby nods his head but still can't seem to form the words, so I say them for him. "He knows."

"I was lost when you were gone. For a long time, all I could see was the pain. I was supposed to protect you. You were so little," Will's voice catches but he draws in a breath, letting it shudder from his lungs as he steadies himself before he continues. "You were so little and there was so much I realised after that I'd wanted to share with you. There's so much we won't have and that hurts. I think it always will, at least a little. It's not fair."

Bobby shakes his head. "I, I—" he stutters.

I squeeze his fingers. "It's okay, take your time," I tell him.

He snuffles as he draws his own breath, copying his brother as he straightens his spine and gives himself a moment to pull himself back together. "I'm s-s-sorry. I didn't mean to make you so sad."

I feel my own composure shaking there because here was this little boy with the weight of all of it on his shoulders too. I tip my head, letting my tears drop as I say the words. "He's so sorry, Will. He didn't mean to make you sad."

Will shakes his head but he's crying too. "Oh Bobby," Will says, his voice part tortured groan part healing sorrow. "You know what I've finally started to really understand this past week?"

Bobby shakes his head, but I know Will doesn't need to see or hear it to keep talking.

"I've realised that this was nobody's fault. It isn't mine as much as I kind of wanted it to be, but most especially it isn't yours either. Not the accident, or what came after. I was sad. Hell, I still am sad. But I'm going to be okay."

Bobby snuffles, lifting his chin. "Really?" he asks. I can tell he desperately wants to believe that's true.

"He needs to believe you, Will," I tell him.

Will drags a breath into his lungs and he turns his body just a little as if sensing exactly where Bobby sits. "I wish I could see you because I want to know that you're really looking at me when I tell you this, Bobby."

Bobby straightens again but he fixes his gaze on his brother. "I'm looking," he says, his voice strong.

"He's looking," I repeat.

Will gazes at the space where Bobby is and there's so much fierce determination on his face that I can almost imagining him piercing the veil to see his brother too. "I want you to hear me."

Bobby nods. Will can't see him, so I say, "He's listening."

"I can't promise that nothing bad will happen. I don't know the future. Who knows, maybe someday Sara will but right now, none of us know everything. But I can promise you. What I did? That won't happen again."

A part of me wonders how he can be so sure. I suspect Bobby wonders too, but he doesn't ask and nor do I.

"This week I realised that giving up isn't okay. Not for me, not for you, not for Dad. Not for anyone who cares about us." Will glances at me. "Grae taught me that."

I swallow and smile because he taught me that too. I nod.

"We have no idea about the ripple of our lives, do we?"

Bobby shakes his head, but Will doesn't need his words. He smiles.

"You rippled so big in my life. And I'll carry you, always, right here." He lifts a hand to thump his chest with his fist.

"I carry you too," Bobby says, copying his brother's action. The little mirror touches my heart because even now Bobby is the echo of his big brother. In every action I could imagine the way he must have worshipped his big brother. He'd walked in his footsteps. It probably drove Will nuts, but I think long from now he'll remember it and smile.

I draw a shaky breath and echo Bobby's words. "He said, 'I carry you too.'" And I mimic the action too which feels strange but makes Will chuckle.

Bobby glances behind him as if he heard something but I look over his shoulder and there's just the lightly lapping waves. Bobby nods, then turns back to me. He reaches between me and Will and links my hand with his brothers.

"He'll be okay now, won't he?" he asks me.

I nod my head. "He'll be okay."

Bobby nods again. "And he has you."

I smile. "Yep, he has me." Will squeezes my fingers and I hear him draw another shaky breath. I lean a little toward him so that our shoulders touch.

"He has to go, doesn't he?" Will asks, his voice shaking. "Like Grae did?"

I watch Bobby and I can already see that same kind of warm glow in him. "I think so," I whisper.

Bobby glances behind him again and again there's this hint as if he's hearing something we don't here. When he turns back to us, he's smiling. He leans close to me and whispers in my ear. "Tell Will, I'm gonna be okay too." I nod my head and my whole body shakes a little as I try to breathe. My heart aches because we'd lost so much already.

Will leans, brushing his lips across my hair and whispers, "Always, remember?" I draw another shaky breath and feel his calm strength around me. There was something truly remarkable about him because he knew a truth so deep in his gut that it left him unwavering. The universe kept showing me that truth, in my Mother, in Grae, and now in Bobby, but I still struggled to believe every time.

"Always," I whisper back as I watch Bobby fade away in the glow. Eventually, all that's left is the sunlight reflecting off the water.

Will and I sit together for ages after, just feeling the sun on our skin and leaning into each other's strength. And then, as the ache of saying goodbye fades a little Will looks down on me. "You okay?" he asks. I nod.

"We have the whole day ahead."

"Just the day?" I ask.

He lifts a shoulder. "A whole life?" he asks. I nod and he grins.

Somewhere inside him he has the strength to grin. I find myself in awe of him again. He stands up and reaches down to pull me up beside him. As we walk up the beach toward the shade of the trees and the green of the grass, he links my fingers with his.

And it's a beautiful day. Touched just a little with sadness, but mostly with a strange light of hope, and wonder, and just a warm sense of knowing that we really would be okay. Both of us.

44

The goodnight I say to Will at my door is kind of shy. There was something more between us now but neither of us was really ready to call it anything yet. Instead, he squeezes my fingers before he lets my hand go and I gave him a wave. I let myself feel the flutter in my belly. And I watch as he walks back across our yards to his own house before I shut the front door and head upstairs.

I sit on the edge of my bed and smile, then glance at the photo in the simple wood frame I'd put on my bedside table all those months ago. My mother's face smiles back at me, full of life and joy. She didn't know what tomorrow held either and the not knowing is scary. But that was okay too.

"Today was a good day, Mum," I whisper to her. I trust she hears me because even though I'm still learning to keep believing it, even though Will sometimes has to remind me, I know she'll always be there. They all will. Forever.

Important Note
From The Author...

Schizophrenia is a very serious and very real illness. In 2019 the World Health Organization wrote that it "affects 20 million people worldwide". It is a condition that can cause significant disability and can affect education, occupation, relationships, even happy, healthy living. However, it is also a condition that is usually manageable. In 2001 the World Health Organisation reported that, "over 80% of people with schizophrenia can be free of relapses at the end of one year of treatment with antipsychotic drugs combined with family intervention."

In Spirit Talker, I contrast this serious mental illness with a spiritual belief in the ability to see dead people. This can be a very controversial topic. As someone who lives with a mental illness (Bipolar) it is a concept I personally have had to struggle with. The question, "Can some hallucinations be real?" is one I still ask myself. But I wanted to define the point in this book that the answer might not really matter.

Maybe Sara has schizophrenia, maybe she is psychic. The point is, her ability to see what she believes are people who have passed over no longer debilitates her. By the end of the book she has been able to claim her life and go forward. She's no longer plagued or disturbed by what she experiences. She is able to live a fully functional life.

I feel like, for the most part, that's all any of us with mental illnesses are striving for. I know there is no cure for Bipolar. I accept my Bipolar as a part of who I am. I've had to learn how my life is impacted by it and adapt my lifestyle accordingly. Sometimes I'm not firing on all cylinders. Sometimes I need to ask for help. Generally, I have a happy, fulfilling, functional life.

But please, if you or someone you know is having a hard time because of depression, mania, psychosis, anxiety, delusions, mental confusion, substance abuse, excessive anger, abnormal libido, or any of a number of symptoms of mental illness, it is important to seek professional help. It is important to trust your care providers, but also trust your instincts. Know that everyone is trying to work together toward your health and happiness.

And most importantly, know that you are not alone. If you need someone to reach out to, someone to talk to, please feel free to contact me at rebecca@rebeccalaffarsmith.com

My love goes out to all of you.

Thank you so much for reading and enjoying Spirit Talker. Please, take a moment right now to leave a review. Your stars, and your thoughts, mean the world to me.

About Rebecca

Born to the magical beauty of her sunburnt country home in Western Australia, Rebecca Laffar-Smith always yearned to explore the wonders of this world and beyond.

After twelve years as a freelance writer and editor, she gave up writing about the non-fiction world in favour of the fantastical creatures and fanciful things she could create and immortalise in fiction. Now she writes in the moments she can steal away from home-schooling her son and daughter, and volunteering as an events coordinator and mentor for her local writing community.

She dreams of someday running a farm-stay writer's retreat on the outskirts of Perth and writing her stories in a detached, hexagonal room with floor to ceiling bookshelves and plenty of natural light.

http://www.rebeccalaffarsmith.com

Acknowledgements

A book is never the work of a single person. There's a whole team helping bring together the final product. This book would not exist without these phenomenal people.

As always, I give unending thanks to my mother, Stephanie Hewitt, and my daughter, Kaylie Laffar-Smith for their unwavering support, shared beliefs, and our true soul connection.

Thanks to a fabulous teacher, Ron Barton for being my inside man checking the ins and outs of the school I opted to send Sara to since I've never had the chance to go there myself.

Thanks to Mel for suggesting Sara's last name and Julz for suggesting Cheeto orange.

Thanks to my brilliant crew of beta readers, Elarra Wylder, Scott E. Douglas, Nici Poland, J Ze Morrell, Heather Salter-Purves, and Imani Benfell. Your feedback, encouragement, corrections, and honesty make all the difference in the world.

And finally, a huge shout out to our Writing Around West Australia writers and National Novel Writing Month. Another fabulous November finally making this book a reality after years of failed starts.

Thank you for reading!